DEAD MAN WAKING
PETER C. CROPSEY

Luke 15:4-7

"What man of you, having a hundred sheep,
if he loses one of them, does not leave the ninety-nine in the
wilderness, and go after the one which is lost until he finds it?
[5]And when he has found it, he lays it on his shoulders, rejoicing.
[6]And when he comes home, he calls together his friends and
neighbors, saying to them, 'Rejoice with me, for I have found my
sheep which was lost!'[7]I say to you that likewise there will be
more joy in heaven over one sinner who repents than over
ninety-nine just persons who need no repentance.

Jesus

My name is Eddie Wilkins. I'm an Orange County boy. So Cal pride
through and through. I live for three things, me myself and I. No seriously, I live for three things, my Harley, heroin and insanity. I am a lost boy
and I am on the run. I am on the run from the law, from the past, from
myself and from God. This is my story.

Jacob,
God bless you bro.
Choose joy!
Choose passion
Pastor Pete
11-12-19

ISBN 145380210X
ISBN-13 9781453802106

This book is dedicated to two people.

First to my wife Dawn who has challenged and continues to challenge me to be the best man that I can be. She is my friend, my confidant, my partner and one very cool character.
She is beautiful, faithful and true and amazing wife and mother.

Also to my mother Patricia who has been my strong advocate even when my life was in a state of total depravity. She always believed in me and never counted me out.
Both of these women are true Proverbs 31 women and a blessing from God.

I want to give special thanks to the congregation of First Love Church for allowing me the privilege of being their pastor, for supporting my family in love and standing behind us through all things. You are all a huge part of our hearts and Dawn and I love you very much.

CHAPTER 1

I can tell by the whimsical melody of the birds on the fence out back that it's going to be a beautiful morning. It's not quite light yet, but the purple of sunrise is starting to creep down the wall across the room. I lay there for a moment putting together what happened last night. Or what didn't happen last night.

This was one crazy neighborhood full of bikers, dopers, and guys either just getting out or getting ready to go back to the pen. Their old ladies would run for them the whole time they were down and then parole day would finally come. The gate money would go in the arm and the crime would commence, continuing until the cuffs went on again. My kind of people, my kind of life, and a perfect neighborhood for Blue and me to hide out.

Last night was a quiet night on Polk Street. Just getting the bikes ready for the run this morning. I don't even think I heard Paul and Debbie beating the snot out of each other in the trailer park across the street. He would come back from picking up dope in North Sacramento and she would accuse him of slamming at the connection's pad. He'd swear he didn't and it would begin.

Sort of made me glad Blue and I were in Sacramento runnin' amok and our old ladies were in O.C. wondering where we had been for the past month.

It started with a call we got from a brother needing some help. Pick up a snitch when she came out of the dope man's house and take her out to the desert so she wouldn't show up in court. We waited in the Caddie for her to come out. She had gone in at about midnight and it was two. She must really be earning that fix.

Blue and I made good partners and we could wait all night. Rolling Stones playing and we're tucked down deep in the seats.

"Wanna do a shot?"

"Oh yeah, indeed I do."

Out comes the little case, precious to behold. We tried to always carry the little case with its dozen prepared rigs all ready to go. Half were just heroin alone and half were heroin and speed. I needed heroin like everyone else needed air. The speed by itself would make me into a tweaking freak, seeing cops in the trees, hearing things and having little people make mischief in the back seat of whatever I'd stolen to drive. However two twenty- five dollar balloons of Mexican heroin added to the speed put me in a perfect place, or so it seemed to me. The heroin kind of defined the insanity, sort of gave the unreal plausibility. It just put a nice cozy blanket of caramel over all of it. It kept me a little more in reality and it drove off the paranoia.

For twenty-three years heroin was my mother's milk. Without it I just wasn't comfortable in my own skin. I felt like I had on socks that were too tight, with one heel creeping down under my foot. She was coming out of the house. I pulled the little hammerless 38 from the small of my back, slipped out of the car and walked down the alley.

"Hey girl what's up?"

"Oh, hey, I know you."

"You're gonna wish you didn't."

Blue pulls up in the Cadillac.

"Time for a trip dear. Get in the back."

She just shrugged and got in. I slipped in behind her.

Dope fiends are a strange lot. We always know that any given midnight might be our last and yet there's this irresistible recklessness and obsession that drives us out into the darkest places, the darkest behavior, the darkest lives. It's like when you flush the toilet and the water starts spiraling real slow. It speeds up as it goes down until at the end it's flying out of the bowl and down the drain. You can grab an accidentally dropped bag of dope out of the toilet if you catch it at the beginning of the spiraling flow.

After that you're done in.

A smart dope fiend puts the lid down before the dope comes out of his pocket. Plug the sink drain too, especially if it's the last you have, that stuff always jumps. Anyway, that's what our lives are like. At first a slow spiral of comfort and numbness, just cruising along, maybe feeling okay for the first time in your life. It later becomes that spiraling torrent. It's a torrent of incredibly grotesque events compounded daily like interest, that seems impossible to get on top of.

We pulled out of the alley and headed towards the 55 freeway. She hadn't said a word but I could hear wheels turning in her head.

"You messed up girl."

She didn't make a peep. I looked at her in the sporadic light of oncoming cars and streetlights. She looked to be a combination of scared, resigned, yet totally still calculating her options.

She had been a pretty little girl. She was somebody's sweet little bundle once. She had been a kindergartner, then a first grader with banged up knees and cute little grin. She read Charlotte's Web and later Nancy Drew. She had her little group of elementary school innocents whom she laughed with, marveled with at the irresistible and yet disgusting ways of boys, and had sleepovers with. She was her daddy's little girl, (maybe his victim, it all starts somewhere). She was her momma's little helper on cake baking day and then one day something started to go way wrong.

Now she was in the back of a 72 Sedan Deville on the way to the desert to pay for an error in judgment. An error brought on by a few too many hours in a cell without a fix and a promise by some nark to let her go if only she would drop a few dimes and show up in court.

She was loaded on speed and heroin that she had purchased with what was left of her feminine charm. She still looked pretty in an after midnight sick sort of way, but if you rolled up her sleeves you would see the ruined abscessed arms of the true believer. I thought of the kind of terrible things a woman with as big a habit as hers had to do every day to stay right and it made me angry and sad. My partners accused me of having a "Captain save a Ho" mentality. That's why I could never afford to slow down long enough to think, it leads to compassion and empathy. Those are two emotions a junky cannot afford. I had my own ape climbing up my back and he demanded at least a few hundred a day. Gotta stay high enough to not see and not feel or the life would plunge you straight into madness. A mammoth paradox iced with the lie that seals your fate. That lie is, "Once a junky, always a junky." That's what makes a true believer, a hope to die dope fiend.

The 55 turned into the 91 and then we went north on the 15. We were headed to a spot outside Victorville. Going up the grade that winds up into the high desert the sky had taken on all the eerie and mysterious hues of predawn. It was so beautiful, the reflected light of the moon and stars playing off the towering slabs of granite and huge boulders lining the highway. I could make out the edge of the ridge above with the pines giving it a serrated look. With the windows down the mountain air carried the blended smells of mountains and desert. Evergreens and pines mixed with sage and just a whisper of skunk threading its way into the tapestry.

"Waste your summer prayin' in vain for a Savior to rise from these streets, well I'm no hero that's understood, all the redemption I can offer girl is beneath this dirty hood, with a chance to make it good somehow, hey what else can we do now except roll down the window and let the wind blow back your hair, well the night's bustin' open these two lanes will take us anywhere."

The Boss was singing the total contrast to what is happening on that 15 freeway northbound into darkness. I just looked out the window at the moonlight playing off of those mountains and I had to harden my heart to keep from plunging into despair. Keep moving, stay loaded, and stay hard. There were those brief glimpses of God's creation, His majesty, which set off a kind of alarm in my head. I knew this life was way south of what it was supposed to be. I knew it was a huge departure from what God had intended, for me, for Blue, and for this dirty- legged dope fiend girl next to me.

Finally she asks,

"What are you gonna do man?"

I slapped her hard across the face and her head snapped back. She looked at me and there was a trickle of blood tracing its way from her lip down across her chin. I saw the little girl with her seventh grade yearbook perched on her lap reading the looping scrawl of well wishing pubescent contemporaries with little hearts over the i's and I died a little.

"Get it together fool." I told myself, "She was probably a slut and a thief by seventh grade."

She just looked at me and she had her little jaw set in stone.

"Hey man, could you pull off at the Antelope Highway off ramp and find a spot to slam?"

"Where bro?"

"You know, the road out to Phelan."

"Yeah sure."

He was grinning in the rear view and shaking his head. He knew my every thought. He mouthed the words,

"Captain Save a Ho.", and we both started cracking up. I slapped her hard three times, grabbed her hair and slammed her head into the back of the front seat. She put her head in her hands and I watched her back heave, she was weeping. At that moment I desperately hated this life I'd made. This is not what the mountains are for. This is not why God created this light, these rocks, and these smells.

"Can't afford the luxury of caring, gotta pay the freight. Keep telling yourself that crap Eddie."

Blue pulled into the base of a fire trail behind some scrub and out came the case. I needed to shut my head off. The little committee up there was causing some anxiety. Why does this have to be a girl? Every Louis L'Amour novel I ever read in lock up clearly taught, "Shoot the guys, save the girls."

Blue went first.

"Straight H for you bro", he said, "I can see your head is a little crossed up. You need to get a little less poetic and a little more pragmatic." We had been running together for 5 years at least and I mean everywhere and every day and we had a good working balance. He knew I was soft in some areas and he needed

that softness to laugh. I needed his ability to overlook emotion and deal with the deal, whatever it took.

I pushed about 2/3 of my load into my arm, pulled it out and handed it to our guest.

"I suppose I could have HIV but the dope is good and it ain't gonna matter to you soon anyway."

She asked if we could turn on the inside light so she could see. I said no but I shined my mini-mag light on her arm. It was heart breaking. I'd seen it all over and over again but sights like that one never failed to dig a huge gouge out of my heart. She pushed that little U100 into what I can best describe as volcanoes of angry abused tissue that went from her wrist to her shoulder. It looked gangrenous.

"Lord what has become of us? We were just little kids once" I thought.

The air in that Caddie got thick with our common plight. I knew the truth. I was nothing but a dead man walking.

We pulled off the highway in Victorville and followed an old wagon trail about 10 miles out in the desert. Blue stopped the car and I told her to get out. I knocked her to the ground and drove her face into the sand and

I could see little broken sticks cutting her cheek. It was so strange to me. She was so compliant. She almost seemed relieved. She knew she was going to die. She just lay there almost as if to say,

"Finally, at last, rest."

We had all embarked on this journey willingly. Not this little trip to the desert on this particular night, but rather this journey into the dark world of drugs and crime. As I looked at this broken creature lying on the ground at my feet I realized she was tired. She was tired of being an outcast, tired of being an enigma. All of us romance the idea that our lives are somehow unique so there's a sick pride in being a junkie.

Still again, every time you go into a store and you know everyone else is there to buy and you're there to steal, there's an outside-looking-in feeling and you know you're living in the depth of moral depravity. I wanted to lie down next to her and have someone else shoot us both in the back of the head. Give us some kind of sweet release. There wouldn't be a soul at the funeral. Everybody we knew would be too busy trying to scam a fix.

I'm torn between feeling lost and broken, despising this life, and a resignation that comes from the knowledge that I can't change a thing. I'm completely insane, living in a capsule of rotting humanity at its worst and the only relief is another shot. It's like being held under water and struggling to reach the surface–the surface is heroin.

I held the muzzle of that 38 to the back of her head. I thought of that toilet-flushing thing. I knew that in a couple of seconds that slow spiraling was going to become a torrent I could not control. I stood up, ground her face into the dirt with my boot, kicked her half heartedly in the ribs a couple of times and busted two caps into the dirt next to her head. I knew when I said it that it was an exercise in futility.

"Don't come back to the O.C. And for sure stay out of that courtroom."

I got back in the Caddie and Blue hit the gas. He was grinning.

"Don't say it."

"I won't Captain."

We started laughing.

I thought briefly about the events of the last few hours and I said to Blue,

"They shoulda called somebody else."

"Nah. They called the right guys."

"Yeah I guess so."

The sun was coming up in earnest now and it was gonna be one hot stinking day.

"I hope she has a nice walk."

"Come on bro she'll be back at the connection's pad by dark and we both know it."

We pulled into the driveway of my house in Costa Mesa about 9 am. My daughter April was in the yard. She was 2. She saw us and yelled,

"Daddy, Uncie Boo, wachoo dooink?" "Yoo waan pancakth?"

"You knew I couldn't shoot her."

"Yeah, I know. Let's eat. I'm starving."

Two weeks later Blue pulls up in the driveway with a trailer behind the Ranchero loaded with his rollaway, a welder and his shovelhead. Everything is loaded on one side of the trailer so I know wherever he's going, I'm going with. He comes in the house.

"I just got a call. She's back and got busted yesterday for under the influence, she's in the county jail. We gotta head up to Stormy's in Sac until this works out. The club will be cool with anything we do but I am worried about a kidnapping and assault case."

As Robin leaves the room she says,

"Don't forget to say goodbye to your kid."

We loaded my bike and my tools. I grabbed some clothes, my leathers, my hype kit and a few hundred bucks.

I break out of my memories and see that the purple of sunrise creeping down the wall has given way to a pale yellow and I can hear the hood starting to come alive. I hear that punk dirt merchant Jack next door starting his car to go pick up the morning package for all the retail smack buyers on the block. He'll cut it twice, re-bag it and sell it to people who trade their food stamps for dope. I've been on both sides of that deal. Sometimes, and sometimes even for a long time, you get to be the champ but in time you always, always, always get to be the chump.

The birds are singing like we live in paradise but the ape on my back is already kicking my brains in and letting me know it ain't paradise until he says so. Blue knocks on the door.

"Wake up bro, it's time to slam, scarf and scram!"

"Come in. The door's open."

Waking up with a heroin habit can go two ways: One, you have a wake up, in which case that first shot of the day is the closest you'll ever get to the first shot you ever did. If you have a good stash for the morning it doesn't matter where you are or what is happening, it's all cool. Or two, you've got nothing put away and you're screwed. You wake up with the Johnes on and anything goes. That's when a dope fiend gets scandalous. If he's got a hustle great, if not there goes the T.V. or the stereo, or the kid's piggy bank. This morning was a good morning. They almost always were for Blue and me; we were a crew. There's strength in numbers.

When you wake up dope sick, and there's dope there it's like Christmas morning at dysfunction junction. Your eyes pop open and you know its waiting. You know how a dog looks when you've been gone all day and you come home and he's starving? You put down the food and he's all shaking and he's gotta go to the bathroom so bad but he's too hungry to leave the food alone. He might dump right there on the floor but he's gonna keep on eating. Very similar.

The dope goes in the cooker, which as soon as you smell it makes you want to take a dump. You're quivering inside from anticipation and the smell is making you crazy. You peel back a little bit of a cigarette filter for some cotton, or you pick some off your socks, and you wad it up real small like a BB and you drop it in that spoon. The tip of that point goes right in the middle of that cotton and you draw it up. Maybe by now you have lost control of your sphincter but that doesn't stop you or even slow you down.

You tie off and slip that rig into your best morning vein, pull the plunger back and watch the blood register in the rig. Swirly, swirl, swirl. Maybe right now you might pause to savor the sickness. Your nose is running like a faucet, your legs feel like they're being stretched on the rack. Your spine is screaming at you, "Push it in, push it in!" You feel like sneezing, gagging, and puking all at the same time. Yeah, I used to wait like that for up to a full minute sometimes. That minute of mini-hell, of a yearning so powerful you're totally incapable of denying it, an obsession so overpowering that you'll sell your rotten soul to make this push—and you do. You push.

I would push it firm and fast and within 3 seconds the wave of warmth and relief would cascade over me like hot honey. Sometimes I would wonder if this one was the one that would kill me. Sometimes I would hope so. I knew that I'd sold out my whole life to the king slave driver, this malevolent demon of demoralization that had a death grip on me 24 hours a day. Once I was loaded I didn't care. It's all right as rain for the next four hours.

CHAPTER 2

"I'm gonna jump in the shower."

"Yeah okay, I need to savor this for a moment; I'll see ya in the kitchen."

I sat there on the edge of the bed for a sec feeling perfect, morning sun lighting the room and the anticipation of a few days riding fast and partying with a lot of brothers. People who knew you, knew what you were about, knew what you were capable of, and overlooked an indiscretion or a fault now and then if you had proven you had salt. In the biker lifestyle being a hype was a total no-no.

You could snort all the speed in the world, take all the reds and rainbows you could gulp down, do mountains of psychedelics, and drink like a fish. If you shot heroin you were out. If you put a needle in your arm you were undependable and weak. Everyone knew you were a liar and a thief.

There were about a dozen of us from Orange County that were excluded from that classification for about ten years. We had hustle, it was organized, we all grew up on Harleys, we all built our own bikes, and rode hard. We never burned our kind of people. Never. We used to say, "There are brothers and there are victims, they are widely separated." We were a crew and we took care of each other and each other's families.

One of the boys had gotten a three-year prison sentence, which left his family in a rough spot. They lost their house and were staying with family. Blue rented them a house and came and got me with a stolen 23-foot bobtail truck. We put on uniforms, and
went to a new housing development on a day when the model homes were not being shown. We broke in and spent the entire day loading every stick of furniture into that truck and we delivered it to the newly rented house.

We had also acquired a home entertainment center from this guy Wes. He owned a pawnshop in Garden Grove and possessed a sweet tooth for meth. He owed us for fulfilling that appetite on credit. I must say it is a beautiful thing to have the owner of a pawnshop in your debt. The guy that everybody owes owing you provides a myriad of opportunities. Use your imagination.

We had a couple of girls working for us that would take forged payroll checks to different supermarkets and buy groceries. The checks would be for a tad bit less than five hundred dollars. If the girl came to the cash register with say a hundred dollars in groceries then she could pay with the payroll check and receive the change. We'd pay the girls fifty dollars to do this. They worked for us regularly, had fake I.D., and would run this game sometimes four times a day each. We would have kids go around the neighborhoods and get grocery lists from housewives and we would fill them for fifty cents on the dollar. We felt good about all of it. Regular Robin Hoods.

We went to some beat up old neighborhood in Garden Grove where the family was staying and picked them up saying nothing. We took them to the new house and Blue gave our brother's wife the keys and the change from the cashed checks.

"Call us if you need us, the rent is paid for six months." We just walked away, all cool and mysterious. We had the look down. It's so easy when you believe your own B.S. John Boy was down for thirty months and the rent was never late. During that time Blue and I did eighteen months ourselves, and the rent still got paid.

That was part of the seduction of it all. We took good care of everybody and they loved us. Real philanthropists. Looking back what we were creating were people that owed and
owed big. It occurs to me that during that time I never had any contact whatsoever with the real world. I was killing myself with drugs and booze. I never earned an honest buck.

Would I have helped anyone if there were nothing in it for me? Yeah, right. I played on everyone's needs. I flirted with them just enough to make them think they were having fun, being mischievous, and I made them think they were doing the right thing.

I drug everyone into this web of dishonesty disguised as romance and excitement and they all paid with the compromise of their integrity. What housewife living in a lower class neighborhood trying to feed a bunch of kids on her husband's meager hourly wage isn't going to buy groceries for half price and have them delivered? How many of those women laid awake at night wondering when the walls were going to come crashing down on this little game?

At one point we had motel rooms all over the place stocked with just beer, cigarettes, disposable diapers and formula. Everything the poor girl with kids always needs, and all poor girls have a gang of kids. Did I care that at any moment one of these rooms might get busted and one of these moms might be there with her newborn, and a couple of toddlers? Did I care if the county held her kids, while she had to call her husband from his nightmare of a no end job? Not much. I was a total scumbag, playing Sir Galahad. For the life of me I could not see past the bottom of my heroin cooker. I didn't know my castle was a house of cards and that the wind would come and blow my world to the wilderness. But it did.

Prison or death were not deterrents, they were part of the life. I knew I had signed up for plenty of cell time and I knew I would die young. For some reason I thought I would die in some flashy way, looking like a gangster with all his game on. It never occurred to me that I would ever be rotting away behind a dumpster during the day, pulling petty thefts and drinking screw-cap wine to keep my withdrawals at bay. I never saw myself sleeping nights in an old wrecking yard, wishing I was in prison, so yellow from Hepatitis I looked like a banana. Yet that's exactly where I ended up.

"Time to get ready",
I said to the walls. I got up and pulled on my jeans, my boots, took my pistol and my buck knife from their place under my pillow and stowed them in my belt. I had kicked in enough doors at sunrise to understand the foolishness of ever leaving the bedroom without my boots on and my weapons handy. Even a midnight piss included boots and a pistol. If you've ever tried to run down a ghetto street in the dark barefoot you understand this.

I walked into the kitchen where Stormy was cooking toast, oats and fried eggs. I lit a smoke from her pack on the counter, took a couple of drags and stuck it between her lips.

"Thanks bro."

"Hey, I'm a gentleman."

"Yeah you are. That is, if taking one of my smokes, hot-boxing it, and sticking it in my mouth when my hands are full, so that smoke gets in my eyes is gentlemanly."
Just then the ash fell into the eggs, and we both laughed.

"Just serve me that one."

"What, you thought I'd do anything else?"

Stormy and Rick were old school Orange County. I'd known them forever. Stormy was one of the funniest girls I'd ever met. She had the quickest wit and the sharpest tongue out of all of us and she could cut you to ribbons. Somehow she did it with a smile and so much love that it never hurt, just made you laugh. She would do anything for the boys and she was treated with the respect due royalty. In fact we all called her "The Queen."

I'd call from down South after she and Rick and the kids moved to Sac.

"How's it going Stormy Ann?"

"Ah Eddie, it's quite good to be the queen."

We'd laugh. Rick was totally into his family. They had two girls, Margie and Ruthie. When things got too hot in O.C. Ricky moved them all to North Highlands. His mom, brother and two sisters all lived there. They were all really cool people. They were not like us but they treated us like family. Ricky was the kind of guy that could leave home with fifty cents in his pocket and no gas in his panhead, and come home with a few hundred bucks by just hitting a couple of local bars.

No one could beat him at eight-ball and he was so funny that people would line up to lose just to listen to him tell jokes. He never made anyone mad, but if you got into a scrap with him you would lose. He was not a big guy but he had the look. Lean, long curly black hair, face full of light and mirth. He carried himself with so much easy confidence it was a study just to watch him move through a bar. He never tried to intimidate anyone and he didn't need to.

Maybe this sounds like a contradiction in terms to the average normal person. "Yeah okay this booze drinking drug using outlaw is totally into his family. What are you nuts?"

Absolutely! It's easy to dismiss us as if we were some feral losers without any conventional feelings of love or family responsibility. That's a lie! We were all created in God's image we all have a heart and we all wrestle with just trying to get by. Is the guy who spends 70 hours a week trying to make partner in some prestigious law firm while his family dies on the vine really that far away from Ricky?

Why because Ricky is an outlaw? That's what he learned. That other guy learned in a very different school. On which man does God pour more compassion? Both are totally lost. God desires to seek and save those that are lost. He said so.

One night some wannabe outlaw was trying to provoke Ricky, messing around disrespectfully with Stormy and generally being a punk. Ricky bought him a pitcher of beer and introduced Stormy as his wife and the mother of his children. Stormy always handled these types of situations with so much grace. This poor fool had no respect for the institution of marriage, so he kept it up. Stormy got up to go to the bathroom, totally setting him up, and true to the idiot's nature he grabbed her rear. Rick set down his pool cue and approached Stupid. I had seen him conceal a pool ball in his vest earlier when all this began but no one else had.

"So I guess we're not gonna be friends?"

"No man we're not!"

The first lick with the pool ball was on his right temple, and then his right collarbone, the second one sounded like kindling snapping. Before the fool hit the ground Ricky hit him quite a few times. Ricky picked up his cue and told a really funny joke.

Blue and I drug the poor fellow outside and threw him in the dumpster. About twenty minutes later we heard a bike start and leave. Sounded like he was having trouble shifting.

A few months later Ricky was riding home and was killed by a drunk woman in a station wagon. She dragged him for a quarter mile and left him mangled in the street to die. She was later caught, pled guilty to some lesser charge and was given probation. He was after all just some stinkin' biker. In fact he was a fiercely loyal man and a king.

Blue came out of the shower and grabbed a plate. I was finishing mine so I took my turn in the rain room. I was standing under the water and I could hear the girls getting up and playing their way toward the kitchen. There was laughter, the tinkling of dishes, the smell of cooking and fresh coffee. The Motels were playing, Martha Davis singing,

"Only the lonely can play."

On the surface it was all so good. Deep inside of me there was a tiny little seed of despair trying to grow into a realization. It would take another eleven years and the death or life imprisonment of almost the whole crew before that realization ever came. It would take the deterioration of Stormy into a thieving lying junkie who never ever laughed before I ever saw through the lie that was our lives.

Rick and Stormy rarely ever did heroin. She was more given to it than he was. Once in a while she would do a hit but she kept a grip and she had

Ricky. Once Ricky was gone she felt she needed a little bump a little more often to get through the grieving process.

The grieving process just kept stretching out and the bumps she needed to get through kept getting closer and closer together.

Jack from next door was seeing to that. It took a couple of days for us to figure it out because she was hiding it from Blue and me. I'd heard her go out of the house when Jack started his caddie to make his run. That's what woke me up. An opening door is an impossible thing to sleep through, especially one being opened quietly, it's a cacophony. A bright light goes off in your head,

"Warning! Warning!"

Jack had gotten busted doing his first armed robbery, gone to the pen, met all the right people, pretended to be a stand up guy, and he was a poser all the while. Women were his hustle and when Rick died he became the helpful neighbor. When we showed up he came on all smiles.

"Hey Bro!"

But he looked like an egg sucking dog caught in the hen house.

"How long you guys gonna be around?"

I thought, *"Long enough to get your stink out of the hood, that's certain.*

I could smell the treachery on this dude.

When I said I was heading to the shower I could see Stormy get a little anxious. I knew she was in need of a fix. Her nose was running and she had little beads of sweat on her upper lip. I let the water run down on my head and I listened to the muffled warmth of what sounded just like a normal household on a normal morning. We were a thousand miles from anything resembling normal and the little seed of despair that had long been germinating in me tried hard to sprout into a realization.

I dressed, looked through my weapons bag, made my choices, a double action thirty-eight revolver for my vest, a 380 for my boot, and a six-inch stainless 357 for my bedroll.

I've rarely had to pull a weapon while on a bike run but I would always hear this little voice in my head,

"Better to have 'em and not need 'em, than to need 'em and not have 'em."

I was once asked after crashing at some people's pad I had met in a bar while on the road,

"Don't you worry, carrying guns on a bike?"

I used to worry not carrying a gun anywhere but the safest place to carry used to be on the bike, on the road. I was taught,

"Keep your license and registration right, and you'll be alright."

There used to be a kind of grudging respect between cops and bikers. If you got pulled over, you shut your engine down while pulling to a stop in a place where the cop would feel safe, you kept your hands on your handlebars until the cop spoke to you and you showed respect.

Once when I was young and cocky, about eighteen, I was pulled over in a pack with some older guys and I got mouthy with a Garden Grove cop. When I thought I was being cool I was jeopardizing everybody. When we got to the Chez Paris parking lot I shut my motor down and kicked out my sidestand. I stood up and stretched my back. I was peeling off my gloves feeling all proud of myself when out of the corner of my eye a fist came like a rocket to the side of my head. I was too off guard to move and it caught me right on the ear. I was knocked over my bike and landed on my head on the other side. I was kicked in the chest and back and ribs, lifted to my feet and punched a couple of times in the face.

I was beaten so badly I couldn't open my left eye or chew for days. I had two broken ribs and a had concussion. I just remember hearing one of the brothers say,

"You'll see that cop when you have a pocket full of something you're not supposed to and then you'll know why you're on the ground right now."

That bit of prophecy was fulfilled forthwith when I was blasting down Brookhurst St. with a big bag of speed and a pistol less than two weeks later. It was around 1:00 am. The red lights reflected off my chrome just before he chirped the siren. I pulled to a stop in a well-lighted place, kept my hands on my bars and when he came up to me I said,

"I'm glad it's you, I wanted to apologize, I was trying to impress my friends, and I guess they weren't impressed.

He looked at my still swollen, bruised mug and laughed.

"I guess you listened to their advice."

"You bet I did."

"Slow down kid."

I wish I'd heard what he really said in those three words, but I didn't. I thought he meant right then, on my bike. Maybe he did, but it would have been good advice for life. As he walked back to his cruiser, he stopped briefly,

"Kid, You know that guy Knuckles you ride with?"

I grew wary,

"Yeah?"

"I've known him since high school. I used to go out with his sister until a drunk driver killed her. I loved that girl, that's why I became a cop. He built my bike too. One night I was right up the street there and I pulled over a big giant guy who decided he wanted a piece of me. Knuckles happened to be going by. He stopped and asked me,

"What's up bro?"

He just sat there looking all fierce like he does until another cruiser showed up.

"That's how it is, you get it?"

"I think I'm beginning to."

"Later kid, stay right."

I sometimes wish I listened better.

I walked through the kitchen and into the garage to find that Blue already had the bikes rolled out to the curb. He was wiping the night dust from my shovelhead.

There's nothing like a brother.

CHAPTER 3

Taking the easy right hand sweeper on to the freeway was sweet as sugar cane warmed in the sun and fresh cut, bleeding juice into your mouth. Two sets of straight pipes full of thunder. Bikes, black and shiny, in perfect tune. Built to ride fast. Blue with ape hangers, and me with drag bars. Other than that, almost clones. Suicide clutch, hand shift, thin little solo seats with pillion pads. Down so low you're looking up and over bed-rolls bungeed to the risers.

The sun is warm, soon to be hot and we're riding handgrip to hand-grip. I hear his head and he hears mine. We move through traffic together like one organism, and hit the fast lane catching top gear, settling in at about eighty. Blue sets his throttle, reaches into his vest and pulls out a pint of Jim Beam. He cracks the seal and gives me first pull. I drink deep and it burns a path to my guts, exploding in my head as I pass it back. We are on the road.

We passed the pint back and forth a few times and then we both went to never-never land. When you ride next to someone for a long time you get so in synch that you go into this no-mind place. The Japanese call this *"Mushin"* and it is a term used by martial artists to describe being so in the zone that every move just happens right. It's a place where you're operating on pure natural instinct. There's no question, no doubt that you're in ex-actly the right place doing exactly the right thing. Everything is suspended in this molasses of perfect contentment. A subtle blip of the throttle or a slight gesture is read and understood without thinking. It's just a link be-tween two men and two machines sharing one heart, one brain. I know that if you have a group of women all move in together that within a short time they will all be going through their cycle at the same time. It's the same with riding with the same guys day in day out, midnight-to-midnight, dawn-to-dawn. After a while you become so in tune that you even have to take a leak at the same time.

We were blowing down the road like a freight train, separating to pass cars and hooking back up like we were choreographed. The sun was bright and fine, and I was perfectly stoned, hours from needing to stop for the little black magic case. I looked over at Blue; he laughed and wicked the throttle. I grabbed a handful too and we shot out into the future. The future wasn't going to be real good. I just didn't know it. What would I have done if I did know? Probably not a thing.

The boys were coming from all over, mostly from So Cal but a good bunch from Nevada. We were all to hook up just East of Modesto and ride out to the club property on the lake together, about a thirty-five-mile ride through the country. We arrived at the rendezvous point first just as we hoped, and parked in front of the little redneck bar.

It was about eleven A.M. and already there was a parking lot full of pick-ups. Lots of local fellas getting off work for a few days and getting ready to kick-off Labor Day weekend. These kinds of entrances are sometimes chancy. We're strangers in town and we look real different from the usual patrons of this fine establishment. Blue smiles and says,

"The mission is stay out of trouble."

"You got that right bro!"

Now this is when you gotta go in and find the similarities between you and whoever looks influential, you gotta make them see them too, establish some common ground, get a handshake everyone can see and get all this done before the drunk jerk, (and every redneck bar, or any bar for that matter has one), can start trouble. Barroom diplomacy, the gathering of allies, an ounce of prevention for something from which there is no cure. The price for failure to do this is someone takes a disliking to us because they are seeing only our differences and none of our similarities and then we get into a big scrap ending in the sheriff having all our gear spread out on the street as we're cuffed in the back of a cruiser. We do not want the sheriff going through our gear.

We step into the cool darkness of the bar still filled with the smells of last night's boot scrapin'. It's a delicate blend of beer, whiskey, urine and puke. It always made me feel comfortable. Blue isn't the diplomat. That's my job. He goes over to the bar, sees everyone is drinking Coors and orders two. He tips the bartender the change from a ten-dollar bill, the bartender smiles.

"Thanks buddy."

So far so good on that end of the bar. He waits until I spot my new friend, then walks to the jukebox and punches in George Strait, (Amarillo by Morning), Conway Twitty, (The Clown), and Merle Haggard, (Workin' Man's Blues). I know exactly what songs he chose because all country bars have the same songs and this ain't our first rodeo.

Five guys are leaning around a standing table that circles a column in the middle of the room.

"Must be a going out dancing weekend."

The cowboy looks at me, and the rest get quiet as he says,

"What makes you say that?"

"Well that's at least a twenty X Resistol hat you're wearin' so I know it's your going out hat and those Hawthorne Packers you're wearin' never had manure touchin' the soles.

"I just wanted to thank you guys for letting us cool off in here and wish you a great Labor Day weekend."

"You carry yourself like you been in the military."

"1st of the 11th Field Artillery, Fort Lewis." I answer.

"Oh, so you did your basic at Fort Sill?"

"Yeah, I can still feel that Hawk in my bones!"

"Yes indeedy that is cold wind country."

We all laugh and my pulse evens out. Blue cruises up with the beers and my new friend Cole says,

"Hey guys make some room!"

I was totally enjoying this company of strangers we had met and so was Blue. That's why he would always say,

"Bro you're the people guy."

It might seem like manipulation I was applying, but the truth is I've always loved people. Somewhere deep inside this burned out broken husk of a young man was a starving heart. Deep down inside of me there was something that gave me a love for people, but here is also a real force whose only mission, whose deepest desire is to kill love and goodness, eradicate it from the face of this earth and the hearts of men. With me that force was winning. Always at times like this the truth would hover trying to break through the fog of deception I lived in. It was always out there far away its foghorn blowing mournful beckoning notes that could not quite penetrate the darkness that was my life. Cole asks,

"What brings you guys in here?"

"We're meeting some brothers here for a bike run."

Just as I finished saying that the sound of thunder in the form of over 100 sets of drag pipes could be heard getting off of the Freeway. It sounded so fine and it raised the eyebrows all around the table.

"Well, time to go! It was really nice to meet you guys, have a great weekend. You ready Blue?"

"Bro, I was born ready!"

As we step out of the dimness of the bar into the bright light of midday it takes a sec for our eyes to adjust. I put on my murder ones against the sun and train my eyes down the street. What greets them is one of the finest sights a Harley riding outlaw could ever hope to see. It's a seemingly endless parade of choppers, mostly black and chrome, their riders looking like raiding barbarians, long hair in the wind, colors blowing out behind, each looking like one with his machine. Perfect unity. We started our bikes as the black and chrome procession rolled thunderously by. We tore out of the gravel parking lot slinging rocks with our back tires and pulled in behind the pack. Many years later I would be in a position at the front of the pack and I would always miss the view from the back.

Riding in a pack of outlaw bikers, all flying colors, is an experience that defies description. It's a feeling so raw and wild, totally addictive. Every patch holder has his own individual style, his bike an expression of that style. Ape hangers for some, left foot on the clutch, left hand hanging loosely by his suicide shifter or draped nonchalantly across the thigh of his old lady. Jaw set, determined, maybe a little cold and calculating looking. Weathered face, long hair and beard, very dark glasses. Another brother might favor the low-down in the saddle look of drag bars and the thinnest possible seat to give that on the ground look. I used to run a piece of sheet metal riveted to the frame for a seat and whoever rode on the back rode on the fender. Comfort was no issue; style was everything. My butt was so hard I could ride that frame from San Diego to Sacramento no sweat.

Blue and I pulled in behind the pack and I just set my mind in neutral enjoying the sound of a hundred sets of pipes going down a country road on a sunny summer morning. I could feel the whiskey and the speed ball of meth and heroin I had done in the bathroom at the bar, and the world seemed pretty fine. We had enough dope for three or four days, enough money for a month and we were headed to the party of parties on the club's lakefront property 35 miles from anywhere.

About 5 miles from the dirt road turn off that led to the property Blue's rear brake wheel cylinder blew and so when we got to the turn off we pulled over. We stopped Danny Mac and told him we were going to wait until all of the brothers were down the steep hill leading in to the campground and then I would help Blue down the hill. I would be his brakes. Danny raised an eyebrow, laughed and said,

"This should be pretty entertaining!"

We had a smoke and listened until we could no longer hear the bikes and figured it was time to go. We positioned ourselves so that Blue's right foot went on my left foot peg and my left foot went on his right foot peg. We both had suicide shifts so we had to do this on the slow roll. We grinned at each other, laughed and dove over the crest of the hill.

The hill was fairly steep with a long sweeping left turn that we could not see around. All we knew was that at some unknown distance around the other side of that downhill turn were a hundred plus bikers waiting and watching. Around the turn we go, Siamese twinned up trying to keep it somewhat slow, me the only one with brakes. Coming around the turn we see the crowd all gathered around a big clearing. I tell Blue,

"About fifty feet from the clearing I'll let go and steer right, you go in and brodie to a stop in the middle. He laughs and nods his head. He pulls it off perfectly, and as the dust clears and he throws down his side stand, the brothers are laughing and Monkey Man comes up with a spoon and a zip lock full of chocolate mescaline and gives Blue a spoonful and I mean *full*. I walk over and grab the bag and the spoon and help myself. Monk whips out a quart of Kessler's whiskey and we all take a long pull. It's going to be a colorful weekend.

It takes a little while for everyone to say their hellos and set up their individual campsites. I watch Monkey Man making his rounds with the Nestlé's Quick and everyone is starting to come on pretty quick. I'm setting up my tent under a big spreading oak tree with Blue setting up between the lake and me.

The setting is beautiful. The lake is about a mile long and about half a mile wide, sparkling in the early afternoon sun. There's a light breeze blowing through the big stand of gnarled old oak trees that surround the lake. I can hear the buzz of insects; kind-of a soft humming that gives me peace. It's blending sweetly with the sound of the breeze blowing through the leaves on the trees. Sunlight filters down through the branches onto our little camp site and is all dappled on the tents and the grass.

I'm beginning to feel a warmth in my limbs and a light gust gives me chicken skin. I can see colors starting to flash around the periphery of my vision, little trails are beginning to follow everything that moves. I reach for the whiskey bottle and a rainbow image of my arm follows in a staccato ribbon of wonder. I'm hoping to see little dragons flying around camp shortly. Psychedelics are always such an adventure. Sensuous, spiritual, hallucinatory, adventure. The only thing that can possibly improve a good hit of acid or some mescaline is a little heroin.

"Blue, you ready?"

He grins as I hold up the case.

"Yeah my brother, it's a grand time to indulge in a little blood boosting."

We slip into my tent and I pull two rigs of pure heroin out of the case. I hand Blue his and we each begin our private rituals. Heroin addiction is very ritualistic; the act of getting high is almost sacred. I tie a bandana around my arm and look at the rope of a vein that goes down the inside of my arm from elbow to wrist. It has a black line of scar tissue about four inches long that is my history.

Aside from blowing up a vein and collapsing it shooting barbiturates when I was thirteen, my veins are in good shape. I was blessed with big healthy veins and lots of them. I've watched people particularly women search and poke for literally hours trying to get a little blood to show in the syringe. It sucks to be them. Right now it's great to be me. The needle goes in and I pull back on the plunger. A jet of blood shoots into the syringe and swirls around with the dope.

If I had just cooked up my shot I would wait a minute for the blood to cool down the freshly heated fix. Now I just pause to feel the mescaline surging through my bloodstream and blowing up in my head. Mushroom clouds of color and feeling. I feel like the top of my head is coming open and the sky is flooding in. A line of heat goes from my head down my neck and through my shoulders.

My legs feel strong and powerful like I could get up and run for miles. The energy passes out my feet and into the earth and I feel totally connected to life. I push the plunger in and in seconds the rush threatens to make me fall back into the rocking chair of lifelessness.

I remember how out of place I felt as a kid. I felt so stripped naked before the rest of the world. Never comfortable in my own skin. Always feeling apart from family and friends not understanding why even though I would try I could never sit in a class room or be part of a group of normal kids doing normal stuff. I was always the loner kid playing it cool smoking cigarettes in the far corner of the playground. Just waiting for the right time to jump the fence and be free. Then I would take my mini-bike up in the hills and ride. The wind and the sound of that little Briggs and Stratton engine were the only peace I knew.

That is until I discovered drugs. Once I got high it seemed as if all my problems, my sense of awkwardness just melted away. I was nine when I really started getting high in earnest. I smoked pot and hash until I was ten, then I took my first acid trip. It opened up doors for me that I had never imagined.

I grew up in Laguna Beach in the late sixties. At the time, it was the epicenter of Southern California's acid culture. The peace and love vibe was everywhere. Gypsies and love children permeated the streets of that little artist's colony on the beach, and I embraced that culture. It was the first place I ever felt that I fit in.

When I was twelve I met a dope smuggler named Max. He was a heroin addict and I thought he was the epitome of cool. He drove a 1950 Chevy low-rider with Lakewood pipes. It was black and slammed to the pavement. Max had hustle and style. He always had a wad of cash and his old lady was beautiful in a dangerous dark kind of way.

I would see Max in the Jolly Roger restaurant every morning with Kristy reading his paper with his murder one shades on. Sitting with his legs crossed, cup of coffee in his hand, black leather trench coat, levis and engineer boots. Way too cool. I had to get next to Max. It took about two weeks of trying to get noticed before he said to me one morning,

"Hey kid, what's your trip?"

"I know you're up to something and I want to work for you."

"What do you think you could do for me?"

They're sitting in their usual booth in the J.R. and Kristy is looking at me with kind of a curiosity. I realize then that she isn't that much older than me, maybe eighteen at the most. I was twelve but really big for my age. Max was twenty seven.

"I don't know, I could run errands or make deliveries."

"What kind of deliveries?"

"The kind you're wasting your time making, that could get you busted, when you could be doing something more important."

"What's gonna keep some dope fiend from slapping you and taking my product?"

"Respect and fear."

"Oh they're gonna respect some punk kid? How old are you anyway?"

"I'm fourteen and no, they're gonna respect you, aren't they? Besides, if I do get ripped off, I promise it'll only happen once and then everyone will know it's not a good idea."

So that's how it started, my first delivery was to a guy named Suede and he took a shine to me.

"Have you ever shot dope kid?"

"No not yet."

"You want to try it?"

"Yeah as a matter of fact I do."

That was my problem see? I never stopped to think of consequences. For me it has always been about the moment. Some fundamental warning system that normal people have was and largely still is missing from my psyche. I never placed any value on my life or thought about the ramifications of what sticking a needle in my arm could be. I never looked at the big picture or thought about the future past next Saturday night.

Suede snapped a taste out of one of the balloons I delivered into his cooker and used an eyedropper with a needle affixed to the end to add a little water. I was mesmerized.

He lit three or four matches and held them under the cooker until the mixture bubbled for a couple of seconds. Then he peeled a little of the filter off of a cigarette and balled it up. Everything was going in slow motion and I felt highly sensitized to the whole deal. He dropped the cotton in the cooker and drew it up with the binky. A binky is a homemade syringe much like an eyedropper on steroids. He handed it to me and said,

"You gotta do it yourself or you're not gonna do it."

He handed me a bandana and I began a process that to me was the most natural thing in the world and would be a part of my life from that day forward. I pumped my fist a couple of times the way I had seen Suede do and I pushed the needle into a vein right at the crotch of my elbow.

At first it went clear through and when I started to squeeze the dropper it bumped up.

"Whoa, pull it out a tad bit."

I did and then the blood squirted up into the dropper.

"Always get a register to make sure you're in the vein."

I nodded my head and squeezed. Almost immediately the rush hit me. It was like nothing I'd ever felt before. Suddenly the world was perfect. Fear and anxiety I didn't even know I had melted away and I felt warm and at total peace. I felt the grin spreading across my face.

"It feels like heaven boy, but welcome to hell."

Within the month I was smuggling kilos of heroin across the border with an old woman who worked for Max and lived in Chula Vista.

Within the year I had been arrested for burglary. I was a thirteen year old felon. By the time I was fourteen I had already overdosed and I didn't give it a thought.

I was jaded and old surrounded by drug addicts and criminals and I'd never even drug a razor across my face. All I cared about was motorcycles, surfing, hustling drugs and first and foremost heroin.

The day by the lake went on with Blue and me pretty much frying in the tent but by sunset we were ready to come out and see what was going on. It was getting dark when I stepped outside and the campground looked like a psychedelic circus. A couple of the old ladies were dancing naked in the clearing; one brother was wiping down his bike with a passion unlike any I have ever seen. Another brother was up in an oak tree just staring up at the sky, and here and there were little clusters of people engaged in deep conversation or just staring in to space. Little John was sitting on the ground on a blanket playing guitar, and Danny Mac was putting the bonfire together. The first day at the run was winding down and Monkey Man's chocolate mescaline had definitely put things in slo-mo.

There was a huge trailer barbecue hauled out by one of the crash trucks and I could smell the ribs and tri-tip cooking making me hungry. I walked around the campground visiting and catching up with old friends. Blue and I were the only guests at this run, meaning we were the only two guys there not flying a patch. We were not members. I was an independent, although I enjoyed a special connection to the brothers through years of affiliation.

The club's National President was like a dad to me. I'd known him since I was fourteen. Blue and Monkey Man had been cellmates in the pen for a couple of years.

Monkey Man didn't hold an office in the club but he had major juice. He had the freedom from responsibilities of a regular member and the power of a very heavy rep.

Everyone knew we were doing business with the club and that we went way back with some of the brothers. So mostly the vibe was pretty good. That is until I saw Crazy Al.

Al had just gotten out of the pen and had been down eight years. He was an unfriendly sort that even a lot of the brothers were not fond of. He was arrogant, opinionated, physically intimidating and a bully. He had been a boxer and for the last eight years he had been locked up lifting weights and cultivating his charming personality. He saw me from a distance and yelled my name.

"Fast Eddie, I thought you'd have gotten a patch by now!"

"No Al not yet."

"Why not? You've been around here forever taking advantage of the hospitality."

Al was baiting me and I knew we were going to have trouble, but not tonight. If something was going to go down it would have to be in the daytime. Fighting in the dark in a fight you can't win doesn't make much sense. Too hard to assess the damages afterwards. I walked on.

The barbecue had a line forming so Blue and I got in it.

"What is Al's trip?"

"He's trailer trash, never had nothing, never will, so he hates you. Think about it, he has no hustle, he lives off of the club."

"Well one thing's for sure: he's gonna want to push this issue and there's no way I can take him. Did you see that guy? He looks like a stack of cinderblocks! I'm done."

"Yeah you are. Well at least he won't be getting a virgin, you've had your booty whipped before."

We both start laughing.

"No kiddin' bro. I'll just stay out of his way until tomorrow and then I'll deal with it."

I got a plate full of tri-tip, potato salad and chili and found a place near the fire to sit down. I was thinking about the thing with Al. The guy was looking hard as a rock and the only way I could win was to creep on him from behind and catch him by surprise with a ball bat or a knife. The problem with that was he was a patch holder and I was a guest so there were political implications to consider. Even though most of the club couldn't stand Al and liked me, Al was a brother. It was simple; I had to lose even if I could win (which wasn't likely anyway, since he'd spent the last eight years boxing and lifting weights while I'd been shooting dope all day every day).

I realized that my butt was gonna get kicked and that there was no way around it except to pack up and sneak out of there like an egg-sucking dog. That was never my style.

CHAPTER 4

The evening was starting to get underway. I had a full belly and the mescaline was fading out of my system. A few colors were still playing around the edges of my vision but I was definitely coming down. The food had leveled me off considerably. The sun had gone down and there was a huge bonfire going in the middle of the campground. Someone had pulled a pickup truck up close and ZZ Top was playing "La Grange."

I didn't see Al anywhere and I was grateful for that. He had been pretty drunk earlier and I was hoping he had passed out in his tent.

"What are you gonna do about Al?"

"I don't know Blue, I'll just have to deal with it tomorrow. It's kind of a no-win situation. I guess I'm gonna get my clock cleaned and with any luck I'll run into him in about six months when he's all strung out on speed and has lost all that macaroni and cheese weight."

"You mean when he's as sucked up as you."

"Exactly my brother!"

That started us both laughing. It was true, guys got out of the pen all buffed out and cocky but if they stayed out any length of time their proclivities for drugs always evened out the playing field. Drugs and time were the great equalizers. If I'd learned anything in life, I'd learned that if you were a bully there would inevitably come a time when you would get yours.

I had learned early on to treat every one with dignity and respect. I was never unnecessarily cruel or thoughtless to anyone. I learned a valuable lesson on the yard at Tracy, or as it had been called for years the Gladiator School.

There was a guy from North Sacramento named Bubba. Bubba weighed about three hundred pounds and was not fat he was just a big motha. He was also a creep. He pushed his weight around and taxed anyone who wasn't affiliated with a clique. Bubba had been down about twelve years and was two weeks away from parole, but Bubba had a lot of enemies. This one day he was benching about four-hundred pounds and just as his training partners gave him a lift off, I noticed this skinny little dude in a big baggy yard jacket, and his beanie pulled down real low, snaking through the crowd. I was standing there with an old Orange County white boy named Lee. Lee said,

"Eddie, watch this!"

I looked up at the gun tower and noticed that the tower guard had conveniently turned to fill his coffee cup from a thermos. Just then this skinny guy I recognized as being from J wing pulled out a piece and as quick as a rattlesnake poked about ten holes in Bubba's chest. That four hundred pounds came crashing down on Bubba's forehead and his head blew up like a melon. Brains went everywhere. Bubba was history and that skinny little dude just faded in to the crowd. Lee looked at me and said,

"Just goes to show ya, if you're gonna be really big, you gotta be really nice."

I never, ever forgot that. I knew that no matter how it turned out with Al tomorrow that I would get my chance to get even when the playing field was level and there was no one around. I would take comfort in that tomorrow as I was getting a righteous whipping from a man who lacked the common sense God gave most people as a matter of course.

Right at that moment I decided to just enjoy the fire and Blue's company. I knew that we were always living on borrowed time. The next time I started my bike could be the last time. The next time we robbed a meth cook could be the end. We were for sure going to get busted at some point, that was a given. It was a precarious life we were living and at that moment there was an opportunity to laugh, be high, to enjoy the camaraderie of like-minded men. I could hear the music, anthems to our way of life, pouring out of that truck.

I could feel the heat from the fire on the front of my levis, and the chill of the night air nipping at my back. Tomorrow and its problems were a long way away and since tomorrow's problems are always coming no matter what you do. Why

worry about them today? The Bible says, *"Sufficient for today are the evils thereof."* Amen.

Blue pulled a pint of Jim Beam from his vest and handed it to me. I took a solid pull and felt the heat of it in my guts. A joint was being passed around the fire and I took a big hit. I usually didn't smoke pot, but hey, this was a party. I had heard that pot led to harder drugs so I tried to leave it alone.

We sat around the fire for a couple of hours telling stories and cutting it up but I couldn't really get this thing with Al off of my mind. I told Blue I was going to crash and I went to the tent and did my good night shot. Sleep came fast that night and I slept the dreamless sleep of the dead. I woke up early and lay there for a minute just listening to the birds and looking at the little droplets of condensation that had formed on the ceiling of my tent. I reached for my wake up and decided to relieve myself first. I pulled on my boots, unzipped the tent flap and stepped out. It was a glorious morning. The air was crystal clear and fresh. The sun was already warming the chill off of the grass and steam was rising from the ground. It was a picture perfect day. Perfect day for a whipping.

I remembered when I was in the pen and something would be ready to go down. If you were hanging with what we called a car, a group, then you were expected to represent that group if there was ever trouble. You reaped the benefits of having a group of fellas, getting stoned, drinking pruno, having a crew to hang out with. If there was trouble you had to stand up and be counted.

There was always the anxiety of knowing that when the doors opened in the morning it was on. Lying there the night before full of fear. Feeling the lump of a prison made shank through a paper thin mattress. Not being able to think of anything else. I don't know anyone who looks forward to getting stabbed so I think if a person says they're not scared they're either lying or stupid. I was scared, but I was also always the kind of person who would jump in first and give it all I had. People mistook this for

courage and I never corrected anyone, but the fact is I just can't take the anxious anticipation of the moment. Let's just get it on and get it over with. If I'm gonna die lets just get to it, please.

That's kind of how I woke up feeling that morning. Oh I knew I wasn't going to die, unless wounded pride had suddenly become fatal. And even my pride wasn't really going to suffer, because the whole scenario's outcome was predetermined. Still, it was probably going to hurt, and I was always concerned about my teeth.

I once hit a guy while he was in the middle of saying something and his jaw just broke like fine china. It also caused him to soil his pants and I remember being astounded at the realization that I'd just discovered the origin of the colloquialism, "I beat the crap out of him." I took note of the open mouth thing and hadn't uttered a word in a fight since. An open mouth means a weak jaw, but I was mainly worried about my teeth. Vanity might be a self-indulgence, even a weakness, but if you have good teeth they're worth worrying about.

I could see I was the first up so I decided to go ahead and do my wake up. Should I do speed with my H or just stick to heroin? Just as I was getting ready to step into my tent pondering my dilemma Blue poked his head out of his tent.

"Wait for me bro, I'll be right there."

I was sitting cross legged on my sleeping bag when Blue bent down through the tent flap.

"Don't be doing any crank this morning it will just mess your head up even worse, and this kind of brouhaha always messes you up. You've got a disease bro, I swear.

Man I have *never* had a more game running partner and I have never doubted your willingness to get serious but you sure do take it to heart!"

"Tell me about it. But hey, at least I can write good poetry."

It felt really good to be understood and Blue understood me well. One time we had been in a bar fight that turned really ugly. I stabbed some redneck that had hit Blue with a pool cue and before I knew it everybody was slashing and stabbing. At one point I slipped on what I thought was beer on the floor and it turned out to be blood. Lots of blood. The guy I stabbed was up under the pool table pouring his life out on that dirty barroom floor.

We got out of there with minor flesh wounds but when we got home I cried like a baby. I don't know why. I never thought to myself, "Why did that have to happen?" Or, "Oh, I wish I could take it back!" We were outnumbered and we did what we had to do and I would do it again in a heartbeat. The thing is I guess that I've never understood violence. I'm not okay with hurting people. It's kind of a paradox though because I've hurt lots of people and I've been badly hurt. I chose a lifestyle full of violent and treacherous people. Maybe I was just a poser after all. I was tripping on all of this, just holding my outfit in my hand and evidently staring off into space.

"Earth to Eddie, what are you tripping on boy?"

"Blue, do you think I'm for real?"

"Oh here we go. The hippie kid from Laguna has arrived on the scene. Bro if you'd have grown up in Bakersfield with an oilfield dad that drank his paycheck and a mom that did the mailman, instead of sitting in a lotus position listening to Ravi

Shankhar and reading The Tibetan Book of the Dead we wouldn't be having this conversation! Are you gonna do your shot or what?"

"Yeah I guess so, it's just that gee whiz, I'm starting to feel a little bit like a junkie."

We both laugh and get busy. About five minutes goes by, five minutes of absolute perfection.

"Eddie?"

"Yeah bro?"

"You are the most for real dude I ever met."

"Eddie get your sucked up little self out here!"

"Man you'd think he would wait until after we had some breakfast or at least some coffee!"

It was Al the early bird.

"I'll be right out, don't get your panties all bunched up."

"Think I ought to take a weapon?"

"Naw it's just gonna be a fist fight. You've got too many friends here for anyone to let it get that heavy. Nobody wants to see this go down except Al."

"Well you gonna come watch the fun?"

"Oh yeah Dog! I wouldn't miss it for the world!"

I unzip the tent flap and step out into the sunlight of an absolutely beautiful morning. One of those sparkly sweet summer mornings. Sunlight like honey dripping off of everything. Slight breeze in the air bringing with it that summery country smell, kind of like wheat. Al looks like he's been doing push-ups, his chest and triceps are all blown up and he's stripped to the waist and glistening with sweat. An attempt at intimidation that would work on a novice is lost on me. The fact is that getting all pumped up before a fight only tightens you up and slows you down, also makes you bleed more if you get cut.

I see Al looking at my arm and I look down to see a little river of blood going from where I just fixed down my forearm to my wrist.

"What a loser you are slamming dope at a club function!"

I'm walking up to him fast saying,

"I know how you feel man it's really an ugly thing."

Just as the words are leaving my mouth I'm throwing a quick jab that catches him totally by surprise and opens his lower lip. I follow it up with a quick right also to the face but it doesn't land as he slips under it quickly recovering from his surprise.

"No point in conversation is there Al?"

It's the only effective punch I land in the next three minutes.

There are probably fifty people watching but I'm intent on what is going on so I don't really even see them. Al comes in fast and hard in traditional boxing style, jab, jab, right hook, jab, right cross. I think he lands them all, the last punch closes my left eye and rocks me back on my heels. I recover a little and he comes in again this time with just a two-punch combination, a jab followed by a right cross. I duck under the right and step in and through, sweep his legs and he goes down.

I'm already done in from adrenaline and forgetting to breathe but I'm determined to make some kind of show. Hitting the ground really pisses Al off and he comes up like a freight train. He charges me and takes me to the ground. I land hard on my back and all the air comes out of me in a rush. He has my shoulders pinned to the ground with his knees and he's pummeling my face. He hits me about five times and blood is filling my mouth tasting coppery as it goes down my throat. I'm fighting choking and trying to steel myself against this rainstorm of fists and someone grabs Al and pulls him off of me. I'm fading out of consciousness but I hear a voice saying,

"That's enough brother. You proved your point."

The dirt feels as comfortable as a big feather bed and the morning sun is caressing me like a lover as I lay there on the ground. I just want to go to sleep right there but I hear Blue's voice,

"Well bro, that wasn't so bad; you actually got a couple of licks in, but your left eye is mangled. You might need a couple of stitches."

Blue gets me up on my feet, and a couple of brothers are there telling me I've got sand and that they're sorry it played out that way. I totally understand the whole deal and it's no big thing. Sometimes the cards are for you, sometimes they're not. I've been on the receiving and the giving end of all kinds of nasty and this was just another in a long parade of incidents that came with the life. A rather inconsequential one at that.

CHAPTER 5

"Blue, I think I'm gonna split."

"Hold still, I got one more stitch to go."

"You cool with me heading back to Sac?"

"Maybe you should just stick around here today and head out tomorrow."

"I don't know brother, this whole thing with Al got me a little riled up and I kinda just feel like takin' a ride by myself and blowin' out the pipes. You're havin' a good time, you should stay. I'll just head back up to Sac and reconnoiter our next move. Ouch punk, that needle looks like it was made for sewing saddles or boots or something!"

"Don't be a broad, I'm almost done. Okay man, so I'm like cool here but don't do anything crazy either on the road or in town until I get back. But really bro, how about you comin' out of the tent with blood drippin' down your arm, what a moron!"

"Man, I guess my blood pressure was up too high to stop bleeding."

"How's your blood pressure now?"

"It would probably be fine if you'd quit poking holes in my face with that stinking harpoon!"

"Hey you don't want a big scar on that pretty face do ya?"

"Scars on a man are sexy."

"Whatever, I'm ready for a shot."

We slammed and the shot took away the throbbing in my face, that was probably more from Blue's sewing job than from the actual injury.

"Hey, are you guys in there?"

It was Monkey Man.

"Yeah Bro we're here."

"Can I come in? We gotta talk."

"Sure, c'mon in."

Monk eased his huge frame in through the tent flap and sat back on his haunches.

"Just thought we ought to touch bases on that thing with the snitch. You guys kind of dropped the ball. You're usually more thorough."

He was looking at Blue and I tried to read his face to determine what he was thinking. He didn't seem angry in the least and the vibe from him had been good when we arrived.

Sometimes it was hard to tell what guys like Monk were thinking or what their reaction was going to be in these types of situations. To tell the truth I'd barely even thought about that whole series of events, even though they were what had taken us out of Orange County in the first place. I was having a good time in Sac, there were plenty of ways to make money and there was plenty of dope. I'd just figured it would sort itself out.

I thought I had better represent our position at that point.

"Monkey Man, you guys were never really clear on whether or not you wanted us to kill that snitch, and I thought about the whole thing and figured it would probably do to just discourage her from testifying. The only testimony she could give was on a few forged checks and anything else she might say would have to be considered hearsay.

Moose was caught dead to rights in possession of a grip of guns and a quarter pound of gag. He's an ex-con so he's gonna get a couple of years for the guns and at least three for the speed. Even if he was convicted on the checks it would only be eighteen months to two years and they would probably run them all concurrent so his time for the speed is all he's gonna do. I got the distinct feeling that this was more about revenge than prevention and frankly I don't feel it was worth us sweating a murder beef just because Moose was riled up about being burned by some skanky slut. It's not like we were getting paid. It's bad enough that we're running from a kidnapping case and hiding out five hundred miles from home. Dude, I haven't seen my kid in three months."

"Yeah well yer right, and the running is over. Moose pled out to possession of the weapons and the crank and the D.A. didn't file on the forgeries. That little girl you chauffeured out to Victorville never implicated you guys in her abduction. In fact it never came up, so you guys are home free. Interesting thing though, she's been writing Moose in county and has started running for him, so again you were right and all's well that ends well."

"So Monk is all this garbage with Al squashed or am I gonna have to go toe to toe with him again?"

"No, Al split about ten minutes after Grumpy read him the riot act for starting a problem with you. Al's been down a long time and he needs to just chill and see what's going on before he just starts stirring stuff up with people that are important to the club. He was out of line and when Grump called him on the carpet for it he got all butt hurt and packed it up."

"I think I'm gonna split too. I got some things in Sac to take care of. Blue's gonna stay here for the rest of the weekend but I kinda gotta go."

"Well you want to do a little of the Cocoa for the road?"

"Yeah sure that'll make for a colorful ride!"

Monk reached inside his colors and produced a big zip loc bag of the chocolate mescaline he was famous for and held it open. I reached in with my knife blade, pulled out about a tablespoon and gobbled it up.

"Bro that's a pretty hefty issue to be ridin' on!"

"Yeah well, high tolerance and all."

We all laughed.

"Just be careful, I don't want to be peeling you off of the front of some semi cuz you thought it was a gateway into another dimension."

"Naw, I can tell fact from fiction, I've had a lot of practice."

"Well Eddie it was good to see you. Hope you come back down South soon."

"Yeah, as soon as we wear out our welcome with the Sacramaniacs."

Monkey Man split and I told Blue I was gonna leave within the hour.

"Yeah well now that Al has taken off there's nothing stopping you, some people will probably think you went after him. That would be interesting.

"I really want to get back and make sure all of our interests are safe and sound. It's goin' pretty good right now and right now might be all any of us have comin."

"True that my man!"

"So, let's split up the dope and the money. I probably only need enough to get me through 'til tomorrow night. By then I should have made the collections of what's owed us. We've got twenty five hundred comin' from the gag we fronted Darlene and Wally owes us a thousand for the tools we took from that pirate body shop in Rio Linda."

We divided the drugs and the money we had and I packed up my bike. Some of the brothers came by to say so long and I was sad to be leaving. I started my bike and talked to Blue while it was warming up.

"You be careful Dog, yer eyes look like saucers."

"Yeah it's comin' on pretty good now. I'll tell you what, if I have trouble negotiating the dirt road up to the highway I'll come on back."

"Ha ha, yeah right, you do that."

We were both grinning as I gave him a hug goodbye and straddled my bike. Blue was one of the few people I ever spent a lot of time around that I never got tired of. He was a very intelligent dude, well read, creative, good looking. I'm not into dudes but no one wants an ugly partner in crime. Your crimey is a reflection of you and a couple of gang bangin', scooter ridin' outlaws ought to look good in my book. Hey, if you got it, flaunt it!

I let out the clutch and shot a little rooster tail of dirt and gravel at Blue.

"See ya later, if yer lucky!"

"Yeah okay bro!"

I was out of there. The dirt road up to the highway was a breeze, my front wheel finding its own way. That's the beauty of living life on a bike, its all second nature.

I could hear every little tic in the motor and envision the parts in there each doing their own job. Pistons going down turning the flywheels, cam lobes coming up on the pushrods opening the intake valves so the combustion chambers could pull in their mixture of gas and air. The mixture getting lit off pushing the piston down, exhaust valves opening to let the spent gasses get blown out my drag pipes.

I could see everything I heard because I'd built it. Nobody had ever laid a wrench on it but me. I built the motor, the tranny, I laced the wheels, I did the paint, and I lived on that bike. That's what made me a biker, the fact that the motorcycle and I were related, married.

I made the left turn from the dirt road on to Highway 132 at about noon. It was a perfect day: about eighty degrees and crystal clear. I was high as could be. Seeing colors and hearing the wind blow by my head had me grinning and I felt like I would start laughing at any minute.

I had been riding for about fifteen minutes when I heard some kind of noise coming from my clutch. I looked down at my open belt drive and watched my clutch hub spinning perfectly. Everything looked totally normal. Again I concentrated on the road ahead. It was slightly curvy and demanded attention. Still I kept hearing an odd sound. I glanced down again and this time I saw a little dragon about the size of a Chihuahua flying right next to my clutch. He was blowing little puffs of smoke that trailed out

behind him like a vapor trail. I thought that was really cool. I couldn't take my eyes off of him. He slowly turned his head towards me and I distinctly heard him say,

"You are going to eat it big time."

Just as he said this I saw the double yellow line curve under my bike and I looked up a second too late. It's true that everything goes into slow motion when you're about to die. I saw the thirty-foot embankment coming up on me and the Volkswagen sized boulders that lay strewn about the landscape appearing hungry to eat me and my beloved bike. The next thing I knew I was airborne at sixty miles an hour. It seemed as if it took forever to hit the ground. When I did, I hit on my front wheel and the impact broke my handlebars right off at the triple trees.

I was driven into the ground still holding my bars and I felt the bones in my right wrist crumble. My right shoulder slammed into the dirt and the pain shot into my brain like a flaming arrow. I felt my collar bone punch through the skin of my chest. I felt my ribs give way as I was punched into the dirt, my bike on top of me now, grinding me into the ground. It slammed me in the back knocking all the wind out of me and then somersaulted over me and landed in a heap, kicking up a huge dust cloud from the floor of the field I landed in. I could smell dirt, hot from the noon sun, and I could smell the weeds that I uprooted as I skid along the ground. And I could feel the pain. It exploded in my brain, intensified a hundred fold by the mescaline. The pain was so intense I could see it, and it looked to have a life of its own.

I lay there trying to take an inventory on my broken body. I could tell that my right wrist was very broken and my right collar bone had punched through the skin on my upper chest. I felt like I'd broken some ribs and my hips were not right. My face was skinned up pretty good and I had road rash all over the right side of my body.

I could hear the ticking of my motor and the sound of one wheel spinning, the brake rotor against the caliper making a little skush skush sound. I figured that any moment someone would come over the embankment to my aid but after fifteen minutes I realized that no one had seen me crash and I was out of sight from the road. What was I gonna do? I thought that if I could get up I could walk but any movement at all sent rockets of red searing pain through my shoulder and my arm. I tried to flip myself over onto my back and it was then I realized that something was very wrong with my hips. I could see my saddle bags about ten feet away in between me and my bike and I desperately wished I could get to them. I needed a shot of heroin right now.

Off in the distance were a few acres of agricultural land and the guy who owned it was putting up alfalfa. I could see his barn and beyond it the farm house. It was then I realized that I'd heard a noise and the reason I noticed it was that it had just stopped. The sudden absence of sound got my attention. It had been a tractor and just then I spotted it. It was sitting off to the right side of the field, a red Farm All with a disking rig behind it. Between the tractor and my forlorn position was a man and he was walking my way. As he got closer I could make out that he was in his early sixties, dressed in bib overalls with a checkered flannel shirt underneath. He was wearing a trucker hat, John Deere green. He had gotten close enough that I could see his weathered features and the stubble of beard that covered his work worn jaws. He looked like a kind man, his concern weighed heavily on his face.

"Hey son, are you bad hurt?'

"Yeah pop I'm pretty busted up but I'll live."

"I was just makin' the turn at the end of my field when I saw you flying through the air. Amazing you ain't dead! Let's have a look at you, do you think you can walk?"

"I'm not sure, I think I cracked my pelvis."

"Okay don't move I think I can get my tractor over here, it will take a minute I have to drop the disker and hook up the flat bed. Will you be okay?"

"If you can hand me those saddle bags I can make it 'til you get back.

"Okay here you go. I'll be right back."

He tossed the bags right by my left hand and turned to start back across the field.

"Sir?"

"Yeah son what is it?"

"Please don't call the cops, I mean I'm not wanted for anything bad I just would rather not deal with the law, ya know?"

"Don't worry son. I ain't callin' nobody you don't ask me to."

He turned to walk away.

"Thanks old man."

He just grunted and walked away.

I fiddled with the buckles on my bags and finally got them open only to discover I had opened the wrong side. Cursing my frustrated efforts I flipped the bags over and began my one handed assault on the buckles that normally took two hands to open.

It took a few minutes but I got it done and I got out an outfit full of heroin. There was no way I was going to be able to tie myself off so I went right for my main vein. I was in so much pain that the mescaline had begun to wear off replaced by endorphins and adrenaline. When the heroin hit me it was such a welcome relief. I positioned myself so I was kind-of leaning my left side up against one of the large rocks I'd narrowly missed on impact. Then, I watched through shimmering waves of mid day heat as my rescuer pulled his old tractor over to the barn and after a few minutes he was headed back my way.

The sound of his old tractor chugging its way towards me was comforting. He had hooked a small flat bed trailer up and I could see that he had put some kind of mattress on it. Thank God for the kindness of an old soldier. He made his way to my location weaving in and out of the rocks that peppered the landscape and before long he was at my side.

"Let's see if we can get you up on the rig. Can I put my arm around you and help you up?"

"Yeah, I think I can handle it, its either that or lay here and wait for the vultures."

"Okay here we go."

He got his arm around my waist and as he lifted I pushed off as best I could with my legs.

I could feel the strength in his old work worn body as he helped me onto the trailer.

Sometimes you run in to people who see a need and just fill it. They don't stop to think about the differences, no prejudice, just a willingness to assist, a core kindness that supersedes any cultural, or economic differences. This was that kind of man.

"You ready to ride? I'll try to stay away from the bumps."

"Yeah I'm good, let's go."

As we slowly made our way across the field toward the house. It occurred to me that I had been in more than a few wrecks in my time, and each time it was like a punctuation mark in my life. Something was gonna change because of it. I was curious as to where this little twist of fate was going to take me. I've always liked unexpected change and I felt through the wall of pain in my body a twinge of excitement, excitement at the coming of the unknown.

I had no idea what the immediate future held, but I was was grateful for this old man. We pulled in to the yard in front of his old ranch style house. It was shaded by a huge old oak tree and there was a gentle breeze blowing through the branches. He had built a fountain out of river rock next to the porch and the combination of the breeze in the tree, the dappling of the sunlight through the canopy of that old tree, and the sound of the water spilling out of the fountain was narcotic. I was deeply moved and I said,

"This is such a beautiful place, how long have you been here?"

"I built this place with my wife when we moved out here in 41. We raised two sons here. One of them, Bo, is thirty five and Billy is twenty nine. We finally got them off to college and the next year Joanne was diagnosed with breast cancer. She fought hard but

five years ago she finally lost the fight. She was a trooper right up to the end. I've been here by myself ever since. Bo and Billy been tryin' to get me to sell the place and move to Fresno but I just can't. We poured our hearts into this place, it's paid off and I make enough farming a hundred and twenty acres to make a little money. I want to die on this old place. Well boy, lets get you inside and try to make you comfortable. I'll have Billy come out and help me get your bike loaded up and in the barn."

"Sir, I sure am grateful for your kindness but I don't even know your name."

"Name is Joseph Miller, originally from Lawton, Oklahoma. Son of a farmer's son and not afraid of a hard days work or a long night alone."

"My name is Eddie Wilkins and I work when I have to and quit when I can. I did my basic training in Lawton Oklahoma at Fort Sill, so we've got that in common."

"Let's get you inside."

Old Joseph helped me off the trailer, up the porch steps and into the house.

It was a very beautiful home that showed pride of ownership and thoughtful design. The floor was oak in the living room, which was sprawling. There were hand-woven rugs throughout which had been made to compliment the rich coffee color of the walls. There were a lot of large windows that invited in the light and warmed the place. Sunlight spilled like caramel over the rich leather furniture and one entire wall was bookshelves filled with hundreds of handsomely bound books.

On the far wall was a huge fireplace made of river rock with a gargantuan mantle of oak. On it and on all the walls was this man's life. Beautifully framed photographs of him and his wife when they were young were everywhere. She was a gorgeous woman with flaming ruby hair and lively dancing green eyes. There were pictures of their sons growing up and then I saw pictures of one of the boys in a cop's uniform. My heart leapt in my chest. Joseph saw my expression and said,

"That's Billy. He's a Modesto cop, but don't you worry, he's a fair man and not likely to ask you too many questions or cause you any trouble."

"Well that's sure good to know Joseph."

I didn't know why this man inspired so much trust in me but he did. I felt safe in this old ranch house. He got a big quilt and spread it out on the huge overstuffed leather sofa and he left the room for a minute and came back with a couple of large down pillows. He helped me move from the chair I was sitting in onto the couch. It enveloped me like my mama's arms as I let out a huge sigh of relief.

"Joanne spent her last days right here at home and I have a lot of her pain medication left. Its all past the expiration date but it might still be good. Do you need something?"

"Yeah that would be great."

I didn't know how long I would be here but there was no way I was gonna shoot dope in this kind man's house. Respect for respect. He left the room and I heard him tinkering around in the kitchen. The refrigerator opening, ice cubes clinking in a glass, a cupboard opening and closing, the unmistakable rattle of pills in a prescription bottle. He appeared with a tray that held several large bottles of meds and a large glass of iced tea, along with some peroxide and bandages.

"Here we go. We'll have you patched up lickety split."

Joseph set the tray down on the coffee table and unscrewed the cap from the peroxide.

"It looks like you were in a scrap before you wrecked that machine of yours."

I told him briefly about my encounter with Al as he worked on my injuries. He had hands as worn looking as the trunk of the old oak in the front yard but they were efficient and gentle. After he had patched me up he sat there for a minute just looking at me. I had the feeling he was going to say something but he just shook his head and smiled a kind of conspiratorial smile. Then he sighed and stood up. At that moment I wanted to talk to Joseph like I never wanted to talk to anyone before. I wanted to tell him that I wanted to be like him but that my life had somehow taken on an inertia of its own and that I was powerless to stop the incoming tide of drugs and crime. I didn't always feel this way.

Sometimes I was happy with my life even dedicated to it but when I was around a man like this, in his home seeing his life in the place, the work of his heart and his hands, I yearned for something different. Joseph turned to leave.

"I'll just leave you to your own devices with these pills. I've got the feeling you know your way around with 'em."

"What no, 'On a scale of one to ten what is your pain level?"

He chuckled and headed for the front door.

"No it's pretty obvious yer way past a ten. I'll call Billy and ask him to come out when he finishes his shift and don't worry there won't be any trouble. Oh that reminds me, you probably want to call someone."

He brought the phone over to me and set it on the end table where I could reach it and headed again for the front door.

"You gonna be okay? I gotta get this disking done."

"Yeah I'll be fine I'm just gonna call my friend and see if I can persuade her to come and pick me up. I'll be out of your hair real soon."

"Don't worry about it, stay as long as you need."

"Thanks Joseph you're a good man. Thanks very much."

"You'd do the same. I can see it in you."

I listened to the clump clump of his boots across the porch and I began to assess my situation. It had been about an hour and a half since I wrecked and the pain had settled in to a slow droning numbed somewhat by the huge shot I'd done when Joseph went to get the tractor but it still loomed large. My collarbone had slipped back under the skin and Joseph had put a bandage on it but my right wrist had swollen to huge proportions. My hand looked like an inflated surgical glove. The ribs on my right side hurt terribly and I knew I was going to need a doctor soon. If I could get Stormy to come and get me I could handle the trip back to Sac and go to the hospital there.

I inspected the bottles of pills Joseph had left me; there were three. One was Morphine Sulphate, one was Demerol, and one was Lortabs, an extra strong version of Vicodin. I shook three out of each bottle, thought about the expiration date, and shook out two more from each. I popped them in my mouth and began chewing them up to release their wondrous powers more rapidly. When I had a mouthful of bitter paste I washed it down with iced tea. Due to my huge tolerance for drugs I considered taking more but thought I'd wait a little bit to see how much strength was left in the meds.

I reached for the phone and dialed Stormy's number. She picked up on the fourth ring.

"Where are you?"

"I left the run early and I had a wreck on the bike."

"What, are you kidding me Eddie?"

I could hear the irritation born out of fear tingeing her voice. Since Ricky's death she had been really protective of the boys.

"I'm gonna be okay I just need you to come and get me."

"Where are you?"

"I'm at an old farmer's house on highway 132 about thirty miles East of Modesto."

I realized I hadn't gotten the address from Joseph and that I'd have to wait until he got back to give Stormy directions. I told her as much.

"Okay I'll wait for you to call, in the meantime I'll hook the trailer up to the Ranchero so I'll be ready. Do you need me to bring anything, have you got enough dope to stay right?"

This was the first time Stormy had ever asked me a question like that and I wondered what she would do if I said I was out. Probably hit up that weasel Jack.

"I'm okay"

"Edward."

"Yeah?"

"I love you, I don't want to lose you. I'm sorry if I sounded pissed."

"It's okay. I understand. I love you too and you're not going to lose me."

"What did you break?"

"My collar bone, some ribs and my wrist."

"You must be in some terrible pain."

"Actually I'm not bad." I said, and I realized this was true because the meds were hitting me like a freight train. So much for the expiration dates.

"Listen Storm, I'll call you as soon as Joseph gets back with the directions, and thanks."

"Don't thank me Eddie, I really do love you. I'd do anything for you."

"Okay, I'll call you in a while."

"Bye."

We hung up simultaneously and I shifted around a bit to get comfortable as the drugs hit my body like a wave.

CHAPTER 6

As I looked around that beautiful room again I got that feeling. It was a feeling of having missed some really important information, some knowledge that had escaped me, a knowledge that most people got at birth. I felt like I'd been left out of the loop on a common understanding about life that had been kept a secret from me. As the pain killer's effects intensified I found myself marinating on the circumstances of my life. How did I get to this place? Why wasn't I like Joseph's son Bo? How had normalcy, whatever that was, so neatly evaded me. I never woke up on a fine summer morning and thought to myself,

"I really want to be a junkie and spend my life doing crime and time."

One rebellious and reckless decision after another had brought me to this place and as I lay there I went back in time sort of trying to take an inventory of those decisions.

I started to drift into a cavalcade of memories and before long I was a kid again about six and I could hear my mother talking to a client downstairs in her little dress shop in Laguna Beach. I was sitting on the floor in our modest studio apartment above.

"I got a call from a woman who owns a boutique in Puerto Vallarta and she has asked me to come and head up her design team." It was my mother's voice.

"That's wonderful, are you considering it?"

"I think so, but there's Eddie to think about, school and the language difference. It's just such a huge change."

"Could you leave Eddie with his father until you checked into schooling and found a place?"

At that point I needed to hear better so I bounded down the stairs and skidded to a stop at my mother's feet.

"Eddie slow down, you'll knock Marion off of the platform."

"Sorry Mom. What are you guys talking about?"

My mother was on her knees holding a pin cushion and was pinning up a hem on a black and gold caftan that was encasing the beautiful form of her high school friend Marion. Even at six years old Marion's tall willowy body and her cascading honey colored hair were a marvel to me.

She had been my mother's dear friend since they were teenagers and had always been a faithful customer. As she stood on the wooden alteration platform in the middle of the shop, he seemed a hundred feet tall. She looked down at me and smiled.

"You might be moving to Mexico my little prince."

"Mom, is that true?"

I could feel an incredible adventure coming on.

"Yes Honey, I have a job offer and I'm considering it seriously."

"Let's go Mom, let's go! It will be great, a great adventure! Is it by the beach? It has to be by the beach!

"Yes honey it's right on the beach, a beautiful beach with water the color of turquoise and as warm as your bath."

"Oh Mom let's go, right now, I'm ready!"

"You know Gail that's what I love about him he's just like me, always ready for anything."

"Yes, he gets it from his father, ready to take off for the unknown at the drop of a hat."

My mother and father had gotten a divorce when I was four. They had met at the college for foreign trade and after school they had married and moved back to where they were both raised in New Jersey. Shortly they moved to San Francisco where my father went to Stanford to continue his education. After that they moved to Laguna Beach California. My father worked for a pharmaceutical company in L.A. and my mother went back to designing clothes, something she had done since she was a model for Neiman Marcus at sixteen years old.

In order to avoid a daily sixty mile commute between L.A. and Laguna my dad had an apartment in Hollywood. He was an intellectual, speaking eleven languages and possessing a very inquisitive mind. His passion was literature and as a result he began hanging out in the coffee houses and jazz clubs around L.A. on the evenings that he stayed up there.

The upshot of it was that he tuned in, turned on, and dropped out.

It wasn't long before his hair got long and his absences even longer. My mom wasn't ready for a beatnik husband and before long their marriage came apart. They remained friends and I remained with mom. It was hard on my mom. She sold our house on Ruby Street and rented a place on Pacific Coast Highway near Wood's cove that had a shop area downstairs and a studio apartment upstairs.

I remember my mom crying one night after she had given me a pan of Jiffy Pop and sat me down in front of the TV. I was happy as a lark getting to eat popcorn for dinner. It took me years to understand my mom had been crying because popcorn was all she had

to give me. This opportunity to work for an established clothing line in a place like Puerto Vallarta was a Godsend.

Within the month my mother had closed down the shop and on a gloomy May morning we were in my grandmother's old Cadillac headed up the 405 Freeway to Los Angeles International Airport.

The line at the check in counter was full of dark skinned people who dressed oddly and spoke a language I didn't understand. I had seen a few Mexicans before but had never really studied them. In front of us in line was a family. The father was wearing a cowboy hat and sandals, which I thought was a strange combination. The mother was wearing a huge billowy skirt and a white blouse with lots of embroidery and from behind the folds of her skirt peered a pretty little brown face. This little girl was about my age and she kept sneaking peeks at me from the folds of her mother's clothes. I raised my hand and wiggled hello with my fingers. She waved back and giggled shyly. Kids don't need to speak the same language, they can communicate on an entirely different level.

I knew right then that life was about to get really, really good.

As we made our final descent to land at the airport in Puerto Vallarta I had my face pressed against the glass of the small porthole so I could see the place. I'd never seen anything so beautiful. There were verdant green mountains surrounding a lush valley floor that opened up to the turquoise ocean. In the distance off to the South I could see a river flowing out to the sea.

As the tires chirped out the announcement of our arrival my heart was pounding in my chest. The plane was taxiing towards the terminal when I saw them.

"Mom what are those?!"

"Oh honey, those are iguanas, I think they must like to lay in the sun on the tarmac. Aren't they beautiful?"

"They are so cool!"

They were only about three feet long, but to me they looked like huge prehistoric beasts and I immediately envisioned myself running through the jungle chasing them with a spear. I was about to go completely native. If my mother had known exactly how native, she would have had occasion to rethink her plans.

As we stepped off of the plane the rush of hot, wet, fragrant air that hit me was like nothing I'd ever tasted before. I say tasted because it went in through my nose and permeated my entire being. It was such a total sensory invasion that it made my heart race with anticipation. I could smell fruit and flowers I'd never smelled before: I could smell tortillas and chicharones cooking, I could smell animals and all the smells of hard working unwashed humanity, sweat, urine, feces, but above it all and taking it's rightful place as king was the pungent odor of rain-drenched, sun-baked jungle.

The rapid-fire staccato of so many beautiful dark-skinned people was a symphony and my head was swimming. My imagination had caught fire. My curiosity was a raging inferno.

After we retrieved our luggage and got through customs we headed out to the front of the terminal. At that time in 1963 there were five taxis in Vallarta but my mother was stunning in her strappy sandals, caftan, Ray Ban Wayfarers, with her hair held back in some piece of fabric she had woven in to it. We were able to get a cab fairly quickly.

"El Rio Hotel por favor senor."

"Claro que si senora!"

The old El Rio Hotel was right on the Rio Cuale next to the beach called Los Muertos. Our room faced the river and we could see all the way south to the end of the Bahia De Banderas. As my mother unpacked our somewhat meager possessions I drank in the scenery out of our window. Women were washing clothes on stones while small children frolicked in the water. Dogs that all appeared related by one trait or another ran about chasing the children and each other. There was a carcass of a very large sea turtle in the sandy bank of the river and huge vultures would land and somehow manage to tear off a meager strip or two before the dogs would chase them away. The thing I noticed most was that all of the people were laughing, singing, or just smiling contentedly.

"Mom can we go out there?"

My sense of curiosity was growing into a huge insatiable hunger.

"Honey, look down the beach, do you see the restaurant with the palapas in the sand?

"What is a palapa?"

"It's an umbrella made of palm fronds."

"Yeah I see it."

"Well we have to meet my new boss there in about fifteen minutes; we can walk across the river and down the beach and while we're talking you can swim in the ocean."

"Allriiight!"

My mom was humming to herself and I realized it was the first time I had heard her do that in a long time.

"Mom?"

"Yes honey?"

"You're happy aren't you?"

"You know baby? I am, I truly am!"

Five minutes later we were walking out of the hotel lobby onto the cobble stone streets of our new home. It was loud but friendly sounding, nothing at all like the busy city sounds of downtown L.A. that I had become accustomed to on my trips to the big fabric warehouses with my mother. That place seemed somewhat cold and impersonal, very grey, but here it was a warm and inviting busyness. We made our way down the street, that before long would be as familiar to me as my own belly button, and out to the river. We crossed on stones spaced just the right distance for an adult to step but a little kid had to hop. Everyone on the river's edge stopped what they were doing to watch us pass. Even the dogs and the vultures stopped their game of chase. The turtle would have been watching as well but his eyes were probably the first morsels to be pilfered after his death. There was a group of young boys kind of keeping abreast of us as we walked and they were taunting me.

"Que pasa gringo?" snorted one who seemed about my age.

"Donde vas cabron?" chimed another who was obviously a year younger than me.

The leader was silent and was watching me with sort of mild curiosity. He seemed the same size and weight as me but a year or so older.

He had the brooding self confidence of a natural leader and acted as if his followers were a nuisance that he tolerated lovingly.

"Toma gringo!"

I heard it at the same time I felt a rock whiz in between my mom and me.

I reacted before I had a chance to think. I charged the leader and even though he hadn't been the one to throw the rock I somehow sensed that I needed to attack the head.

I went in with my head low and caught him in the midsection and we both tumbled into the river. The next thing I knew I was at the bottom of a pile of young boys flailing arms probably landing on their compadres as much as on me. I heard the clatter of hooves on the river rock and suddenly the boys scattered. I looked up and saw a beautiful horse and atop that horse was a vaquero, a Mexican cowboy, he looked down at me and once he determined I was okay he turned immediately to my mother and said in halting but clearly understandable English,

"I am so sorry Mrs. lady, please forgive these young boys, they are too wild and have no manners."

My mother replied in perfect Spanish,

"Todo esta bien senor, y muchas gracias, eres muy amable."

"Everything is fine sir, thank you very much, you are very kind."

With a sweep of his sombrero he said in Spanish,

"Your Spanish is very good, allow me to introduce myself, my name is Jesus Rodriguez de La Cruz."

"My name is Gail Wilkins and this is my son Eddie."

"Ahhh, Eduardo, much gusto, eres muy macho!"

That day I had a new hero. Jesus pointed to a stand of trees where a herd of about twelve horses were tethered.

"If you ever want to ride my young fighter you can find me there every day at this time."

"Gracias senor, I would like that very much."

The boys were headed off toward the beach in a raucous little tribe and I noticed they seemed to be heading to the same place we were. We said our nice to meet yous with Jesus and made our way across the hot white sand to the restaurant bar known as La Palapa.

Mom's new boss was waiting under a palapa where she had commandeered a table and a few chairs. La Palapa was a hangout for artists, actors, expatriates, and bohemians who had for whatever reason left the United States in favor of the laidback tropical lifestyle of Puerto Vallarta. It was full of very tan, relaxed and half drunk gringos carrying on very cerebral conversations, reading very thought provoking literature, or just scanning the beach through Ray Ban Wayfarers with the smug expressions of someone who knows a secret that you wish you knew. I asked my mom if I could swim.

"Of course dear I'll wave for you when your food arrives."

In all of the excitement we hadn't eaten since we were on the plane and I was a bit hungry but the perfect little waves breaking in the bay were much more alluring than the thought of food.

I ran across the scorching sand and it felt so good on my feet. I dove in the water under a wave and exhaled a stream of bubbles through my nose. It was wonderful to feel the warm crystal clear water as my body knifed through the shore break. I felt the surge of resistance as I passed through the body of the wave and then the release as I emerged into the trough behind it. I broke the surface and the dazzling array of thousands of droplets of water sparkled and shimmered as they flew through the sunlight. Life was perfect.

I looked to my left and found myself face to face with the leader of the little tribe of antagonists from the river. Tentatively he smiled at me and turned to launch himself into a wave. He body surfed it expertly to the shore and stood up in the soupy, sandy foam at the water's edge. I immediately noticed that he had ridden the wave straight in to the beach not angling across the face as I'd learned to do from the surfers at St. Anne's Street in Laguna.

Another wave came and I launched myself into it turning hard to the right and flying fast across the face, getting inside the curl being effectively barreled. At the last second I ducked out the back of the wave and emerged feeling like I had made an impression. The young boy swam back out and without a word he caught another wave and duplicated my performance. The smile on his face was so magnetic and full of joy that I began to laugh.

"My name is Vicente, you are very good in the waves."

"I grew up in the ocean, and my name is Eduardo."

We had a definite language barrier but for the next hour we traded waves and laughter and a mutual respect began to develop. We were quite a pair. Vicente with his mop of hair so black it looked blue and his dark, dark skin, so dark in fact that when he smiled it made his teeth look an impossible white. Then there was me, golden brown from the sun with hair bleached white by the California sun and surf.

"Eddie, come on out now you need to eat!"

"Come on Vicente are you hungry?"

I pointed to my mouth then my belly.

He shook his head no but his eyes said yes. I got out of the water and ran up the beach to the palapa where a feast of tortillas, carne asada, pescado, and pollo were waiting.

"Did you make friends with the boy from the river hon?"

"Yeah mom, his name is Vicente."

My mom stood up and took a few steps toward the water.

"Vicente! Ven aqui por favor, hay comida para usted tambien!"

Vicente bounded up the beach and unabashedly gave my mom a big hug, laughed and then stuck his hand out for me to shake. In that moment a bond was formed, and I had made probably my very first friend.

CHAPTER 7

In the first month living in P.V. I was enrolled in a Catholic school on the North side of town and we had rented a little two bedroom house in the Colonia on the South side of town, the South side of the river. It really was the Barrio. We were the only white people in the entire Colonia, which suited me fine. It turned out that Vicente lived around the corner and our back yards faced each other.

Vicente had a beautiful sister named Maria who was my very first crush. Their house was made of hand-made brick with a palm frond roof; the floor was just very densely packed dirt. They had a gate and a curtain for a front door. Their mother cooked on an open hearth that was fueled by wood chips and there was always a big pot of frijoles simmering there. I would go by there and Vicente's mom would always grab me a tortilla, warm it and fill it with beans.

She was a happy woman running a happy family. Her husband was a laborer who worked long hard days mixing concrete by hand for the construction of commercial buildings and private homes. In those days there was no concrete plant, no concrete trucks. Sand was hauled up from the beach in burlap sacks atop burros. The man who had the string of burros was considered a big shot, a man of means. Vicente's father would remove the sand from the burro's backs and empty the sand into a pile.

Each sack probably weighed a hundred and fifty pounds and the man was not a big man. He would then shovel it into a trough where it would be mixed with gravel, calcium, silicon, lime and water, and hauled in buckets to wherever on the job it was needed. Vicente's dad Victor did this ten hours a day, six days a week and yet I never saw him raise his voice to his family or fail to be a loving father and husband. They had nothing but each other and a strong faith in God and the church and they were happy.

My first day of school Vicente and I walked into town together. As we walked other kids joined us until there was about six of us. I could sense the trepidation of the other young boys about the friendship that Vicente and I had formed. I wouldn't say there was a racial prejudice just a suspicion of something they didn't understand. I was dressed in a uniform exactly like theirs but I was as different as I could possibly be. I heard a dour faced boy talking to Vicente with a decidedly bitter inflection in his voice.

The other boys were batting at rocks with sticks as we walked along and didn't seem to be paying much attention. Suddenly the boy who had been talking with Vicente lunged at me and head butted me just under the chin. He was yelling a bunch of stuff I didn't understand and we fell onto the cobblestone street in a heap. We wrestled and I ended up on top but I sensed this was not a time for me to best my young adversary.

I knew I needed to make a good showing so as not to appear weak but it seemed prudent to let this boy win. I realized that in the ten short days I had been in P.V. I had learned quite a bit about myself. I found that I was an open hearted boy who genuinely liked people and that I didn't feel the least bit uncomfortable with this cultural change. I seemed to just understand what was going on with these confrontations and there was no fear of physical altercations and even though I had never been in a fight previously I possessed an unusual calm and clear headedness.

I was willing to fight but in my heart I wanted to make friends and learn everything I could about these people, their customs, I wanted to know their very hearts. I had fallen under a spell the moment we landed at the airport and I had a sense of being on a precipice about to launch into flight. I was about to be born into an adventure that would form so much of my character both good and evil and would shape my way of thinking for a lifetime.

The boy I fought with ended up on top and Vicente pulled him off of me, I had a puffy knot under one eye and my clothes were covered in dirt but other than that I was fine. We continued on with that boy staying ahead of us about a hundred feet but occasionally glancing back to lock eyes with me. It was very difficult to read his expression but I didn't really sense any malice just a kind of curiosity and maybe a little suspicion. As far as I knew I was the only white kid in town so it stood to reason that I was going to have to prove myself. I felt like I was doing a pretty fair job so far.

Vicente elbowed me and when I looked at him he simply said, "Maria." Suddenly it was clear, this boy was jealous of the fact that I lived so close to the object of his affection. Why would I be a threat? At seven years old it was something I didn't understand.

I walked into class dirty, bruised and torn and the nun who was attending to the dozen or so boys looked at me with at first surprise and then compassion. I really didn't understand the point of my being in this class in the first place. The lessons were all in Spanish and I had mastered all of maybe five words and relied mostly on hand gestures in communicating with Vicente. The nun pointed to an empty desk in the middle of the room and I sat.

The day went by and at first I tried to pay attention and soon the teacher's voice turned into a steady droning and I found myself wandering deep into my imagination. I was thinking of the beautiful green verdant jungle that surrounded me and this beautiful little pueblo. I dreamed of following the river up deep into the mountains. I imagined discovering deep pools with a canopy of jungle vines and swinging out over the water and plunging into the crisp clear water.

I made up my mind that day that the classroom was not the best place for me to get an education. This turned out for me to be a lifelong sentiment. I would always prefer to be out in the world learning through experience rather than in a classroom learning from the experience of others. I was always a voracious reader and later on would often ditch school to go to the library. That hunger for the written word has saved me and until I went to Bible College I really had no formal education, only what I learned from reading.

After school I separated from my new crew most of whom were still filled with trepidation about me. I made my way through town weaving through the throngs of people who were mostly on their way back to work after the afternoon siesta. It was hot and people were moving slow. The afternoon had a dreamlike quality to it.

I walked toward the river hoping to find Jesus and his string of horses and I hoped he was still keen to teach me to ride. As I approached the river I saw the grove of trees where he said he would be and I saw them. About ten horses were languishing in the heat, heads drooping down, catching a nap on their feet.

Jesus was nowhere to be seen and I assumed he had gone home for lunch and siesta.

I introduced myself to each of the horses and I felt something quicken in my heart. These horses were so beautiful to me. Their eyes were so expressive, liquid brown and appearing to hold some precious secret. The rhythm of their breathing was very calming to me and they smelled good. I was lost in my mind somewhere, my hand absent mindedly stroking the neck of one of the horses. I felt someone behind me and turned to see Jesus watching me with a big grin on his face.

"Te gusto los caballos." *"You like the horses."*

"Yes very much."

"They seem at ease with you."

"They are very beautiful."

"Si, which one do you want to ride?"

I took to horsemanship the way a duck takes to water and it wasn't long before I was sort of working for Jesus. I'd show up at his house in the morning, groom and saddle the string, grain them up and then line them up at his front gate. Then I would go into his kitchen and his wife would give me a boleo, which is kind of a mini loaf of bread crunchy and chewy on the outside, soft and fluffy on the inside. She would slather it with butter, sugar, and cinnamon right out of their brick oven and then she would pour me a cup of strong coffee with a wedge of chocolate dropped in.

I was learning Spanish quickly and had at home begun refusing to speak English.

No one asked me why I wasn't in school. Vicente told the nuns at school that my family had moved away suddenly. I had developed a relationship with one of the horses, Maya, a sorrel colored mare who had as adventurous a spirit as I did. Jesus would let us leave at siesta time and I would bring Maya home at sunset.

My trouble with the ditching school thing began and ended in the course of one morning. It was about ten o'clock and I was riding Maya through town on the main street.

Jesus had needed to shoe horses and when I got there early in the morning he had Maya done already and told me to just take her out and ride, he'd see me at the river in the afternoon.

I had been spending my days with Jesus and the horses for about a month and every one in town was used to seeing this brown skinned, blonde headed little white boy riding Maya, either bringing up the rear of

Jesus' string or just the two of us headed to the river where we would follow it up into the mountains to explore.

Maya was prancing and I was riding tall straight and proud, whenever I was on her she was all spirit, full of life. We were deeply in love.

I saw the taxi coming up the street and I had a sense that it was a bad omen. It began to slow and then my mom's face appeared out of the back window. She was literally speechless.

"Alto! Alto!", she yelled at the cab driver."

"Uh, hola mama."

"Don't you 'hola' me young man, what are you doing on that horse and why aren't you in school?"

"I don't go to school mom."

"What? What are you saying Eddie, surely you go to school?"

"No Mom, I haven't been for a month."

"But why? And how could you pretend to be going to school all this time?"

By this time I had swung down off of Maya and we had started walking towards the river, towards the spot we had met Jesus almost six weeks previously.

"Mom what is the point of me sitting in that classroom all day when I don't understand enough Spanish to learn anything? I'm learning ten times as much helping Jesus. I'm learning Spanish so much more quickly out here in the town and I'm learning about horses. Jesus has practically given me Maya and in the afternoons we ride up the river and I meet people and explore. I'm learning way more out here that I could in some classroom. Can't I just stay out of school at least until I can speak Spanish enough to make sense of what the nuns are saying?"

"Is Jesus at home Eddie?"

"Yes Mom."

"Let's go, I'll swing up behind you."

My mom introduced herself to Maya and when she swung up and on it didn't seem to bother Maya a bit. My Mom had grown up on the back of a horse and I was hoping the ride to Jesus' house would bring her around to my way of thinking.

As we made our way through town we passed a great deal of people whom I had become acquainted with.

"Hola Eduardo, Buenos Dias senora!"

"Que Tal nino?"

"You seem to have won over the locals Eddie."

"I love it here Mom, I'm learning so much about people, and Jesus is teaching me so much about horses."

"Well we'll just see what we're going to do about this school thing after I talk to Jesus."

CHAPTER 8

We got to Jesus' house and he was just finishing shoeing, he had a smile on his face that said he had been waiting for this.

"Well I was planning on being mad at him but I can see that's going to be impossible.

What is it about him?"

"He has a pure heart Mom."

"Where do you learn these things?"

"From Maya I guess, she sees people for what they are."

We were at Jesus' house for a couple of hours and by the time we left my mom had made a deal with Jesus that she would pay him fifty dollars a month for him to tutor me in reading and writing which we would accomplish using whatever presented itself during the day. Street signs, advertisements for merchandise painted on windows, the text on a cookies wrapper, whatever printed word presented itself.

This was easy for me due to the fact that I was a sponge for any kind of knowledge and it soon became a great game that Jesus and I would play as went about our day. Jesus would read something that he saw and I would try to figure out where it was written and I would repeat it. My mom was to teach me math in the evenings.

I was with my mother at the beach one Saturday and all of the ex-pats were hanging out talking about John Huston's film, The Night of The Iguana. The film was being shot just south of Vallarta at a place called "La Jolla de Mismaloya."

Due in no small part to the presence of cast member Richard Burton and his wife Elizabeth Taylor, the set, attracted large numbers of paparazzi, made international headlines, and in turn made Vallarta world-famous. This was all the buzz and there were heated arguments.

One view was that of the die hard ex-pats who felt that their idyllic Mexican hideaway would become Hollywood-ized. The other faction believed that the attention brought by the renowned director and his stellar cast somehow made them special. Kind of like,

"Yeah we were in P.V. when Huston came, we were part of the deal."

Although they didn't express it in that fashion that was the impression I got. Total posers.

There was one man who stood out to me and he sat a little apart from the group.

He looked like he was mildly amused by all of this controversy. He sat back with his Kent cigarette and his glass of Oso Negro Vodka and just listened with a smirky kind of grin on his face. He had the face of an adventurer, handsome in a rough way with one eye damaged in some way. I would later learn that in fact his eye was glass and that he had blown it out as a child with a cherry bomb.

Later as the sun had set spectacularly on the Bahia de Banderas the group dispersed.

It was kind of a tradition for as many as possible to hop in a cab and ride-share to their various destinations around town. We ended up in the cab with that same man. I remember thinking it was no accident. His name was John Stewart and he was an architect who came to Mexico on a diving trip and fell in love with the culture and the lay of the land. He saw rightly an opportunity to create magnificent residences in a place where contstruction was cheap and an architect could build with incredible vision not constrained by beaurocratic limitations. That is, if a man had incredible vision, which it turned out John Stewart did.

As the weeks went by and my mom and John spent more time together I learned that he was a real macho man. The locals called him El Rey, The King, or El Oso, The Bear. He held the records for the deepest free dives and the largest trophys one of which was a fifteen foot long Saw Shark which he shot at sixty feet. He had a reputation for treating his workers with great respect and dignity, for which he was adored by the local obreros. In fact his superintendent over all construction was a man named Sauternino who would stay with Mr. Stewart until his death in 1993.

I could tell that my mom was in love with John and it wasn't long before they got married. I think I amused John Stewart. I know he saw in me that same recklessness and lack of fear that he himself had, the difference being that he had learned how to harness his in a positive way. He was a hard worker, a hard player, and a hard drinker but his vision to build and create maginificent architecture kept his demons under control.

I would be almost thirty six years old before I ever had a vision or a plan. I have to say that during those long years I did my level best to ruin my life and that while he was never an affectionate man he was always there for me. Enough said about that for now.

After I had been in P.V. for about six months I met Jesus' nephew, also named Jesus. He went by the nickname Chuy, pronounced Chewey. He soon became my second mentor. He taught me how to spear fish and to make a lobster gig with a stick and a large fish hook. He taught me how to choose the best branches to make a bow and arrows and he forged arrowheads out of metal and taught me how to assemble the arrows, fletching them and matching the shaft to the head for the best balance. He taught me how to live off of the land, what in the jungle was edible, what was medicinal, what was poison. Then he filled me with a poison that would forge my behavior for many years to come.

We were at a shack used by hunters deep in the jungle and we were eating tortillas and beans that we had brought along. Chuy reached over and touched my leg, then he leaned in and kissed my neck. What happened next was very confusing for me. I was seven years old. I had no idea or knowledge about this sort of thing. This was someone I trusted and loved. He had taught me so much and yet there was something very scary and strange about what was happening to me.

It felt good to be touched but it also somehow felt wrong. I didn't want to say anything that would jeapordize our relationship and right then I made a compromize. As long as he didn't hurt me I would do what he wanted so I wouldn't lose him. This went on for six months and during that time I did my very best to not think about it. Most of the time I was succesful but there were times when I would be alone and some still small voice in my head would tell me this was evil. It would tell me that I was evil. I was evil and I would always be evil.

One day I was riding Maya through town and it was on a religious holiday. I don't recall which one, but as I was passing the beautiful Catholic Church in the middle of town I saw an old woman dressed entirely in black making her way up the stairs to the front doors of the church on her knees. Half of her face had been disfigured by some disease. There must have been hundreds of stairs, because the distance between the street and the front doors of the church was probably fifty yards. I swung down from Maya and I walked over to get a closer look.

This was my very first experience with anything spiritual, my first ever thought about God. I looked up at that church, which was very imposing, beautiful but imposing. There was something very majestic about it and as I looked at this old frail woman making her way on her knees up those steps. Something touched me in my heart and I began to cry. This deformed old woman who must have suffered so much in her life was having a love affair with God.

By now at eight years old I was already a wanderer, detached from my family, a little island unto myself hurtling through life like a meteor. At eight years old I had already been drunk on Tequila, stoned on pot, smoked cigarrettes, and now I was being used as a toy by a thirty year old man. There I was watching that old woman in her act of love and worship with tears pouring down my face and for the first time, I felt the presence of God. In that moment I felt Him speaking to me saying,

"I love you my child and I will always be with you."

CHAPTER 9

Two weeks later I was on a plane touching down at LAX. It was the end of the Summer of 1964.

1964 gave us the Beatles, Lyndon Johnson, Vietnam, and the first Ford Mustang. 1964 gave me an attitude. My father and his second wife Faith picked me up at the airport. I remember walking up the jet way, into the terminal and seeing my dad with long hair and a beard. He had flowers woven into both.

He was wearing a Neru shirt with a leather vest over it and jeans tucked-in to knee high boots. He looked cool. His wife Faith was beautiful and she had a smile on her face that told me she was happy I was coming to live with them.

My only real memories of my dad started on my fifth birtrhday. He picked me up at a little citrus ranch that my mother and my uncle had in Vista, California. We lived there, my mom, my uncle, and my grandmother who was really my main caregiver. She taught me etiquette, taught me to read, to speak properly, (she was very proper), and she taught me to swim. My mom had purchased the place from a family whose daughter was an olympic swimmer and they had put in a twenty five meter pool. By the time I was four and a half I was swimming like a fish.

My dad drove down from Hollywood to take me out for the day. We got into his little square back VW and took off.

"Where are we going Dad?"

"We are going someplace really special but you have to keep it a secret, can you do that?"

"You mean not tell Mom and Grammie?"

"That's right my boy something just between us men."

"I guess I can do that."

We drove for about an hour and after the small talk was out of the way it was eerily quiet. What did we have to talk about? I was a five year old boy and he was an absentee father living the life of a single man in Hollywood. We drove for a little more than an hour until we reached back roads that wove in a meandering way through groves of oak, fields of planted alfalfa, and pastures with horses and cows. It was beautiful country and the summer heat brought a syrupy laid back quality to the day.

We turned off the road into a long driveway that was flanked on either side by oak trees and after about a quarter mile we came to a very tall wall made out of wood.

It reminded me of the outer perimeter wall of a western fort. In the middle of the large front gate there was a man sitting in a chair under an umbrella. I couldn't see beyond the gate because about ten feet inside there was a free standing section of wall that was to shield anyone at the gate from being able to see inside. You had to drive to the right after entering. The man under the umbrella had a clipboard and as my father pulled to a stop he was already checking something off.

"Hey Charles, good to see you!"

"It's good to see you too Mike."

"So that's the little man, eh?"

"Yes, Eddie this is Mike."

"Hello Sir, nice to meet you,"

"Nice to meet you as well young man. He's very polite Charles that's a good thing."

"Yeah he's a good kid."

I was wondering what was going on and what kind of a place we were going to. I could hear lots of people on the other side of the wall. I heard kids and in the distance I thought I heard the sproing sound of a diving board followed by the unmistakable sound of someone executing a cannon ball. I was getting excited and was beginning to expect some kind of huge amusement park like Disney Land or Knott's Berry farm.

My father put the VW in gear and we made the little jog to the right to get around the wall. The sight that greeted me caused my jaw to drop and my heart to pound in my chest. I felt the blood rushing in my ears, and I thought I was going to pass out.

There were people everywhere. There were old people, young people, kids, babies. There was a woman who was so pregnant she looked ready to burst. People playing horseshoes, people playing volleyball, people setting up picnics on the grass, people were just lounging in the sun on blankets and in lounge chairs, and every single one of these people was stark naked!

"Welcome to The Swallows Club son, happy birthday!"

I began to cry. I think maybe I was scared because I had promised to keep this a secret and I didn't know if I could. You see I desperately wanted to please my father. I knew for sure that I was the reason he left, that I had done something to drive him away. I rarely saw him and when I did I tried to behave like a perfect kid. Please and thank you, yes father, no father. I watched my posture and tried hard not to be a bother in any way.

He seemed strained like he didn't know what to do with me or how to talk to me.

His father had sired him at sixty years old and he was sent to boarding schools from an early age so he really had no idea how to do the "Dad" thing. So there I was crying and hating that I was crying.

"Eddie it's okay, really. I know this is kind of a big surprise but this is a totally natural thing. These are all totally normal people. Look at them and forget for a moment that they're naked. Do they look like weirdos or freaks to you?"

"No dad I guess not."

"Son they're just people who love to worship the sun and express their freedom without clothes."

"But why can't I tell mom we came here?"

"Well Eddie there are some things that I am going to teach you about life that your mom wouldn't understand. There are ways of looking at life that your mom would never approve of but that doesn't make them wrong. Can you trust me on this?"

"I guess so dad, but do I have to be naked too?" "Not until you're comfortable my boy."

We pulled into the parking area and got out of the car. There was another couple who were arriving at the same time and they had a son about my age

"Hey Charles you brought your boy, outta sight!"

"Yeah it's pretty far out but I think he's a little shocked. Jim, Donna, Donny this is my son Eddie, and today is his fifth birthday. "

"Nice to meet you Eddie, my boy Donny will be five in two weeks that makes you both Leos, you should get along just fine."

I looked at Donny and he was already shucking his clothes as fast as he could.

I looked from him to his dad and then to his mom. She was very beautiful, dark skin, very long black hair. They were a beautiful family.

"Hey Eddie can you swim?"

"Yes I love to swim."

"C'mon lets go, the pool's right up there."

I looked to my dad who by this time was wearing only tennis shoes, very weird.

"Sure go ahead. I have a volley ball tournament starting pretty quick, Donny will take good care of you. Donny if you guys get hungry just put lunch on my account okay?"

"Okay thanks a lot! C'mon Eddie let's go to the pool!"

I felt really strange at first. I had never been naked around anyone but my grandmother and my mom. I had also never seen adults naked, or little girls, or teenage girls. Donny and I spent the entire weekend in the pool. At night we camped out under the big sprawling oak trees trying to scare each other with scary stories and talking about how different boys were from girls. By the end of the weekend I was totally comfortable and it all seemed quite normal.

The only problem was that it was anything but normal and so began a trend in my life that allowed me to gradually and incrementally become accustomed to almost anything no matter how far south of "Normal" it was.

So in 1964 my mom shipped me to live with my dad and his wife Faith whom I fell in love with immediately. She was beautiful and when I walked toward them coming off the jetway she ran to me and scooped me into her arms. She buried my face in her hair and it smelled like jasmine, patchouli, and sunshine. She said,

"I feel like I've been waiting for you my whole life!"

In the years that she and my dad would be together she would pour her heart in to me and I know now that she desperately wanted a child of her own. My father was not really father material and realized that about himself after being saddled with the responsibility of me. Tragically for lovely Faith, who would have made a wonderful mother, as she was to me, after she and my father divorced she married a man just like him who also had no interest in having children.

It's incredible to me how people will continually make the wrong choices in their lives and suffer the consequences and yet return to the same mistakes time and again. People who are intelligent and forward thinking in many areas of their lives just somehow have a proclivity for disastrous choices. That in fact is exactly my life story.

"Eddie I feel like I've been waiting for you my whole life! Let's go home okay? I've got your room all fixed up. I hope you like it!"

My father seemed very uncomfortable, his smile seemed kind of pasted on and as we walked down the corridor he put his hand on my shoulder and it felt like it was done with a great deal of trepidation. Faith had my hand in hers and because of her I felt that everything would be okay.

We made our way through the hustle at LAX and finally got through customs and out to the parking structure. My dad still had the cool VW sqare back, only now it had a symbol painted on the door.

"What is that dad?"

"That's a Japanese word, "Ronin."It means a wandering Samurai, who has no lord to serve. A ronin was a masterless samurai during the feudal period of Japan. A samurai became masterless from the ruin or fall of his master, or after the loss of his master's favor or privilege. Since a ronin did not serve any lord, he was no longer a samurai, as the word samurai came from the verb saburau which was the Japanese for "to serve."

The word ronin literally means "drifting person." According to the Bushido Shoshinshu (the Code of the Samurai), a ronin was supposed to commit seppuku or suicide upon the loss of his master. One who chose to not honor the code was "on his own" and was meant to suffer great shame. However a ronin was given equal respect to master-sponsored samurai by the general population and were actually preferred by Zen masters, artists, philosophers over their more obedient and faceless samurai counterparts. As thoroughly bound men, most samurai resented the personal freedom enjoyed by wandering ronin.

Ronin were the epitome of self-determination; independent men who dictated their own path in life, answering only to themselves and making decisions as they saw fit. Miyamoto Musashi was a famous Japanese samurai, who became a ronin and is considered by many to have been one of the most skilled swordsmen in history. Musashi became legendary through his outstanding swordsmanship in numerous duels, even from a very young age.

He was the founder of the Niten-ry style of swordsmanship and wrote <u>The Book of Five Rings,</u> a book on strategy, tactics, and philosophy that is still studied today. I am a ronin, a wandering man lending my sword to whatever cause seems right and true."

"Oh, okay, Thanks dad, that's cool,"

That was my dad, a genius with very little to say until you got him going. He truly was a ronin. He wandered through life alone no matter who he was with and he lived in the vast caverns of his mind which were huge libraries of languages and literature. He thought outside the box and was often misunderstood but he didn't care. He was a genius with a camera and at that time in his life that was how he made his living. His camera was his sword and he lent it out to whatever cause seemed right and true.

CHAPTER 10

I had no idea where we were going, I had never been to Los Angeles before.

I had only the memories of this being the place that stole my dad out of our lives.

We had been a family and something had gone wrong. I often felt as if somehow it had been my fault but my mom had explained to me that my dad had to follow his dream and because of that they had grown apart. This was the place where his dream lived and now it was a place where I would live. Somehow I knew I wasn't a very big part of the dream.

In the car Faith was twisted around in her seat gushing all over me and I sensed that she was normally not a gusher, but I was a big part of her dream. Her dream was having a family and no doubt if she could show Solo Guy her mothering skills he would fulfill her dream. But I know she was always all the way real with me in the expression of her feelings and in the next few years she became my mom, my confidant, and my best friend. Still, looking at my dad's face in the rearview mirror he looked like a man who had just been sentenced to death.

He hated the idea of this intrusion in his life and to his credit he faked it fairly well most of the time, but I always knew. He had absolutely no clue about fathering or family and seeing his wife take to it like a summer wind scared him right down from the joint they no doubt smoked on the way to pick me up.

We went north on the 405 to Sunset blvd and meandered through Brentwood and Beverly Hills. I marveled at the huge homes and wondered what Vicente and Maria would think. There were gazebos in the yards of some of these homes that you could fit three of Vicente's house in. As we came into Hollywood I got my first picture of the 60's in full swing. Sunset Blvd went in the blink of an eye from the homes of the rich and powerful to the haunts of the young, rebellious and loaded.

It wasn't the full on hippie scene that it would be by the summer of love, 1969, but it was in that embryotic state where you could sense change in the air.

"He's already been to the Swallows club and McConville what's the big deal?

He's seen a woman naked before.

"That may well be Charles but he's never seen me naked before and it's important that I make the right impression from the start."

"So what, we're going to change our lifestyle because my son has come to live with us?"

"We may have to make some adjustments yes."

"Do you think there is something wrong with the way we live our lives? These are fresh new times and the old, straight conventional way of living is like a prison. I want to raise my son in the same way I've been living, in freedom."

I felt like saying,

"I don't care what you people do, I've got my own deal and you aren't part of it.

You don't have to change a thing for me in fact just pretend I'm not there."

I was so angry at having been sent away so my mom could pursue her life with John Stewart that I was determined not to allow anyone or anything behind the walls that I was constructing in my heart. Seeing the tenderness on Faith's face and the life sparkling in her eyes made me think it might be a difficult task.

The following Monday I was enrolled in Wonderland Avenue School and in spite of my seething anger I felt a certain excitement. One of the main causes of this excitement was a vision of beauty with long blonde hair and the ungainly but somehow graceful motions of a colt. Her name was Jenny Thorton and I would later learn that she was the daughter of popular afternoon music show host, Floyd Thorton. Wonderland Ave school was teeming with the children of people in the, "biz."

There I was suddenly plunged into this big school that seemed to move at great speed. In my obstinacy I had refused to wear the American clothes that my dad had bought for me and was wearing totally Mexican garb complete with huaraches. I think my father allowed that little bit of rebelliousness being fairly sure I would be ridiculed into conformity. I had sworn I was going to refuse to speak English but my resolve in that arena disappeared the minute Jenny said,

"Hi!"

She was astoudingly pretty. Her eyes were completely and totally blue not one irregularity. Her skin was like silk, her teeth perfect and she just came up to me and started telling me all about herself. I was mesmerized. She talked for five minutes, and then said,

"Okay, see ya later."

She never spoke to me or looked at me again.

Watching this exchange was a young girl who was about to become my first and best friend. Her name was Michelle and she too was very pretty but in a completely different way. No, you know, I wouldn't say Michelle was pretty she was alarming. She carried herself like a much older person. You hear people described as old souls, well that was Michelle. She had long sandy brown hair and green eyes. She had a sprinkling of freckles across the bridge of her nose and she had a livid scar, very deep and very cruel that ran from the corner of her mouth all the way down her chin and onto her neck. She carried that scar on the very front of her face, almost proudly daring you to stare at it. Jenny Thorton faded into the distant past like a meteor.

"So you met our Jenny."

It was said with no malice whatsoever, just a kind of affectionate amusement.

I was incapable of a response, I just stared at the way her lips moved around that scar which caused her to stick it out even further.

"You're really dressed kind of weird."

"I'm from Puerto Vallarta," I managed.

"You're not Mexican."

"Yes I am."

"Say something in Spanish then."

I described riding my horse on the beach.

"Wow. What did you say?"

"I described riding my horse on the beach."

"You don't have a horse."

"I do, her name is Maya. Well I did, but I'm here now."

"I love horses."

"I love your voice, I love your face, I love your scar."

What I really said was,

"Where do you live?"

"Up Lookout Mountain Road."

"Me too."

"Good we can walk home together."

She was waiting for me by the gate when school let out, she was scrubbing little circles in the dirt with the toe of her PF Flyer.

Her tennis shoes were grimy from adventure, one of her socks was up and the other was down. She had little golden hairs on her legs that glistened in the sun. She had a bad scrape on one knee that had recently scabbed over but she had picked that off during class and it was bleeding a little. Her dress was clean and sleeveless and she had that same little furry thing going on on her arms. She had a couple of freckles on her shoulders and when she looked up from where her toes were drawing in the dirt she flipped her hair back with an expert flick of the wrist.

It happened in slow motion and my prepubescent, didn't even know I liked girls, frozen in the realization that I did, little mind was suddenly a cavalcade of emotions.

Yes there had been Maria, Vicente's sister but that was more of a curiosity, this was an avalanche.

"Jiminy Christmas haven't you ever seen a girl before?"

"Sure, lot's of times."

"Coulda fooled me! You ready?"

"Yeah sure."

"Okay close your mouth and let's go."

She took off ahead, I would have followed her anywhere. It seemed to me that she was always ahead, always kind of leading the way. Yeah, I was a stranger in town and she knew every shortcut and every cool hiding place so it was natural that she would lead in the beginning. But even a year later when our twosome had grown into four kids and a dog she was still out in front. I was content to let her lead because she always had the best ideas and found the best adventures but mainly because she always looked at me in a way that asked,

"Is it okay with you? Am I doing the right thing?"

One day on the school yard playing handball some kid asked me in an effort to embarrass me,

"What are you her slave?'

She jumped up and got right in his face and said,

"No he is not my slave, he is my knight errant, my protector, my guardian and I am his princess!"

She had quite an imagination....

But on that first magical day of Spring when the hills of LA were all green and the mustard plants were in full bloom and the anice weed was sweet to chew we walked up Lookout Mountain Road and I began one of the deepest sweetest friendships of my young life.

Her fingertips lightly brushed across my forearm and she said to me, "Eddie, talk to me in Spanish."

I told her in Spanish all about Chewey and what he had done to me and my confusion and I talked for a while and then I cried. She took my hand and held it tight and didn't ask me what I had said.

One day before long I told her everything in English and she held me then as well.

CHAPTER 11

The next morning she was standing in front of my house when I came out to go to school.

"Hey! How did you know where I live?"

I had dropped her off at her house yesterday and hadn't told her where I lived.

"My dad knows your dad, he's a photographer too."

All the way down the hill she was telling me who lived where.

"The Association lives there."

"Who's the Association?"

"You know the song, 'Everyone Knows its Windy."

I shrug my shoulders and shake my head.

"Oh, the Mamas and the Papas live there."

I look confused.

"Oh that's right you're a Mexican and don't know anything."

"I know plenty."

"Yeah like what?"

"I can ride like the wind, I can find lobsters in sea caves, I can spear fish and catch iguanas big enough to eat little girls from L.A. like you!"

She laughed music and ran ahead. There was so much light in her.

"You have to come over after school and listen to records."

The day I told her about Chewey we were sitting Indian style in a vacant lot that was all tall green grass and mustard plants and we were totally concealed.

"You want to know about my scar?"

"Yeah okay."

"Car accident."

"Yeah?"

"That's it, car accident, I went through the windshield because some-body stopped in front of my dad and he ploughed into them. Now I have this scar, which I used to hate, but now I use it to tell me about people. I get a bunch of money when I grow up and that's it.

"What do you mean tell you about people."

"Like you."

"Me?"

"There you were talking to Jenny Thorton the prettiest girl in school and afterwards I walk up. First thing you do is look right at my face, you see my scar but it doesn't seem to bother you I even stick my chin out a little to be sure. Yeah, you don't even flinch. You look right at it, not trying to pretend you don't see it. You didn't compare me to Jenny."

"Yes I did."

"You did?"

"Yeah I did, and then I forgot all about her."

She thought about that for a minute, reddened just the slightest little bit and then she used her middle finger to comb a stray strand of hair into place behind her ear, even her ears were perfect, she said,

"Anyway that's when I knew."

"Knew what?"

"That's when I knew you."

"Michelle, I have a scar too I think."

I told her everything, where he touched me, what he made me do. How it started out almost innocent and how it progressed to a series of more and more demanding episodes, intimidation and fear replacing the trust and love I had once had for this man. When I started talking we were sitting side by side and before it was over she was laying on her back and my head was on her chest. I could feel and hear her heart racing as I spoke.

I could feel and hear her breath catch in her little chest as I poured out my guilt and my shame. She had my head clutched tightly to her and my tears had gotten the front of her dress soaked. We fell asleep and when we woke up she held my face in her hands and she kissed me on the lips. We were just children and yet we both had experienced pain way beyond our years.

She hadn't told me everything about the scar and maybe she never would but she had heard me in my pain and in that kiss was more compassion and love and understanding than I had ever known.

All the kids were at the handball court, it was lunch break and there was a line waiting to play. Michele and I were at the back of the line. I was still the new kid from Mexico with the weird shoes. I had given in and had begun to wear jeans and t-shirts but I refused to give up my huaraches. I had been there for about three weeks and there were some comments being made about my only hanging out with the scar faced girl. I was ripe for retaliation but Michelle kept me from several potential scuffles. I didn't care what they said about me but to refer to my friend in that way made my blood hot for a fight.

I was beginning to understand what she meant when she said she used her scar to tell her about people. From what I could tell so far from my short tally of experiences most people basically were no stinking good. We were standing there waiting our turn when I see two large boys physically throwing another boy out of line.

"Get out of here piss-pants, we don't want you getting the court all wet."

The subject of this cruel dialogue suddenly comes flying out of the line and tumbles to his back on the asphalt. One of his assailants straddles him and then kicks him in the ribs. I see a little trickle of blood drip from the kids elbow and blossom into a tiny crimson flower on the ground. Everything goes silent and the only things I can hear are the sound of my lungs sucking in huge amounts of air to compensate for the massive dose of adrenaline injected into my system and the pounding in my ears as my heart distributes that adrenaline to every nerve ending in my body.

This boy standing over piss-pants is one of the louder punks at this school who ridicule kids with differences, like Michelle with her scar. He's probably two grades above me and twice my size. I spot a steel lunch box under the bench on the side of the handball court. Michele is too mesmerized by the action to see me grab the box. Before I've even thought about the consequences, that boy is unconscious on the ground with a very large laceration on the back of his head that somehow looks like a big toothless grin.

The next thing I know I'm in the principal's office with my teacher, the playground monitor, and a police officer. The principal is on the phone with my dad making arrangements to have me picked up. For the first but not the last time by a long shot, I'm expelled from school. I don't even care. I did what I thought was right and I'd do it again. I looked out the window and about fifty yards away pretending to be in line for the drinking fountain to avoid going into class is Michelle, and she's looking right at me. I am her knight errant, her protector, her guardian, and she is my princess.

It takes an hour for my father to get there and when he arrives he seems calm and he doesn't say a word on the way home. We walk in the front door and Faith is waiting. She tries to give me a hug but my father shoves me aside and tells me to go to my room. I can hear them talking at first and then the converstaion becomes more tense. Soon it becomes heated and they're yelling. Then I can hear Faith crying. I have no idea what is said but I know that Faith was defending me. The only thing I did hear was at one point my father shouted,

"He's my son I'll do as I see fit, you stay out of it."

Shadows begin to cross my room as evening comes on and I fall asleep.

"Wake up son."

The light goes on in my room.

"Take a bath and get ready for bed."

"Okay dad."

I am in the bathtub wondering what is going on. My mind is reeling with questions, questions that are born out of a serious lack of stability in my life.

"What time is it? Are we having dinner? Am I out of school for good? Will I be sent away? Have I ruined things here with my dad for good?"

My father walks in to the bathroom with his belt in his hand.

"Stand up and grab the towel rack."

The first lash hits my wet skin and my knees buckle from the pain, but I stand there. By the fifth lash, I've bitten through my bottom lip and my mouth is full of blood. I swallow it because I'm afraid to make a mess. I don't know if I cry out but I manage to keep my feet and finally it ends. He turns and as he walks out he says,

"Be sure you brush your teeth."

The backs of my legs and my butt are covered with angry welts some a half inch high.

I climb into bed hungry, hurt, and confused and I fall asleep.

I feel someone next to me in the middle of the night and I know by the smell and the breathing that it's Faith. She is pressed hard against me, with her arm wrapped around me and I'm so glad she is there.

My hurt and angry tears fall on my pillow in silence and I think about Puerto Vallarta, Maya, Vicente, the sea, and the heat. I don't think about Chewey. I'm learning to stuff that into some secret dark locked place. Just before I fall back asleep I think of Michelle. She is standing in a field of mustard blossoms, smiling at me, for me. Her measuring rod, the scar on her perfect face has taken my measure and it has found me true. Our lives are woven together by hope and pain. In each other we have found some light and in that light has been born a measure of hope. If not for the hope that we found there perhaps the pain would have been too great. For me on that dark night that pain tempered slightly with that tiny whisper of hope was all I had.

A week passed with me sort of getting used to what later would become a lifestyle, doing time. I stayed in my room and I read four Sherlock Holmes novels by Sir Arthur Conan Doyle.

"Your little friend was by again."

"What did she say?"

"She's rallying support to defend you and get you reinstated in school. She's really some girl, isn't she?"

"Yeah mom she is."

There it was. It just popped out and the room went quiet, all breathing stopped. Faith had a startled look on her face. Then her eyes filled with tears, huge tears and they cascaded down her face and the next thing I knew I was in her arms, my face all crushed against her chest. She smelled fresh and clean and she was warm and soft and I melted into that safe place. I could hear her heart and her breathing and I thought of the last time I had my head against the chest of a female. Faith's full soft woman's body, a comfort and a refuge and then Michelle's bony little girl's chest, something I felt a deep need to protect and cover. Both of their hearts beating under my head and both of their hearts beating full of love and mystery.

She held my head against her breast and slowly her breathing became regular and her heart began to beat normally.

"I love you."

She had one arm around me and her other hand was stroking my hair and I could have stayed right there forever.

"I love you too. Is it okay if I call you mom?"

"Oh yeah, it's more than okay."

That was it. Our relationship was defined.

Later that evening we were sitting at the dinner table. I called Faith mom and she quickly looked at my father to gauge his reaction. He looked scared. I was immediately sad for Faith but she seemed to be way too high on being my mom to be concerned. A deep need in her had been filled and her contentment was unassailable.

"The boy he was protecting was Paul Moskowitz. The boy he hit has a long history of being a bully and getting in trouble for picking on kids who have differences."

"What is this Moskowitz boy's difference?"

"He wets his pants at school."

"That's a tough one."

"Eddie's little friend Michelle called Mr. Moskowitz and told him the whole story.

It seems that Paul hasn't wet his pants since that day. Nobody ever stuck up for him before and his father believes that Eddie's intervention somehow gave his son a measure of confidence."

"What about the boy Eddie hit with the lunch box?"

"Michelle called his parents too."

"And...."

"The boy's father called the Moskowitz family and made his son get on the phone and apologize. Michelle came to the door today and she really wanted to see Eddie but I told her she'd have to wait and ask you but she told me this whole story and so I called the school. The principal called both families and the point is that Eddie can go back to school tomorrow."

I was elated! And even more my level of appreciation for the value of Michelle's friendship went up astronomically. I couldn't wait to see her. It was amazing to me that a little girl had taken control of the situation where a bunch of adults had failed and had brought solution to bear on the circumstances. But then she was no normal little girl. She was my beautiful scar face girl who could measure a person in a glance and was only looking for the pure in heart and she had found me.

Over the next two years our little band of gypsies, including me, Michelle, Paul Moskowitz (formerly known as piss-pants) and one dog, (a huge Doberman who had adopted us but really belonged to some actor down the street) shared a magical time in the Hollywood Hills. There was music in the air and everyone was high on the life that was developing.

Singer-songwriters and rock and roll bands were moving into Laurel Canyon in droves and there was a kind of innocence in the way every one was exploring the limitless possibilities of community creativity and artistry. People were all smoking pot and hash and experimenting with psychedelics. It was a new frontier that appeared as an avenue to freedom. There was a spiritual aspect to this searching and seeking. It all seemed so natural and so pure that it was common for kids to get stoned with their parents. I started smoking pot with my dad when I was nine and took LSD with him the first time when I was ten.

Under the sink in the kitchen there was a huge tupperware container filled with pot.

My dad sold weed to a lot of people and kept larger quantities in different places throughout the house but the under the sink stash was for the family. I would roll a few joints and head out to meet my crew. We would run up into the hills and get high and explore all the trails and paths that ran through the open areas that were everywhere in the canyon.

Laurel Canyon was country by L.A. standards. L.A. seems to have a higher water table than say Orange County and so there are lots of trees and growth. It was a perfect place for a bunch of stoned kids, full of hiding places in the little canyons and meadows that ran throughout the foothills. We had a tree house in a gnarled old oak tree, just a platform really. It had pieces of two by four nailed up its trunk for a ladder. There was a very chubby kid in our crew named Howie. One day we were all up in the tree house stoned to the gills and Howie decided to go down and take a pee. Me I just peed into the

wind but Howie was bashful about his body so he started to climb down. You know it's strange but I remember telling Michelle afterwards that I had the feeling that something monumental was going to happen.

Well, about halfway down the tree one of the two by fours split under Howie's weight and as he plummeted to the ground his poor little privates got caught on the nails sticking out of the tree where the wood had been. It was instant pandemonium. We were all very stoned and we looked over the edge of the platform and there was Howie laying on the ground screaming, writhing in agony with his hands gripping his torn and mangled testicles, blood just pouring out.

Everyone was screaming except me and Michelle. We just looked at each other and scrambled down to see what we could do for Howie. Michelle pulled his hands away to assess the damage and it was really terrible looking. What I saw convinced me that from then on Howie was going to be singing with the castrati. He was wearing a huge army field jacket and we were able to get it off of him and then slip it under him. It made a kind of stretcher and we all grabbed hold of a corner and humped poor Howie out of there. I don't know what mortified him more: the thought of growing up without gnads or the realization that Michelle had seen his secret places.

Fortunately the doctors were able to put all of Howie's parts back in their proper places and as far as I know they worked fine.

CHAPTER 12

At ten years old our conversations weren't the conversations of the ten year old kids today. We were the products of a very stoned and yet very cerebral culture. Our parents were artists, scholars, writers, and musicians. By the time I was ten I had read Kafka, Hesse, The Bhagavad-Gita, The Tibetan Book Of The Dead, and many more of the popular philosophical flavors of the day. So there I was in like 1965 living in the epicenter of the, "Turn on, tune in, drop out", movement.

I had in my short little life already seen and done way too much. My father had basically abandoned me. I had lived in a foreign country and learned its language. I had been betrayed and sexually abused for the better part of a year. I had seen a lot of grownups naked and doing things no kid should ever see. I had out of body experiences on LSD. I had read more and heard more than my level of emotional maturity could properly process. I had been left to fend for myself by parents who were too busy for me, with the exception of Faith who was my salvation.

I was stoned all the time, and I had one relationship apart from Faith that was real. It was selfless, genuine, pure and innocent. It was love in its truest form.

But there was a love that was mine that it would be years before I came to understand and it was the love that God had promised me that day in front of that church in Puerto Vallarta,

"I love you my child and I will always be with you."

No matter where I have ever been, no matter what suffering or pain I have ever experienced whether self-inflicted or not, He has been true to that promise.

But on a human level from the last time I saw Michelle until I truly came to know Jesus almost every relationship I ever had was a counterfeit.

It was mid August and I had just turned twelve. We had all signed up for a summer camp through school and the camp was doing a weekend trip to a recreational park somewhere in San Diego. We all loaded on the bus and our little crew lined up across the entire back seat. I was against the window and Michelle was crushed up against me. She was uncharacteristically quiet and reserved.

She should have been talking up a storm about what we were going to do all weekend but she was contemplative and melancholy.

Howie had a transistor radio and it was blasting KHJ the AM rock station of the sixties.

They were playing all the summer songs like, California Dreamin, Do You Believe in Magic, Hang On Sloopy, and then they played Michelle by the Beatles. She laid her head on my chest and when they played Just Like A Woman by Bob Dylan and he got to the part, *"And she breaks just like a little girl"*, the floodgates opened and the tears just poured out on to my chest.

Then came the heavy caught in your chest kind of sobbing that only deep soul weeping can produce.

"My dad got a job in New York and we're moving, maybe even in two weeks."

I felt a lump the size of a grapefruit form immediately in my chest and our tears mingled together as they would do many times in the coming days. It was the last night of the trip and we were sitting on the grass next to a man- made lake. There was music playing through speakers that were attached to the trees and the song, "I Think We're Alone Now", by Tommy James and The Shondels came on and we knew this was our goodbye, our last time together. There was only the song, the sound of our breathing and the smell of jasmine on the warm night air. Those things and the taste of the salt from our tears. We just held each other.

"Good bye scar faced girl."

"Good bye my knight errant, my protector, my guardian, my prince."

No words were spoken, there were none needed.

Sure enough two weeks later they were gone and during that two weeks we saw each other only twice. I think I was already developing an, "Its gonna end so I'll just end it now", mindset, and I know she was wired just like me. I seemed easier just to cut it off, get it over with. I would learn this was a very handy skill to have when I began getting locked up. I would see guys whining on the phone in the County Jail or getting all freaky about what their girl friends were doing. I was like, "Dude, just let it go. You look like a punk all tied off waiting for the phone."

I'd always see these guys on visiting days sitting on the edge of their bunks waiting for their names to get called and when they wouldn't they'd be all crestfallen. I'd say,

"Cut it out man, this is your life now and if you can't handle that then quit doin' the stuff that gets the cuffs put on you. Why do you want to make it all hard on yourself? It's not like you can control anything out there."

For me I didn't use the phone, I didn't write letters and unless you were sending me money or a quarterly package I'd rather not hear from you. I'll see you when I get out.

I never saw Michelle again and I have no idea what ever happened to her. I hope she didn't choose the same road I did. Women don't fare well in the life. I will confess that in the weeks following her departure until the new family moved in her house I would go and sit on her porch or stand outside her bedroom window and I would feel. I would feel it all.

"Eddie your mom called, they're moving to Laguna Beach and they want you to come live with them. Oh, and you have a little brother. I think she said his name is Paul or something. Faith can help you get your stuff boxed up next week and I'll drive you down."

That was it. No,

"Son, how do you feel about it?"

Or,

"I'm really going to miss you but we'll keep your room ready."

Ten days later we were driving to Laguna to drop me off. Faith cried the entire time. In fact, she climbed out of the front and into the back seat to smother me with hugs and kisses. I really loved her and knew I would miss her deeply. My dad was quiet and was obviously uncomfortable, but he knew relief was just a short time away.

My dad and Faith were divorced within the year and he quickly replaced her with a younger but far inferior model.

We pulled up in front of the house in South Laguna but only after driving down Coast Highway from Corona Del Mar during which time I got to see my new stomping grounds. Laguna was jumpin'. Lots of trippy people. Guys with surfboards, girls in bathing suits, and a whole lot of long-haired seekers of the eternal cosmic vibration. In other words stoners or as we called them back then, "heads." I was quickly warming up to this move.

It was a beautiful hot summer day, and the air was alive with promise. I felt my heart beginning to pump in my chest with the anticipation of fresh new adventure. As we pulled in the driveway my mom and John came out to meet us and holding my mom's hand was this little blonde haired guy, my brother. He was two years old and I felt an immediate sense of love and connection, the kind only blood can bring. I had a brother! I had always felt alone in the world and suddenly I wasn't. I just wanted to meet him and hold him and be his big brother.

My mom was smiling but she was nervous, after all this was a really big deal. I had only seen her once in a couple of years and where she had only had to be concerned about John and Paul here comes this kid and a carload of boxes. New husband, new baby, and now a new person injected into her life. How would I fit? How would her husband feel? John just stood there stoically aloof as was his way and when my dad went to shake his hand and say hello he actually grunted.

In Mexico they called him, "El Oso", The Bear. It fit perfectly. But when I grabbed my little brother up in the air and he squealed with delight out of the corner of my eye I saw John smile. Just for a second but it was enough. I knew he was going to be okay.

It was still a few weeks until school started and three days later my grandma came to stay, mom and John took off to Mexico for business the next day. There was a young Mexican housekeeper named Rosa and Paul kept her and my grandmother busy. I was left totally up to my own devices. I had a virtual cavalcade of devices. Oh yes indeed I did...

CHAPTER 13

"Bye Grammie, I'm gonna walk down to the beach."

"Okay, have fun dear!"

I hadn't been in the ocean since I left P.V. and man it felt good! I had made my way the half mile or so that it was from the house to West Street beach and what I found after walking down the four hundred and forty two steps to the sand was amazing. The beach was huge, at least a mile long and very wide. The water was cobalt blue and there was a nice little swell running but the waves were just closing out right on the sand. Not good for surfing or body surfing.

Then I spotted a little cove at the South end of the beach that was set apart by a natural rock jetty. It ended on its Southern most side at a huge cliff. The waves would come into the cove and bounce off of this cliff and run sideways across the beach. They would meet up with the waves coming straight in and then they would jack up into a huge wedge, doubling in size. This is the same phenomenon that takes place at the famous body surfing spot in Newport aptly named, "The Wedge."

The entire beach was covered with people and most looked like they were from out of town but this little cove set apart from the main beach was where the local kids hung out.

There were all kinds of kids from my age up to early twenties hanging out in different groups but they all knew each other. They were all wearing real bathing suits, Hang Tens and stuff like that and I was wearing cut off pants. They were all tan and I was white from living in L.A. I felt way out of place, but by this time in my life I was totally accustomed to feeling out of place having moved around so much. As I laid down my towel I felt what seemed like a thousand eyes on me and the beach had gone kind of quiet.

I made a quick survey of the area and I observed that the kids were divided in two main groups. The larger group was comprised of what were probably the jocks and the cheerleaders, and the smaller group, (though not by much), were shaggy and had a cloud of smoke hanging over their area. I had made a third group of one off to the side, which was soon to become a lifestyle.

I sat and watched the waves for a while picking out who the dominant body surfers were and making mental notes about the take off spot and the timing of the sets. The really big sets just closed out across the whole beach, just big bombs, great for getting oohs and aahs from the beach if you dropped into a big one and took the free fall, ducking out the back at the trough. The medium size waves however could be picked up as sidewash off the cliff and you could be slingshotted into a big A-frame that would barrel all the way down the beach.

There was a cluster of older guys, I mean like high school guys, that were dominating the take off spot by the cliff. It was time to make my entrance and probably end up in a fight. Learning to fight is important if you're always the new guy. I ran down the beach self-conscious about my shorts and my white body but I dove into the shore break with confidence. I had always been a fish and on the big South swell days in
Puerto Vallarta I was always in the water. I felt more at home in the ocean than on the land and as my body knifed through the shore break I let a long stream of bubbles out my nose and I was grinning.

During the next few years it may have been the ocean and surfing that kept me alive because I was about to pursue insanity in earnest, pushing the envelope in every conceivable way.

I swam over to the little knot of heads bobbing in the water in the take off zone I had chosen and the first thing I noticed was that all of the boys had on fins. That was okay I had really big feet! I let a couple of sets go by to show some respect and then I swam deep into the peak as a set wave approached us. I was in the spot, by myself and the wave should have been all mine. That's the etiquette. A local guy swam in front of me and cut me off, which is totally par for the course. You'll see the same thing from Trestles to Pipeline; you gotta earn your spot in the lineup. If you're an idiot and don't get how it works you might as well go home.

If you're an idiot at Pipe you'll meet my friend Kala Alexander, the enforcer of a group of local Hawaiian boys called The Wolf Pack. They're the boys who keep the kooks where they should be, out of the water. At times their counseling methods will include the breaking of a board and the breaking of a face. Pipe is a very heavy wave and the consequences of a kook in the water could easily cost a life.

The guy drops in right in front of me and gets in trim and I ride right up his back and launch myself into the barrel using his shoulders as a catapult and that's it, I'm in. I hear hooting from the beach and I know when I get out of the water it's not going to matter that I'm really white and am wearing cutoffs. I swim back to the lineup and the guy who dropped in on me and is several years older has a big grin on his face and he splashes at me. All he says is,

"Nice!"

That guy was fair skinned with freckles and his name was Mark Klosterman. He would later become the head lifeguard in Laguna and a legend as a waterman.

I stayed in the water for hours and when I finally got out I had caught a whole lot of waves. As I walked up the beach I got nods of approval from the guys and the girls all giggled and whispered to each other. I saw a kid lighting a smoke and I walked over and asked him for one. The whole beach was waiting to see where I was going to land and when I moved my towel over to Stonerville I had sealed my fate.

I've often wondered what it would have been like if I would have decided to hang with the "NORMAL" kids. My life might have been completely different. I might have become a doctor or an attorney or played football. People often say to me today,

"You're really big, did you play football?"

I always reply, "Nah, I played hooky."

I never did fit in with the straight kids. I was always drawn to the reckless, the risk takers, the restless ones. I could no more sit in a classroom or show up every day to practice some sport than I could fly. I could sit for hours and read or if something interested me I could pursue its every nuance until I knew everything there was to know about it but I was absolutely incapable of taking education, or anything about life for that matter, in the prescribed manner.

There were times when I would resolve to conform, I would dig in my heels and try to sit in a classroom and participate and I would last maybe a week. Then my heart and my mind would take flight and the classroom would become a huge python squeezing me and choking the life out of me and I knew I was being devoured.

"Thanks for the smoke, what's your name?"

"Philly, what's yours?"

"Eddie."

"Where are you from, man?"

"Well, I don't really know if I'm from anywhere. I lived in Laguna until I was seven and then...."

I told him about P.V. and Laurel Canyon,

"And so now here I am. My mom and her husband and my little brother just moved from Puerto Vallarta and I came to live with them."

'Where are you living?"

"On Brooks Street."

"Cool, I live on First."

"Can I bum another smoke?"

"Yeah but I've got something besides cigarettes."

"Well then, fire it up!"

Laying there in the sun a couple of hours later and realizing that I might have a serious sunburn, I notice that people are leaving the beach. I'm stoned, I'm feeling comfortable in my own skin and it's Saturday afternoon.

"Do you know your way around here at all?"

"No, I rode through Laguna coming here but this is as far South as I've been."

"Well when you go up West Street from the beach the street that goes to your house is Monterey. You go left to go to your house. If you went right it would take you into the center of South Laguna. There isn't much here: two gas stations, two liquor stores, a hair salon, and a real estate office. But there's still plenty to do, trust me. Can you come out tonight?"

"Yeah my grandmother goes to sleep about eight and the nanny is downstairs with my brother. I can definitely get out."

"Okay come down Monterey past where you turned right to come to the beach and go two more blocks. You'll see a vacant lot with a big Avocado tree in the middle of it. I'll meet you there about eight thirty."

We walked up those four hundred and forty two stairs that seemed like a thousand and I was pretty sure I was gonna die. In fact the beach is named Thousand Steps and I know whoever named it named it on the way up and not the way down.

"What's up little man?'

I had known my little brother for only a few days and already we were completely in sync. He followed me around and if I stopped to sit down he would just automatically climb up in my lap. I had never felt anything like what I felt for him. He would put his head on my chest and I would smell his baby fine blonde hair and know that I would die to defend him. He would look at me with such adoration that it would just bring out huge tears. I knew that no one was ever going to do to him the things that had been done to me and if anyone tried, I would not hesitate to kill them immediately.

After dinner my grandmother was sitting on the couch finishing her highball, a single cocktail that she had every night all of her adult life. I was on the floor with Paul and a pile of Tinker Toys. I would build something and he would tear it apart and he'd push the pile over to me and say,

"Do over! Do over!"

I was so content that I almost forgot about Philly. Paul started slowing down and so I went and poured a bottle and hauled him up on the couch next to my grandma. I had him in my lap and was giving him the bottle and he was just staring up at me, sucking on the bottle and he reached up and wound the long hair on the back of my neck around his finger and soon he fell asleep.

My grandma was just watching us and she said,

"Its really good you're here Eddie. He needs you."

"Yeah, grams, he's great isn't he?"

My grandmother was the most aristocratic woman I've ever encountered. Perfect etiquette, perfect speech. She possessed a regal bearing that could make even John Stewart treat her with deference. You would never know that she was the very first lady ever licensed to sell cars. She sold Packards in Florida. My mom was the youngest of four kids and her dad died when she was just a couple of weeks old. My grandmother supported those kids through the depression selling cars and then she loaded the entire family in a twenty two foot camp trailer and hauled it all the way to California. She took no guff off of anybody and she was the coolest woman who ever lived.

"Can you take the baby down to Rosa honey? I'm going to bed. Oh, and don't get your dirty sneakers all over the window sill in your room, that's fresh paint!"

As I said she was the coolest woman who ever lived. I didn't feel the need to use the window for an exit so I just went out the front door. I made a mental note that when I was leaving the house secretly when my folks were home I would keep the window sill clean.

I stepped out into the night and was immediately enveloped by sensations that still today give me a sense of ease and comfort. Late Summer, a full moon and about a mile to walk. There was a light warm breeze and it carried the sweet fragrance of Night Blooming Jasmine. There's a slightly purple cast to the night that I've never seen anywhere else. It must be caused by the way the hills just spring immediately up from the sea. Something in the combination of the sea mist and the abundance of sage on the foothills causes the moonlight to be refracted in purple in the shadows and on the trees. The pavement of the road has a definite purple hue to it.

Back then, there were no streetlights in South Laguna. As I walk up the street bathed in just pure moonlight, I'm absolutely filled with a sense of adventure. I feel completely free. Every step I take is a step towards uncharted territory. I'm caught up by the smells of the night, the sounds of life going on in the houses as I pass, the whisper of the soft warm breeze in the trees and the lonely cry of a coyote somewhere in the hills. I'm absolutely at home in the unlimited possibilities of the unknown, the uncertainty of the not yet revealed. I wither in the status quo, I die in the familiar. I am a stranger to the hearth and home with its days and nights smothered in predictability.

I see the cherry from Philly's smoke from about a block away, brightening every time he takes a pull. He's standing under the canopy of the biggest Avocado tree I've ever seen. As I draw closer I take note of his demeanor, and the way he carries himself. He's leaning against the tree and has about him the casual catlike elegance of the detached heart. The cynicism in his face is tempered by deep amusement. I understand and I can read his thoughts.

"I see you people, all of you. You're cruel and selfish. You betray to gain, and you smile as you plunder, and I myself am amazed at how funny I think it all is. It's all one big joke."

I don't know who has done what to Philly but I know him and I knew him the minute I laid eyes on him. Just like Michelle, Philly and I share the fate of all those who have seen way too much, way too young. Our hearts are way too closed and our eyes are way too open. We have been seared by the hot iron of man's depravity and have retreated to a place where trust is only given to those who bear the same scar tissue. Scar tissue that only the scarred can see.

My study of Philly is interrupted by the smell of a hot motor and I look around to find the source and I see it. Behind the tree is a black mini-bike. To me it looks like a Roman war horse. My desperate love for two wheels was born that night.

"Hey Eddie, what's up?

"Yer town, you tell me."

"When do you have to be home?"

"By morning, I want to be there when my little brother wakes up."

"You ever sniff glue?"

"No all I've done is pot, hash, LSD and peyote."

"I've never tried acid."

"Oh well we definitely have to fix that."

Philly begins to dump stuff out of a paper bag onto the ground. A pair of socks, a couple more paper bags, and two tubes of Testor's model glue.

"Just copy me."

He unrolls the socks and hands me one. I give it a cautious sniff and find it's daisy fresh. He flattens out the sock and squeezes the entire contents of one of the glue tubes down the length of the sock. I do the same. He then rolls the sock and places it neatly in the bottom of the bag.

"Mission control we are ready for blast off!"

With that he puts the opening of the bag over his mouth and nose and begins breathing very deeply from the bag, and so do I. After a few breaths I begin to hear what sounds like a helicopter, whop, whop, whop, whop, but at the same time my body feels like it's pulsing with this vibration in time with the helicopter.

"Okay stop, not too much, we got stuff to do. Like for example, we gotta smoke this joint and then I want to show you something or I should say someplace."

There's a phenomenon I've noticed with real dope fiends and alcoholics. No matter how stoned we get, almost right up to the moments just preceding death we have this ability to function. Now of course there are exceptions to this, say for example the serious tweaker or cokehead in whom the psychosis brought on by lack of food, sleep and the serious misfiring of synapses for extended periods of time has rendered them a blithering idiot.

Looking inside the VCR for, "Them", or staring for hours out a crack in the blinds at the empty car parked across the street being certain "They" are in there. "Them", could be law enforcement, aliens, demons, or maybe demon aliens in law enforcement.

I knew a guy who completely demolished his entire house looking for listening devices and cameras. Every sheet of drywall off of every wall. His wife was out of town at a family funeral and he got a hold of a big bag of speed. She was more than a little surprised when she came home. I've also seen fall-down drunks, rambling incessantly on about their misfortunes to anyone who will listen and when that fails to themselves. I do think these are somewhat of an exception. The dedicated, practiced, professional substance abuser is way too concerned about getting to the next ritual of his addiction to ever totally lose control. It becomes a matter of resetting the default on the brain computer. Somehow we will our limbs to follow our orders.

Philly and I were way past stoned as we wheeled his little Briggs and Stratton powered mini bike out to the road. He reached down and grabbed the pull rope and gave it a good pull. That little motor came to life and to me it sounded as good then as a big Harley motor with straight pipes sounds to me today. He had taken a ten inch piece of ¾ inch pipe and threaded it directly into the cylinder head for the exhaust and it gave it a most incredible sound. Kind of like an M-16 on full auto being shot in a tunnel.

Now the smell of exhaust and gas had pressed themselves into the fragrances of the summer night. Sea air, jasmine and the smells of a motor have always been able to take me right to my,

"Good place."

Even now in my fifties I will sometimes ride my Harley down to Laguna on a summer night and find a place in the village to park and recapture that sensory impression. I'll ride the streets until I hit a place where the jasmine is in the air and I'll pull over under a tree and shut down my bike. I'll just sit there listening to the clicking of my engine cooling and drinking in the blend of sea, jasmine and engine and I will just go to that place of no time.

Nowadays I pray and I thank God for His mercy and His grace and I am amazed at His faithfulness. But on that first night with Philly I was far from thinking about God though I fully understand now that He was always thinking about me.

"Hop on, just put your feet on top of mine but don't forget to move 'em off when we stop, okay?"

"Yeah I got it."

Now that little bike had a top speed of maybe thirty miles an hour on a good day but to me it felt like we were flying. We tore up West Street, made a left and followed the winding road up the hill and through the neighborhood. The houses began to thin out toward the top and the road ended in a cul-de-sac. Philly turned into a place where the curb and gutter had been poured to make a driveway entrance but as of yet no driveway or house was there.

There was just a wide trail and we took it into the hills that just rolled infinitely out into the distance. Philly knew the way and he wove his way expertly around all the potholes and dips. We rode for a while and I fell into the rhythm being played out by that little motor. The trail was winding its way out onto a landscape that was eerily lunar and the white sandy surface of the trail was illuminated by the moonlight.

I was in total peace. The anger and the fear, the feeling of being alone in a world that was always somehow so foreign to me was gone and in its place was a sense of awe. The sky was alive with the dancing light of the stars and the moon was so big and bright that it seemed close enough to touch. I felt a kinship with Philly. I didn't even know his story yet but I knew he was another one of the broken ones. An alien in a place that made no sense.

He was another lost boy cast adrift on this sea of life that for most seemed to be charted. For us there was no true north, the compass wheel spun like a top and no matter which way we tillered our vessel the bow seemed always to be entering a tempest. A hurricane named Jezebel whose eye was uncertainty and in the ravaging winds that that tore mercilessly in their path around that core of doubt were anger, fear, suspicion, mistrust, pain and a deep insatiable hunger for love.

But in that moment, on that bike, riding across that surreal and beautiful landscape, covered by this blanket that is the universe, vast and unsearchable and yet close enough to touch, in that moment there was peace. Something was calling to me and just for that brief moment I heard it again,

"I love you my child and I will always be with you."

CHAPTER 14

The next day I met Philly at the beach and he had another kid with him. I was a tall kid but this guy was huge! He towered over me. He had huge hands and feet, a shaggy bowl haircut and a bad case of preteen acne. He immediately reminded me of Steinbeck's Lenny. He carried himself as if he were in someone else's body and was unfamiliar with how it worked. He just looked very uncomfortable. At first I thought he was just a big lummox but then our eyes met and in his eyes there was so much light, and mirth, and in those eyes was a deep intelligence. His eyes said,

"I know I look ridiculous, I've been the butt of all the jokes for a long time. I'm a lost boy. It's okay because I know things none of you will ever know. I know the secret things."

"Eddie this is Drew. Drew this is the new guy I told you about."

His hand swallowed mine like a Boa swallows a rat.

"Hey, nice to meet ya."

"Yeah you too."

The connection was immediate, an alliance formed, we all sensed it and we looked at one another and grinned. Philly got out a joint and proudly proclaimed,

"Oaxacan Sensimilla!"

That was as good as it got in those days. We passed that doobie around a few times and Philly said,

"Drew's dad owns the liquor store."

That's what started it, just a couple of chuckles at first and then it picked up steam. The laughter came rolling over us like a freight train. We laughed until my sides hurt and I thought I was going to puke. It was the sense of making a connection.

"Man we're not alone."

For a lost boy few things are more horrifying, than the end of summer. Prison never scared me, but going to school scared me to death. All of those people and they're all just fitting in so nicely. They sit at their desks in their neat little rows and apparently they can hear what the teacher is saying. They can actually sit still for the entire period. I simply cannot. School is the ultimate exercise in futility for me. I begin to suffocate before I even get there. Then there's the whole girl thing. Michelle was only my friend because she initiated our relationship and she found my clumsiness endearing. The sad truth is that I'm the guy who if there is a cluster of girls standing around outside the bathroom I will always emerge with a six foot tail of toilet paper dangling from the back of my jeans.

So we laughed hysterically knowing that we were not going to do it alone, we were gonna be a crew. Outwardly we would display a confident bravado.

"We don't give a rip."

We would hang by the back fence of the playground smoking cigarettes and pot and at least twice a week we would climb that fence and be gone, glorying in our daredevil attitudes. Inside we would wonder what was wrong, so deeply desperately wrong with us.

We spent the day baking in the sun, body surfing, and getting stoned and as the sun began to lose its hold on the day, the sand began to cool under our bodies and the breeze raised goosebumps on our scorched skin, we headed up the steps agreeing to meet at the avocado tree later that night.

There was a house on Monterey street that was set back from and up above the road that whenever I walked by I could hear music. Jefferson Airplane, The Byrds, or John Lennon. Occasionally if the wind was right I would smell weed. I had seen some of the people coming and going and they were definitely into something that I wanted to know about.

On this afternoon they were having a party and so I walked up the long flight of wooden stairs to the porch that was cantilevered from the front of the house. The porch was furnished with a couple of couches, some beanbags and a huge Persian rug. Sitting in the middle of that Persian rug was the biggest water pipe I had ever seen. It was actually a table and it was made from one side of one of the giant cable spools the utility companies used and in the middle of it was a large Pyrex funnel connected to a Sparkletts bottle underneath. There were four large clear plastic hoses coming out of the top of the table.

Around this massive device were three guys and one woman sucking passionately on these hoses. The technique was to first load the bowl, which held about an ounce of buds. One person would hold a torch over the bowl and all four people would begin inhaling and exhaling deeply and quickly to fully charge the system. It took about four large breath cycles and then the volume of smoke belching out of those hoses would envelope the smoker and after a couple of more long pulls they would fall back into the bean bags coughing uncontrollably. I had to try it!

No one asked me what I was doing there or who I knew, the woman just passed me the hose and motioned for me to take a seat. I took a couple of really big hits and I saw immediately two things. One, that it took a huge amount of product to operate this contraption so there was obviously plenty around this pad and two that this thing was insanely effective at rendering you very high. I was lounging back in the beanbag with my eyes closed as Marty Balin was singing,

"Today—you're making me say that I—somehow have changed."

I was floating on the beautiful melody of Jefferson Airplane's music and I felt a gentle squeeze on my shoulder.

"You made yourself right at home."

It was the woman` who had given me her place at the table pipe.

"My name is Hope, and who are you?"

"I'm Eddie, I just moved in down the street."

"Well Eddie I'm going in the kitchen to make some tea, want to come along?'

With that she turned and walked through one of the two huge sliding glass doors that faced the porch. I got up and followed. The inside of the house was cool from the breeze that wafted in and it smelled like the same incense I had become so accustomed to in L.A. There were stained glass skylights in the ceiling and the room was awash with color.

The room was large and open and furnished with a lot of stuff from places like India and Morocco. In one corner there stood a huge Buddha at least five feet tall. The kitchen was just part of this large great room separated only by a bar with stools running down its length.

I was standing in front of a bookcase perusing the titles and noting that I had read a number of them.

"Do you like books Eddie?"

I told her that I did and told her which ones of hers I had read.

She tilted her head and arched an eyebrow.

"That's astounding, you're so young." Hope pointed to one of the stools, "Have a seat Eddie."

I popped onto one of the stools as she poured hot aromatic tea into two cups, or bowls actually since there were no handles. There was a bowl on the bar that held a pile of sugar cubes and as I reached for it she quickly snatched it out of my reach. She replaced it with a jar of honey, gave no explanation and said,

"So tell me a story young Eddie."

Hope was probably thirty years old and had a very powerful presence about her. As I got to know her over the coming months I came to think of her as the queen and her house was the center of her kingdom. She seemed to always be holding court, and even in the laid back party atmosphere of that first day everyone paid deference to her. I must have talked for a half hour or more. I told her my life story, the whole thing. She just sat there with her chin resting on her hands listening attentively. She had a conspiratorial smile and her eyes sparkled and danced and I knew she listened to every word I said. I ended my story with my appointment to meet the boys later and I realized that it was getting dark.

"Can you come back again Eddie? I like you very much and I need someone like you to take care of little things for me."

"Sure I can come back, when?"

"Tomorrow morning would be good."

With that she stood up, went to the kitchen counter and retrieved the bowl of sugar cubes. She opened a drawer and got out a roll of foil cut off a tidy strip and placed three sugar cubes in it. She folded it neatly handed it to me and said,

"LSD 25, very pure and very sweet, tonight is the full moon, take it with your friends and wander under the stars.

"I should go now."

"See you in the morning then little man."

I looked up as I reached the street and she was standing at the porch rail watching me.

John and my mom had come in from LAX that morning and had been at the house long enough to freshen up and leave again for a business meeting in Newport Beach. I came in the house just after sunset and they were just leaving again, all dressed up to go to an art show at the Newport Harbor Art Museum.

"Oh hi honey did you have a good time at the beach?"

"Yeah mom it was fine."

"Grammie said you made some new friends."

"Yeah I met a couple of guys."

"Do you feel at home here Eddie?"

"Yeah Mom, it's just great."

"Okay good, well we're going to run off now. Gramms has some dinner for you in the kitchen. We'll probably be home late so I'll see you in the morning"

"Okay have a good time you guys."

I wolfed down my dinner, showered, put on jeans, a t-shirt and ran out the front door.

"See ya later grams."

I got part way out of the driveway and turned around and went back. My little brother was sitting in his high chair and as I approached he held out his arms for me to take him.

"Hey little guy, I almost forgot to love ya up!"

I spent about fifteen minutes wrestling around with him and then I gave him to Rosa.

"Buenas noches Rosa, ya me voy."

I could still hear music as I walked past Hope's house and I wondered what kind of things she had that she wanted me to do for her. I was late to the avo tree and I could see the twin cherries of Philly and Drew's smokes glowing in the dark. Yeah, I was late but I came bearing gifts. In my hand I had the neat little foil package that Hope had given me and I held it out as I joined the boys. I unwrapped it and held the three cubes in the open palm of my hand.

"I know Philly hasn't but Drew have you ever taken acid?"

"No.", he said as he popped a cube in his mouth. Philly followed suit. No questions asked. Nothing like,

"What does it do? How long does it last? Will it kill me?"

That's how we were. No fear, no sense, just a live for the moment kind of mindset with no thought of consequences. I ate mine and Philly said,

"Hey let's hitch down to the hot springs in Ortega Canyon."

We crossed the Coast Highway and stuck out our thumbs. It took a while to get a ride but finally a big Olds pulled over and I hopped in the front while Philly and Drew hopped in the back.

"Where are you guys headed tonight?"

"San Juan Capistrano," Philly said.

"I can get you as far as Del Obispo Road."

I turned around to look at the boys and I could tell they were coming on. I could feel it too. Hope was right; it was pure and sweet. There was no invasion of the senses just a gentle thrust of power and color. I could feel every vibration of the car and the landscape going by began to get extremely detailed and beautifully intensified. I also began to sense a strangely familiar vibe coming from the driver. It was the same vibe I got from Chewey, and it was lust. I began to feel an anger welling up inside of me but it was tempered by a sense of control.

He didn't know that I knew and that gave me the advantage. I reached up onto the dash of the car for his pack of cigarettes, which concealed my right hand and gave me the opportunity reach into my pocket for the folding knife I always carried. Funny, it was Chewey who taught me to always carry a knife.

"Can we get a couple of smokes?"

"Sure help yourselves."

I could feel his sick desire coming off of him like a stink as I got closer to him while reaching for the pack. I turned to Philly and Drew and handed them each a Parliament.

"Here you go guys."

I tried to convey to them what was going on in the front seat but they were lost in the wonder of their first psychedelic experience. Well it was promising to be a wild one.

We had gone about five miles and were passing Monarch Bay when Sicko reached over covertly and put his hand on my thigh. We were going seventy miles an hour and there was nothing I could do except fight down feelings that were rising through me like a volcano. Feelings and thoughts I had buried very, very deep inside. I felt a rage building in me as his groping hand burned into my thigh. He must have mistaken my inaction as acceptance because he moved his hand higher.

The bile rose in my throat in proportion to my rage and my sweet taste of LSD 25 was turning bitter as my mind involuntarily recalled the past, the worship, the trust, and then the betrayal and the pain. About a mile ahead I could see a stop light and I really hoped that it would be red when we got to it.

Sicko was saying something inane presumably to keep everything he was doing hidden and I didn't hear a word of it. I was completely focused on the traffic signal getting closer and closer and the feel of the blade in my hand. The light turned yellow and I prepared myself, his hand fully in my crotch now. When he brought the car to a stop I yelled,

"Jump out now!"

I slammed that four inch blade between his ribs as fast and as hard as I could and then I did it again and again. The door was locked and it took a second for me to find the unlock button. Sicko was holding his side and screaming and I was screaming too.

"Get out of the car! Get out now!"

My two partners were paralyzed in the back seat. Their mouths frozen open in twin expressions of shock and dismay. The light was still red as Sicko punched the accelerator and I dove out of the car. I saw the red pickup barreling through the intersection as the Olds shot out directly into its path. The pickup caromed off of the Olds and piled into a bus stop bench and the Olds rebounded in the other direction and came to rest with its rear section sticking out of a hedge.

The back doors flew open and relief washed over me as I saw my friends come tumbling out onto the street. We ran, and we ran turning off of the highway into a residential neighborhood and strangely enough we were laughing. On the right I saw a dark house with the garage door open and we ducked inside. As quietly as I could I let down the door behind us.

I realized that I still had the knife clutched tightly in my right hand. There was enough light to see that there was blood covering my hand and the sleeve of my windbreaker. I didn't know what to do. Suddenly reality came crashing down on me like a big wave pinning me to the bottom and depriving me of air. I was spinning and I was close to passing out. The adrenaline that had coursed through me and charged me with enough fury to make so vicious an attack was gone and it left me feeling wrung out and small.

I was really high and that I had just inflicted multiple stab wounds on a predator that caused a major collision. Were the people in the pick-up hurt? Was pervo alive? Did anybody see us? Were we going to hear the screeching of tires as cop cars stopped in front of our hiding place? Where could I wipe the blood? What should I do with the knife and my jacket?

I snapped out of my reverie and became aware of Drew and Philly, they were clearly shocked. Their eyes were as big as saucers from the acid but the gravity of the circumstances we were in was bringing them down quick. Many kids that age or many adults for that matter would have panicked and done whatever it took to distance themselves from culpability.

"I don't know what happened he just gave us these sugar cubes and the next thing we knew he was stabbing that poor guy."

I was standing in the middle of the garage when as one they came to my side and huddled with me. I knew right then that these two guys would ride this train with me wherever it took us.

"Wow man...."

That was all that was said and Drew said it, and then we all just kind of stood there staring down at my bloody hand still holding the knife. I turned my hand over and then back again trying to figure out if the blade was long enough to kill. It definitely was.

"What do we do now?"

Philly asked.

"I guess we should just wait here for awhile."

We huddled in the corner of that garage for a couple of hours petrified with fear and high as could be. The garage was full of stuff. Surfboards, an old golf cart, a couple of old beat up Fender amps and a Baja bug under a tarp. We heard a car out front and light slipped in under the crack of the door. The occupants started talking,

"Did you shut the door man?"

"Nope sure didn't."

"Well open it up would ya?"

We scrambled up under the tarp and climbed into the Baja bug just as the door came fully open and headlights flooded the garage. They had the stereo on in the car and the Yardbirds, *"Heart Full of Soul"*, was playing.

By now it had to have been midnight and we were on the downside of our peak on the LSD. Two guys got out of the car. They were surfer stoner types and I could tell they had been partying hard. I was watching them through a little hole in the tarp. One of them reached over into the back seat to retrieve a shopping bag and I heard the clink of bottles. They weren't done with the evening's festivities yet.

They trudged out of the garage and when they did they left the door open. At least we would be able to sneak away quietly. We waited a half hour and then we emerged from our little sanctuary and began rummaging around stealthily. In the back corner was an old Coldspot refrigerator. In the dim recesses of the unlit box I spied a gallon of Red Mountain wine and I pulled it out, cleared my throat to get the boys attention and hoisted it high in a mock salute to Bacchus the supposed Roman god of wine and intoxication.

In a whisper Drew said,

"I don't think we should take the highway home."

"Could we try to make it on the beach?"

"There might be a lot of rock climbing involved."

With that we set out. Our plans for the hot springs had been tragically derailed by circumstances from which the consequences were as yet a mystery, and a scary mystery at that but I began to feel the resurrection of our adventure climbing up out of its grave as we walked down that quiet street under a bright full moon. We made it to the beach and stopped to smoke some pot and drink some of the pilfered wine.

I still had the matter of the knife my blood stained hand, and windbreaker to deal with. I cut the tags from the inside of my jacket and burned them. Then I walked down to the water and used my jacket to scrub the blood from my hands and the knife. Giving the knife one last long look that probably should have chilled me but didn't, I wrapped it up in the jacket.

Finding a suitable spot where the iceplant hillside met the beach I began to dig. Philly lent a hand as Drew kept an eye out for anyone who might be watching. We dug a three foot deep hole and I placed the bundle carefully in its belly. That bloody bundle represented my first encounter with a desire to kill that was borne out of wounds inflicted on me. Wounds that were a kind of killing of a much slower and more insidious nature.

I was feeling strangely detached from the events that led me to this hole. I did not yet know the origin of man's depravity, his ability to step so far outside the light that he could expend the energies of his twisted passions and lusts on a child. I only knew that I had survived this soul sickness so far and if it meant killing to protect myself then I would live with that just as I lived with the wounds that this age old battle of good and evil had been carved so deeply in my heart. I began to throw sand in the hole.

"Wait!"

It was Philly.

"Do you think we should say some words?"

He was grinning and at that moment as we all burst into laughter I thought that this night would bind us together forever.

I had thought the better part of the acid had left our systems but as we smoked and drank it renewed itself with vigor. It had some seriously long legs. The beach stretched out to the north for about a quarter mile and ended in a cliff with very large and very expensive houses lining its top edge like the decorative filigree around the edge of a birthday cake.

We smoked and drank for a while and then we began walking. The moon was so bright that the sand was glowing impossibly white and the ocean was full of a kind of green light I had never seen before. I learned later that there's a luminescent bacteria called dinoflagellate that when tumbled in the breaking of a wave emits a beautiful green glow.

Often when I ditched school I went to the library to find answers to the questions that presented themselves in life. We walked along that beautiful beach and I realized that the entire universe was alive. Nothing stayed still. The stars sparkled and twinkled in space, meteors soared the heavens, and grains of sand were lifted and moved by the breeze at our backs.

The sea! The amazing sea! Swells came in generated by storms thousands of miles away and then crashed on the shore after their long journey saying to us,

"We are mighty warriors born out of distant violence and we have marched across many seas to die here in this final assault, would you honor us in our passing?"

As each of these fallen warriors retreated back to the sea spent and docile in its wake was a cavalcade of life. Thousands of sand crabs hurried to hide themselves in the wet sand, their tiny little antennae sticking up to create little v-shaped wakes that in the luminescence and the moonlight sparkled like vast field of diamonds. It would explode at the retreat of each wave and then quickly diminish, brightly refreshed as the next wave died on the sand. Each time was a celebration of that storm warrior's journey.

CHAPTER 15

I snuck in the front door of the house and the clock on the entry way wall said 3:30.

I almost didn't see her as I passed through the living room but there she was sitting in the big wing back chair under the soft glow of a reading lamp, afghan covering her from the waist down and a book open on her lap.

"Wake up Grammie."

"What time is it Eddie?"

"It could be early or it could be late depending on how you look at it."

She just chuckled softly and shook her head.

"Come on Gramms I'll help you to bed."

I gently helped her to her feet and walked her to her bedroom door.

"Good night Gramms, I love you."

"I love you too boy."

She stopped in the threshold of the door.

"Eddie?"

"Yeah?

"I know you're on a journey but don't get too far from home."

"I don't even know where home is Gramms."

"Home is wherever I am Eddie."

She held her arms open and I slipped into her embrace. All of the madness of the night came tumbling into my mind like a cavalcade of disjointed and somehow strangely intangible thoughts, real and yet very unreal. Then suddenly it all crystallized into the certainty that as much as Gramms loved me I had no home except my own mind. It was the only place I was completely free. No one could ever intrude upon my intellect. No one could invade the core of my being unless I let them. At that moment the walls I had built around me of stone and mortar became covered with armor plate. I put Chewey out of my mind, I threw out the loss of

Faith and Michelle, I buried the events of the night, the stabbing, the car wreck, all of it. I planted my feet and set my jaw. I would not be moved. Then I heard it again, that voice,

"I love you my child and I will always be with you."

And just as it had the other times I heard it with it came this soft caress of comfort and safety, like and oasis in a desert of waterless, lifeless uncertainty. But for the first time a question arose in my mind. Do I trust myself, my strength, my tenacity, my own survival instincts or do I trust this mystical voice that I couldn't touch or see.

I climbed into bed and slept like a dead person but at the crack of dawn I woke up with a start. I went quietly to the living room since everyone was still asleep and I turned on the local news. No report. I went out to the front yard and grabbed the morning paper.

There was nothing yet. That was the very first time I ever opened a newspaper. I went back in the house and headed for the kitchen to get some cereal. I had a couple of hours to kill before I was expected at Hope's.

Rosa came upstairs with my little brother and set him in his chair at the dining table. He was too big for a high chair and too small to sit at the table without a booster but having made the transition from his high chair was obviously a source of great pride for him. He didn't like to be fed but he was still pretty awkward with a spoon so watching him try to eat his cereal was a riot. He tried so hard to copy me. He'd watch me intently as I would take a spoonful and put it in my mouth, never taking his eyes off of the spoon. He was a very analytical little guy, watching the exact angle of the spoon as it went into the bowl and emerged loaded with cheerios.

He couldn't get the angle right and if he got any at all they would fall off of the tipping spoon and land on the table or the floor. He would do the exact same thing time after time and with each failure he would shrug his little shoulders and emit a heavy sigh. Finally he would give up and drop his spoon and just reach in the bowl with his hand and stuff a handful of sopping wet cheerios in his mouth. Our eyes met as his hand was in his mouth up to his wrist and we both started laughing.

It was a very good time and I felt almost normal except the nagging expectancy of a knock at the door. A knock that would bring the events hidden in the darkness of the night into the bright light of a beautiful summer morning. I lived most of my life like that, waiting for the door to get kicked in or the red lights to go on behind me. It seems it was always like that. There was always something I had just done behind me that put the consequences forever in front of me.

On that particular morning no knock came, but I knew it could be days before investigators found one of us if they ever did. I replayed the events over and over and it seemed unlikely that any of it could come back on us. Still someone could have seen us get in the car or something. I thought we were in the clear but we were really high and I easily could have missed something.

"Good morning honey."

She was always so cheerful.

"Good morning mom."

"You weren't in your room last night when we got home."

"Yeah I got in kind of late. Did you and John have a good time?"

By answering the obvious query,

"Where were you?", with a question of my own I gave my mom the option of dealing with a disciplinary confrontation or changing the subject and I had learned that she would always much rather avoid confrontation. I was unaware of the guilt she harbored in her heart for having sent me away so that she could pursue her relationship with Mr. Stewart and that weighed on her a great deal, but she was always a person who would rather keep up appearances that everything was all right and sweep anything uncomfortable under the rug.

As long as things looked okay then they must be okay or at least not terribly damaged or in danger. This morning she chose to avoid confrontation.

"Oh the art show was wonderful! They exhibited ten of your dad's, I mean John's paintings and everyone loved them, blah, blah, blah."

I had already checked out. I didn't have a dad, didn't want a dad, and didn't need a dad.

"Where is John?"

"Oh, he went to the gym early and then he's going to the office."

This man was truly an enigma. He drank like Earnest Hemmingway every night. Judging by the amount of bourbon he consumed he had to have been buzzed, but he really didn't look it. He would become more morose and his eyes would take on a very intimidating look but he never actually looked drunk.

You would think he was about to get mean or say something cruel, but often he would look at you with a very intense glare and say something hysterically funny (at least to me it was funny). Looking back, I think I was one of the very few people who laughed. I think that's one of the reasons that while he never really participated in my life, he was always there for me in a way. We got each other.

As I was saying he drank every night and yet he was up at six AM and in the gym and at the office by eight. He would work until six in the evening and then come home and do it all again. He was a machine.

The kitchen clock said 8:30.

"I'm going to meet some friends mom."

I was out of there like a spirit, gone in a flash. As I walked down the street to Hope's house I half expected to see a sheriff's cruiser coming the other way.

The first thing I noticed was that the big water pipe table was gone from the porch.

"Come in young Eddie. You're punctual. I like that!"

"Good morning Hope."

I felt as if I should be saying Miss Hope. There was absolutely no evidence of the debauchery of yesterday afternoon. The house was spotless, in perfect order. It smelled wonderful, a combination of pot, incense and baking. Hope, I would come to find out was a complete contradiction in terms. She was a homemaker, she was always baking or cooking, her house was always perfect, she actually wore an apron, and yet she was a cunning and sometimes ruthless business person.

She stayed at the top of her game and was absolutely intolerant of any ineptness or bungling if you were in her inner circle. She was all of that and she was dangerously beautiful. She had a smile that would radiate such benevolence and was so calming and inviting that it would completely disarm you but she also had a look that could make the hair stand up on the back of your neck. I was never the recipient of that look but I saw plenty who were.

We were all at a party in the canyon on Woodland Drive at the Red House and there was a fellow there who had been bragging that he had bested her on a deal for a substantial amount of pot. Woodland Drive was also known by its inhabitants as Dodge City and it was the home and headquarters of the Brotherhood of Eternal Love. The Brotherhood was responsible for the importation and distribution of the bulk of pot, hash, and LSD in the Southern California area and on that day all of the hierarchy was present.

Hope walked straight up to this fellow and by the time she was done he was standing all alone and was left no choice but to concede defeat and restore what he claimed to have beaten her out of. The beautiful thing was that in his bragging he had pumped up his take considerably more than what it had been and so he repaid probably triple what he had actually gotten.

"Would you like some tea Eddie?"

"Yes please, that would be nice."

"I made two kinds of brownies Eddie. You may have one of the special batch and as many as you like of the normal batch. Any more of the special ones and I'm afraid you would be rendered incapacitated."

She said this with a wicked grin that started my heart pounding. Oh but she was beautiful! Her hair was gold with hints of strawberry and it was very long and fell in lazy ringlets to her waist. She had almond shaped eyes that were a striking blue, almost purple. She had aquiline features that spoke of aristocratic origins and ridiculously full lips that needed no color. She was tall and willowy and she carried herself with a catlike grace and a self possessed dignity. She was the first deeply sensuous woman I had ever been this close to and it had a very powerful effect on me.

I knew she could sense my raging hormones and it seemed to amuse her.

"Eddie we're going to LA airport to pick up my husband who is coming home from Mexico.

"Oh, I didn't know you were married."

"Of course you didn't silly we only just met yesterday."

She said this as she retrieved a photo album from the drawer of a credenza in the living area. She showed me pictures as we sipped our tea and ate our brownies. Just one of the special ones and several of the regular ones. They were delicious.

"His name is Wayne. We met on Maui three years ago. I was over there exploring my options. I had been at Berkeley in school and I just felt like I needed to go. I had a girlfriend in the islands and I went there to visit. One night my girlfriend and I went to this little cowboy bar in a town called Makawao to see a friend of hers who had a band."

"Wait, wait, wait! A cowboy bar in Hawaii?"

"Oh yeah, there have been cowboys in Hawaii longer than there have been in Texas or Wyoming."

"Tell me about it, please."

"Okay well, in 1867 the first cattle drive here on the mainland went up the Chisolm trail from Texas to Abilene Kansas and it was out of that time the American cowboy was born, but in the early 1800's a ship captain named George Vancouver made a gift of some cattle to King Kamehameha and they rapidly bred and began wreaking havoc. About 1812, John Parker, a sailor who had jumped ship and settled in the islands, received permission from Kamehameha to capture the wild cattle and develop a beef industry. The industry grew slowly under the reign of Kamehameha's son Liholiho.

Later, Liholiho's brother, Kauikeaouli visited California, then still a part of Mexico. He was impressed with the skill of the Mexican vaqueros, and invited several to Hawai`i in 1832 to teach the Hawaiian people how to work cattle. Thus the Hawaiian cowboy came to be and became called a Paniolo. The name Paniolo comes from the word Espanol after the language of the Vaqueros. The Parker ranch is maybe the biggest working cattle ranch in the United States along with the King Ranch in Texas. But there are working cattle ranches on all of the islands. On Maui it's the Ulupalakua ranch. Then there are the Robinson ranch and the Wilcox ranch on Kauai."

"Hope, how do you know all this stuff?"

"Well as soon as I saw a cowboy hat on a real cowboy and he was Hawaiian I was as surprised as you and I had to know. You and me Eddie, we're people who have to know. So I did what people who have to know do, I read."

My mouth was dry and I didn't trust my voice so I just nodded in agreement. We were sitting on a low couch in the living room area and by this time I was very stoned. As we talked hunching over the photo albums that were arrayed across the coffee table we began to slip closer together until her bare leg was touching mine. It was unintentional as far as I knew but its effect on me was astounding. I was so engrossed in her story that I hadn't noticed her closeness but suddenly it was consuming me. She seemed to sparkle like some ethereal siren and I was drunk with the nectar of her beauty.

She had a scent coming off of her that was light and fresh, traces of lavender and vanilla. Her hair cascaded in golden ringlets down over her shoulders and ended trailing out across my forearm. I could see fine golden hair on her upper thigh and her long legs were tanned and sinewy with a dancer's muscle. As she turned and smiled at me her teeth sparkled an impossible white and her lips, full and red, parted in a twisted little grin that made my heart pound.

"Earth to Eddie!"

"Oh I'm sorry I was just, uh thinking about your story."

Her smile was mischievous but pure and without a trace of marital treachery. That she was aware of her effect on me I had no doubt but it was more cute to her than anything else, after all I was twelve years old and I believe that she sensed that I had never been around a truly beautiful woman before.

"Ahh I see. Well I was telling you about Wayne. He was playing guitar in the band and between sets we started talking. He was shaping surfboards, selling pot up country in a little town called Olinda and living in a house with a bunch of surfers and musicians.

He sat out the next set to talk to me and we talked until the bar closed. Afterwards we went for a ride on his motorcycle and we've been together ever since."

As I looked through the photo albums I got a picture in my mind of a man that I wanted to know, had to know. Any man who could capture the heart of this amazing woman and hold her love was a man from whom I could learn much. There were pictures of them in Hawaii, pictures of him and his boys at a surf spot I would later fall in love with myself, Honolua Bay. Then she turned another page and there it was. It was black and polished aluminum and sitting absolutely still in the picture it looked fast. Wayne and Hope were standing behind it and it looked like they were in Mexico. Sitting on the ground next to the bike were two duffel bags and I gathered they were on a road trip.

"This picture was taken in the Yucatan. We rode that bike from Topanga Canyon through Mexico and into Central America. We were gone three months and when we came back we stayed on the Coast Highway as much as we could and we ended up at a little surf spot in town named Thalia Street. We were tired and dirty but we were so alive.

The waves were good that day and as we sat on the top of the steps I watched Wayne's body move with each surfer as he rode. He was completely unaware that he was doing it.

Riding through town I felt a call on my heart from this magical place and as I sat there watching Wayne I knew I wanted to spend the rest of my life with him and I thought I'd like to spend at least part of that life here. He was thinking the same thing because he turned to me and said",

"Hope, I could surf this break every day and be content. You wanna live here?

I laughed and said,

"Yeah I do."

"Good, you wanna be my wife while we're at it?"

"Nooo, I don't really think so."

"He looked taken aback for the briefest instant and then we both started laughing and when we kissed I knew it was that one kiss that promises forever."

"We had sold every last thing that we had to make that trip, which turned out to be quite a bit. When we got under way we had a whole lot of money in traveler's checks.

On the way South an idea began to form itself in my mind and when I mentioned it to Wayne it came over us both like a landslide. We decided to make it a buying trip. We bought art and furniture, jewelry and clothes. We sent money home to a friend who procured us a warehouse in LA and so on that day at Thalia Street we had a respectable

inventory in storage and now we had a place where we could make a home and start a business.

"Does he still have it?"

"Does he have what Eddie?"

"The bike."

"Oh Eddie you're such a man. Have you even heard a word I said or has it been the motorcycle the whole time?"

"I could say it all back to you word for word I bet."

"That's good Eddie because one thing you should learn about women is that we like to talk but more importantly we like to know we have been heard.

"I'll remember that, I promise."

She tousled my hair and laughed music, a beautiful melody.

Now I was the little brother and that was both tragic and a great relief at the same time.

"Come on we need to get going. We'll stop in the garage on the way to the car and you can see the bike.

The garage was large for the period in which the house was built, many of its time having only single car garages. It was full of imported goods waiting to go to their shop, which I had only just learned about and had yet to see. Off to one side was an object covered in a tarp much like the tarp that covered the Baja bug that had been our hiding place the night before. I felt a momentary anxiety, but it was instantly rinsed away when Hope pulled it back and uncovered a sculpture of black and polished aluminum that literally weakened my knees. Oh but it was beautiful!

"It's a 1948 Triumph six fifty. Wayne doesn't ride it that much now and I haven't been on it since our trip. My back side is still out of sorts."

Something in the way Hope spoke harkened back to a more proper time. She always chose her words carefully and was not given to colloquialisms or slang and I never once heard her say a foul word. Many people might easily have said,

"My ass still hurts."

But not Hope.

I was not yet very familiar with bikes but even my untrained eye could see that this one was not entirely stock. For one the seat was thin and low and was hand stitched. I commented on this and Hope laughed and said,

"Oh he made that. It's his solo seat. That couch hanging on the wall over there is the seat we had on the trip."

And indeed it did look like a couch.

"I know what you're thinking Eddie and trust me after seven thousand miles even that behemoth of a seat was agony."

The pipes were fashioned in a way that they came down gracefully in front of the engine and then tucked up under the bike in a way that somehow said,

"I am both loud and fast."

The gas tank was void of any emblems whatsoever and the black paint looked hand rubbed with care.

"You ready? Put your tongue back in your mouth and quit drooling on my floor. Maybe he'll teach you to ride it."

There was a very easy camaraderie developing between us and as we got into Hope's Land Cruiser I was smiling in my heart and yesterday's problems seemed far away and tomorrow's not worth the trouble of worrying about.

She slapped my feet sharply,

"Get your feet off the dash please."

"Hey, I'm twelve remember."

"Oh yeah, it's easy to forget; you're such a man of the world."

She gave me that smile of hers which was just a little bit crooked. It had the power to completely disarm or completely lift me up and I was sure I'd do absolutely anything to stay in the light of that smile.

She pushed in a four track and Jimi rocked us on down the road. Hope pulled a joint out of the pocket of her blue chambray shirt and held it out to me with long exquisite fingers.

"We might not be quite yet stoned enough young Edward. There are matches in the glove compartment."

We headed North on the Coast Highway and when we got to the bridge at Victoria Beach she turned off onto Alta Vista Way and we were soon cruising down a street parallel to the Highway called Glenneyre Street. This was my first time in the village since I was seven and I knew I was home. We followed Glenneyre into the heart of town, turned right up Park Ave. and made a left on Third Street.

"That's Fat Annie's house right there."

She was pointing to an old two-story shingled house covered in vines, which sat right on the corner of Third and Park.

"She has a son named Stevie who is your same age. You'll meet him in Dodge City. He's a very soulful kid. He was born with something wrong with his hips and so he walks with a very bad limp in fact one leg just kind of drags along so he can't play sports or surf but he rides a surf mat."

I was thinking, "Lost Boy."

"I would like very much to meet him."

"I think you two would get along very well. He's like you, he's different from most kids, it's as if he's not a kid at all. I guess he's what you'd call an old soul. So are you Eddie; you're an old soul."

I took a long pull on the joint and held it out for Hope and again I was captivated by the grace in her long fingers as she took it deftly from my hand. We were getting out of town toward the mouth of Laguna Canyon road passing the Festival Of Arts. The canyon is really country and the people who have lived there the longest tend to be a slight cultural departure from the people in the village.

Back in the day Laguna was largely a Bohemian culture. Artists, writers, musicians, and a large gay community, but the canyon, while it had its share of those kinds of folks was where the pick-up trucks were, and often they would have a couple of bales of hay in the back. It was where the guys that made their living with a back hoe and a dump truck called home. I later had a friend whose family owned some stables in the canyon and they had a lot of horses, dogs, cats, and birds. The canyon was that kind of place.

We pulled up to the international terminal and Wayne was outside at the curb. He looked like a hippie surfer version of the Marlboro man, just very cool. He had a Mexican Indian bag slung over his shoulder and at his feet was a duffel bag. I jumped out of the Land Cruiser ran around and opened the tailgate, grabbed the duffel bag and threw it in.

Hope was in his arms and his shoulder bag had slid to the ground so I grabbed that and threw it in too. Hope broke away from his embrace and announced,

"Wayne, this is Eddie."

"I'm Eddie."

"So you must be Eddie."

"Uh huh, Eddie."

"You guys are so stoned right now. Let me guess, a little eaten and a little smoked."

He put his hand out to shake but not in the manner of my parents friends when I met them, but in that brother handshake.

"I've heard all about you Eddie, it's really good to meet you. Did you guys smoke all the weed on the way or is there a joint for me?"

Hope ushered him to the car, squeezed his butt and said,

"Maybe a brownie too, if you've been good."

"Mama, I'm always good!"

I hopped in back through the tailgate and we were off.

CHAPTER 16

The last couple of weeks of summer before school started I spent almost every day with Wayne and Hope. The first few days I would show up at their house at about 8:30 in the morning and we would drink coffee and smoke a little pot. That is, Wayne and I would drink coffee and Wayne would tease Hope about her herbal tea. We would then head down to their shop, which was on Coast Highway between St Anne's and Cleo Streets.

They had an import export business and they brought in all kinds of merchandise from Mexico and Latin America. Clothes, art, furniture, sculptures and anything Wayne found that looked interesting: a set of old wooden doors from a church, or a wrought iron gate, all kinds of cool and eclectic stuff. They had a pretty diverse clientele. There were the hippies but they were the ones who had some money, and I would later learn that many of them were from the periphery of the Brotherhood so their money was funny, if you know what I mean. They also catered to some interior decorators and wealthy folks from Emerald Bay, Monarch Bay and Newport Beach.

But it was at their warehouse out in the canyon where they stored whatever wouldn't fit in the store or things that needed a little repair that I learned what was really happening with Wayne and Hope.

About four days after Wayne got back he announced that a shipment was coming in that day and we would be working at the warehouse.

"Eddie, you want to surf with me tomorrow morning early?"

"Yeah man that would be great!" "Do you know how?"

"I body surfed a lot in Mexico."

"Be at the house at six then, and Eddie?" He said this as he was pulling up the big rolling door on the front of the building.

"Yeah Wayne?"

"I'm about to let you into my private world. Keep it to yourself and don't screw it up, okay?"

"I won't Wayne, I promise."

I had shared with Wayne and Hope the story of my short life and I knew that they cared for me and understood me in a way that no one else had. They didn't have any kids and I think I kind of filled in a blank spot in their lives. Of course they weren't my parents, nobody had any illusions about that. Had they been in the position of being authorities in my life I would have surely rebelled against them as fiercely as I did any authority.

The relationship was serendipitous. I wandered into their lives one summer day and in me they discovered a curiosity. A precocious boy with a fierce hunger and a quick mind already scarred and jarred by life but still with some sense of innocence. In them I found a door into a world that was beckoning me, seducing me. In Hope's deep and ethereal beauty and intelligence and Wayne's cavalier and optimistic outlook on life which expressed itself in his music, his wandering, his surfing and his love for Hope, I found a place where for a brief time I fit.

I had fit with Maya, I had fit with Faith and Michelle, I fit with my little brother Paul, but I had learned not to hold too tightly to fitting. As soon as I fit well enough to be comfortable I was caromed off to some new place with new people. Mostly I felt homeless…

Wayne walked through the warehouse to the little office space in the back and I followed more than a little curious about Wayne's private world.

"There's a little carved wood box in the center drawer of the desk, twist up a doobie and I'll make some coffee."

I had been rolling joints for quite a while, my dad used to set me at the kitchen table with a shoebox full of weed and I would roll twenty or thirty joints at a time when he was having a party. The technique was to take the lid of the shoebox put in a handful of pot still on the stems and break it apart removing all of the stems and breaking it all up into a consistency that wasn't too fine and not too coarse. If it was too fine the joints would run, burning down one side and you would have to spit on your finger and then apply the spit to the side of the joint that was burning too fast. If it was too coarse little sticks would punch through the rolling paper and you would end up spending time making little paper band-aids.

After all the stems were gone you would gather all of the pot down to one end of the lid and using the folding back of the rolling paper booklet or a business card, (didn't see a lot of credit cards back then), you would tilt the box top at an angle and with the card kind of winnow the pot so the seeds would roll out and down to the other end of the box, I could clean and roll an ounce of pot in about forty minutes. That's pretty fast for the little hands of a ten year old kid.

I had been noticing since I had come to Laguna that the pot looked different than it had in LA. I pulled a little knot of green out of the box and held it up to the light. No seeds and covered with sparkly little crystals. As I broke it apart it had a fresh almost piney smell, strong. Rolling it was so much easier. It was sticky and rolled as if it couldn't wait to be a joint. Wayne was standing by the coffee pot watching me.

"You've been smoking that old kilo weed huh?"

"Huh?"

"Yeah, dried out old weed full of stems and seeds and pressed into kilo blocks. It's all there was until we started exploring around and found the sensi."

"Huh?

Yes, I was as sharp as the edge of town at times.

"The sinsemilla little brother! Sinsemilla, know what that means? What am I saying? Of course you do you're a little Mexican."

"Yeah, that means without seeds."

"Right, but to us it also means a much higher quality, much higher in THC content, never pressed and only the buds get picked and packaged. We're right on the cutting edge of this stuff, and we're exclusively importing it right here into this canyon."

Wayne was often animated when he was excited about something but he was really pumped about this and many years later as I watched the pursuit of higher and higher grades of marijuana developing I realized I was a witness to a first pioneering effort.

From trash weed in kilos to the seedless cannabis sativa from Oaxaca and Michoacán, to the even more potent Columbian. Then the hashish movement, America's first experience with cannabis indica.

Places like Kabul, and Lebanon, and Morocco became the travel destinations of the Brothers. Then hash oil and the Thai invasion. Thai sticks that would blow the top of your head off. Finally to the importation of the seeds from the indica plants and the establishment of domestic plantations in places like Hawaii, Humbolt County and later Fallbrook California.

We were sitting there smoking a little and drinking some really good coffee when the phone rang.

"Yeah, what's up?"

I could hear Spanish on the other end.

"Bueno somos seguro aqui." *We're good here.*

More on the other end that I could not hear.

"Que te parese, como una media hora?" *What, about a half hour?*

The other end, blah, blah, blah.

"Okay, Buena suerte." *Okay, good luck.*

I commented, "I didn't know you spoke Spanish."

"You're not the only white Mexican in Laguna little buddy. C'mon let's take a walk. You can bring that doob along."

Wayne grabbed two folding chairs and went out the door. I followed grabbing the joint and a book of matches off of the desk. We walked to the end of the driveway and under the shade of a big Pepper Tree Wayne set up the chairs and plopped down in one.

"Let's just see what the weather is like out here today, sit down and light that up."

"Is it cool?"

"Trust me little brother anybody who might take notice of us smoking isn't interested in us just smoking, but we're going to sit out here and watch to see who might be watching."

"Who might be watching and why would they be watching?"

"Well there are actually four guys who might be watching but I think I'm still flying under the radar. Those four guys are supercops. Neil Purcell, Norm Babcock, John Zapparito, and Bob Romaine. They're trying to bring down Dodge City and the boys and they're very crafty. They aren't just cops though, they're real people and like with Neil Purcell, he and his family live right here in town, right up on top of the world. He reminds me of Wyatt Earp. You know he's out to get you, wants to bring you down but you can't help but respect him.

Anyway they could be up on the hill in which case I'm looking for the reflection off of a pair of binoculars or a puff of dust kicked up from a slip on the trail. Down here it's easy. The canyon is one road, no place to hide that can't be seen. It's hard for them to set up surveillance from a car. I know all the cars that are supposed to be here and it's easy to spot anything out of place. As far as why they would be watching, that you're about to find out.

I guess I should ask you because you can walk out of here right now and no harm done, but if you stay, you're definitely in the deal."

"No, I'm definitely in the deal, all the way."

"Yeah, I thought you would be. Hope said you were a game kid."

"She said that?"

"Well not like that, but that's what she meant. Check it out buddy, here come the boys with the toys."

I looked up the road and saw a big bobtail truck coming. About fifty yards away the turn signal went on and they were close enough for me to see two Mexican guys in the cab. They made the turn into the driveway and the guy riding shotgun yelled out,

"Hola mi hermano, que pasa?"

He was a big giant guy with a huge grin and one gold tooth in front. The driver was a lean wiry guy with the look of the predator. Behind the truck was a four door Ford that could have been a narc car but it sure wasn't. It had three guys in it who didn't look all that nice to me. They pulled up to the roll up door and all of them hopped out. The big guy from the truck came up to Wayne and grabbed him in a bear hug.

"Everything went perfectamente, muy tranquilo, smooth sailing all the way. We didn't see anybody following and there was no one at the harbor."

"Well good, let's unload the goodies."

"Bueno! Abre la puerta Juanito!

"Open the door Juanito."

One of the guys from the sedan went to the back of the truck removed a lock and threw up the door. On the floor of the truck were wooden crates stacked two high and covering all of the available deck space of a sixteen foot truck.

"Aqui esta mi amigo, quinientas libras de el mejor producto que ofrece Mexico."

"Here it is my friend five hundred pounds of the best product Mexico has to offer."

The truck was backed right up to the door and so we began the unloading process. Two of the guys were up in the truck and they would go to the front end of the truck's box and bring a case to the back. One of them had a cat's paw and a hammer and he would pry the lid off of the crate and they would then hand the large black bag of pot to me and another of the delivery guys. They would then take the empty crate back to the front of the box and then repeat the process. We would carry the bag to Wayne and, you'll never believe it, Chewey and they would put it on what I assumed was a big laundry scale and record the count in a ledger.

We were almost finished when Hope whipped in the driveway in her Land Cruiser.

"Hey guys lunch break! Or maybe I should say dinner break since its almost sundown. I brought cerveza and, tortillas, pollo, frijoles, and pico de gallo."

By this time the guys that had seemed so heavy at first were my old compadres. They were amazed at the fact that I had lived in Mexico and spoke fluent Spanish and the vibe was very cool as we stood around the big bowls of food and stuffed tortillas full of chicken and beans and salsa. Wayne had broken open one of the big black bags of pot and had been weighing out one pound bags and he had taken a couple of ounces out to play with. The smoke was the sweetest I had ever had, the beer was cold and good and the release of tension as the initial importation and delivery of five hundred pounds of Zacatecas Red Hair Sensimilla was complete had everyone grinning.

It was a little after dark when the truck, the almost cop car and the smugglers got underway and then it was just Wayne, Hope and me.

"Did you bring the twelve gauge baby?"

"Yes my sweet husband and a box of shells as well."

Sometimes Hope would sound like Julie Andrews in the Sound Of Music.

"Good baby, I'm going to stay here with the load. I bagged up ten individual pounds for you to take to Dodge so the boys can sample what we got. Just take them to the Red House and leave them with Bobby.

"Okay babe. What about Eddie?"

Wayne looked at me and smiled.

"You did good today partner. I know I said we'd surf in the morning but we might have to do it later. Can you come back and help me bag all this up tomorrow?"

"Yeah Wayne that's fine, and thanks for trusting me. I won't let you down."

"Hope, take Eddie with you and bring him back in the morning."

"Oh, is that an order, captain?"

"Yeah, don't make me spank you right here in front of our protégé, and bring me eggs sausage and a waffle from the Jolly Roger when you come."

"Si Senor, mi capitan."

"Oh so what now everybody speaks Spanish? I'm just not feeling very unique right about now!"

Wayne and Hope look at me and then each other and they just bust up.

"Oh you're quite unique Eddie, trust us on that one."

Then their arms are around me and it's awkward but it feels good.

There's a feeling that you get when you're in the middle of doing something that's way out on the edge and it's going well. Giddy. It's quite a different thing when the door of success slams shut and you're caught, thrown in the back of a cop car and taken to a cell. The sinking gut, the weak in the knees feeling, then the resignation and finally stoic acceptance, and a set jaw. Put on the tough guy hat. There was a song writer back in Laguna when I was a kid and his name was Les Moore. He used to say,

"Hope for the best, expect the worst, and be at peace with what you get."

That's a good motto for a criminal. Right then, in that moment we were in the giddy place.

"Are you ready to go Edward?"

My grandmother called me Edward and I hated it, with Hope it was fine, intimate, made me feel a part of her. I was surprised at how much I wanted to be a part of her, and now of them.

"I was born ready!"

We loaded the pot in the Land Cruiser and we were off. This was to be my first trip to Dodge City, Woodland Drive, the iconic home and headquarters of the Brotherhood Of Eternal Love. Law enforcement characterized them as organized crime, however that's not how they characterized themselves. They were in their minds seekers of a spiritual truth. This truth was in the teachings of all the prophets from Jesus to Mohammed. Also in the teachings of the Eastern mystic religions from Buddhism and Hinduism to the Tao Te Ching.

They believed that the use of marijuana, hash and LSD opened doors of perception allowing easier access to these spiritual truths. Initially the motives for the importation of pot and hash and the manufacture of LSD particularly Orange Sunshine were pure and innocent. There was no profit motive, there was a movement motive. Eventually that changed. There were individuals who didn't share the spirit of the movement and they saw the potential for huge amounts of money and they knew how to play the part. They might not have been as successful in the perversion of the heart of this era if it weren't for one thing.

While looking for higher and higher potency marijuana and other mind altering substances in South America somebody stumbled across the substance that brought the hippie culture to its knees. That substance was cocaine.

This is just my personal view but I believe that cocaine opened the gate and let the wolves in among the sheep. This isn't to say that cocaine was a new thing at that time. It had been widely used for various reasons, medical, psychological, and recreational from as far back as the 1850's. By the early 1900's its use had reached dangerous proportions, and then in early 20th-century Memphis Tennessee cocaine was sold in neighborhood drugstores costing five or ten cents for a small boxful. Stevedores along the Mississippi River used the drug as a stimulant, and white employers encouraged its use by black laborers.

By the turn of the twentieth century, the addictive properties of cocaine had become clear, and the problem of cocaine abuse began to capture public attention in the United States. The dangers of cocaine became part of a moral panic that was tied to the dominant racial and social anxieties of the day. In 1903, the American Journal of Pharmacy stressed that most cocaine abusers were "bohemians, gamblers, high- and low-class prostitues, night porters, bell boys, burglars, racketeers, pimps, and casual laborers."

Not much has changed, right?

When cocaine arrived on the scene of the heretofore comparatively benign Southern California drug culture it dealt a blow that transformed what had been a spiritual quest into, for many, a tortuous road of addiction and ruin. I've seen firsthand that this is always the way. The calm before the storm, the sweet seduction before the betrayal.

Dodge City was still holding down the New West.

Woodland Drive was an idyllic setting. It had all the charm of a sleepy little village. Little cottages laced throughout, nestled sweetly amidst towering eucalyptus trees. It definitely had a vibe all its own. Sitting on the porch of one of the first houses on the lane, a dulcimer perched on his lap, strumming contentedly was a young man with long black hair and a dark long beard. He was wearing muslin pants and a shirt of the same material that was tie died in rich purple, red and orange. Security.

"Hey Hope, howsit?"

'It's good Horse. Is Bobby at the Red House?"

Horse set down the beautiful stringed instrument that had such a beautiful mournful tone and came out to the Cruiser. He was impossibly tall and moved with the grace of a cat.

"He should be."

He leaned against the window frame, which bent him nearly double and glanced in the back at the piled-up bags of pot.

"Ahhh Hope, you come with treats. Is this the Zacatecas sweet bud with the pretty red hairs we've been salivating about since Wayne got home?"

"Indeed it is my long brother."

"Head on up and as soon as I can get someone to relieve me I'll be up there. I can't wait to roll a fat doob!"

"And indeed you shall Caballo, indeed you shall."

The Red House was at the end of the drive and sat at a higher elevation than the rest of the houses on the drive. We parked and walked up the stairs to a large patio area and there was that table pipe or its clone. The patio was carpeted in Indian and Persian rugs and there were wind chimes everywhere. On the edge of the patio there was a drum kit, a few amps and a P.A. system. Sitting on one of the amps and noodling on a Gibson acoustic guitar, a Hummingbird, was the quintessential hippie.

Long golden hair and beard framing an angelic face. When he looked up and saw us his smile was probably the most genuine smile I had ever seen on a man in my life. There was absolutely no guile in it, just a great kindness and honesty. This man was John Gale the main shot caller for the Brotherhood. He handed the guitar to a young boy about my age who had been sitting at his feet and got up to greet us.

"Hope, the queen. Om sister."

"Hello Johnny, how are you this fine evening?"

"There's jasmine in the air, bread in the oven, and music everywhere so I'm exceedingly well! You looking for Bobby?"

"Yes I am, I brought the sample LBs."

"Oh that's good, we've all been waiting. Stevie, fetch Bobby would ya bro?"

It took a minute for this kid to get to his feet and as he began walking he kind of hobbled dragging one leg behind him, but he moved quickly. I thought,

"So this is Stevie."

He walked up to us and stood directly in front of me.

"Hey bro, howsit, I'm Stevie."

"I'm Eddie."

I put my hand out for a handshake.

"I know who you are."

He put his arms around me and gave me a hug.

"Welcome to Dodge City brother."

He stood back and we just looked at each other for a moment then he laughed and limped off.

"I'll get Bobbie, John."

I had met Hope and found in her a perfect person. She was pure and seemingly untainted. Then I met Wayne and he was just as pure as Hope. Now Hope had brought me to this wonderland of bohemian bliss and I had entered into a microcosm of the world that I never would have thought existed. Why did that kid hug me? How can a man have a smile so real? What is happening here? Stevie was absolutely beautiful. Like Michelle with her scar, he wore his defect as if it was an asset.

I never had a romantic or sexual attraction to another person of my same gender and I didn't at that moment, but I was immediately and completely in love with Stevie. He looked like an angelic being with long honey colored hair to the middle of his back. His face was lovely, almost feminine except for the strength that poured out of his eyes, piercing, inquiring, and answering all at once.

It may well have been that I saw myself as the antithesis of who Stevie was. I was capable of great rage and I saw that rage as a tool, a strength. I was the runner, the loner, and as I had displayed not many nights earlier, potentially I was the killer. I counted on no one but myself and I trusted no one but myself. I was not a joiner, didn't want to be a part of. But what was all of that but a carefully constructed perimeter of defenses I had constructed to protect myself against further demoralizations like the ones I had experienced in my life up until now? What was it that I was both powerfully repelled and attracted at the same time to what these people had here?

I didn't even fully know what it was but I sensed a strong sense of community and a common thread that was binding it all together. I had never been bound to anything that didn't end up hurting with the possible exception of Michelle and Faith and they were torn from my life, uprooted.

Presently Stevie came back with someone I presumed to be Bobby, he was shaped like Buddha and had a baby face, a quick smile, and merry inquisitive eyes.

"Hey Hope, you brought the samps?"

"Yeah Bobby, they're in the Cruiser. Wayne sent ten pounds, separately wrapped so you could get them around to everybody."

"Cool, we should be good for a few hundred pounds by next week. Just takes a minute for the samples to get out and let people see the quality. Is it as good as we hoped for?"

"Better I think, very tasty and very pretty. If the rest is anything like the bag Wayne unpacked the buds are very well preserved, very little broken and very little shake."

(Shake is what falls off of the buds during transport and is normally made up of shade leaves that are dryer than the resin filled buds or flowers and so they fall off. The result is that shake is less potent and less desirable. The perfect pound of weed would be all fat buds, unbroken and uniform in appearance with almost no shake in the bottom of the bag.)

"Could you guys hump that stash up here?"

John was speaking to Stevie and me.

"Sure!" we chimed, and then looked at each other and grinned.

Stevie and I walked down to the land Cruiser and Hope, John, and Bobby disappeared into the house. Ten pounds wasn't a lot of weight but it was a lot of bulk, however each of us was able to carry half. We unloaded the bags onto the ground first and as I was taking the last bag out of the car, being careful not to be too rough on our fragile cargo, Stevie turned around with an ornately carved wooden box in his hands. Taped to the box was a little card with the Om symbol on it and my name.

"Looks like someone left you a gift bro."

"I took the box and looked at it. It was the height and width of a shoe box and only about half as long. It was the box from the desk at the warehouse. I opened it and the smell hit me immediately. Fresh bud. Atop the approximately three ounces of high grade sensimilla were a one hundred dollar bill and a note. The note said,

"Learn well, choose wisely."

Time would show that I did neither.

"Nice gift."

"Yeah but I don't know what to do with all of this pot."

"You sell it bro."

"I don't know anybody."

"You don't need to know anybody brother. The brothers own a shop called Mystic Arts World. It's really a base for our church. Right across the street is Taco Bell and every hippie tripper in the area is posted up there either selling or scoring. This pot, it's the new thing. You go down there and give away about a quarter ounce worth of pinner joints, nah, maybe eight or ten doobies and you wait an hour. Then for the rest of the day you sell joints for two bucks apiece as fast as you can pull 'em out of a bag, guaranteed."

"Can you help me?"

"I'll go down there with you and show you the deal and then you're on your own. I used to do just what I'm telling you to do but I've moved up to selling the pounds. I'll get them fronted from John and Bobbie for seven hundred and turn them for eight hundred, seven fifty if they buy ten or more."

As we carried the payload up the stairs my mind was very busy. I used to roll about fifty fair size joints from an ounce of weed. If there were three ounces in the box that was one hundred and fifty joints. At two dollars apiece that was three hundred dollars, plus the hundred Wayne had given me which I presumed was for my labor for the day. My mind was reeling with the possibilities.

It didn't take long for Hope to wrap up her business with John and Bobby. Crazy Horse and another guy who had only one arm had come up and everyone was high both from the smoke and the prospects of this venture. We said our goodbyes and headed out.

"Did you have a good day Eddie?"

"I had a great day! I learned a lot and Wayne left this box for me in the back of the Cruiser under the pot."

I opened the box and showed her the contents.

"Oh, that box! I haven't seen that for a while. We found that box in a little shop in the Yucatan. I'm glad he gave it to you. Wayne is a wonderful generous human being but he doesn't normally take to people the way he has taken to you. Do you know what a mentor is Eddie?"

"Yes, like a teacher but more personally involved, right?"

"Good description Eddie but I think invested would be a better word than involved."

I thought about that for a minute and asked,

"Why would he want to invest in me?"

"Eddie, we live in a time like no other time that has ever been, at least here. People are questioning everything. Politics, religion, the status quo. This war in Vietnam has awakened the angst of the young people of this country, and they're growing increasingly dissatisfied with the government their parents have supported. Thousands of young people are forced into military service, given guns and sent to die in the jungles of Southeast Asia. I'm against the draft Eddie but I'm also against not doing your duty to your country, I have to say that. But there's unrest Eddie. War, civil rights, questions about the role of the government in the lives of the citizens, so many things.

With it all is this quest for meaning of a higher nature. The brothers are looking for God in getting high, opening the doors of perception, tuning-in to the God consciousness. Their motives are pure but they're naïve. I was raised in church Eddie. I had a military father and a God fearing mom, and while I too question religion and dogma, I also question the concept of a god who is pleased with his worship being brought to him on the wings of LSD, or peyote or pot I'm sorry Eddie I talk too much sometimes."

"No, no, Hope please, I love to listen to you."

"Well Eddie the quest for God is a beautiful thing, it's what we were created to do, seek Him. But this quest for the perfect drug to use to find God is a Pandora's box of wickedness."

"How do you mean?"

"I said the brothers are naïve. What I meant was that they have ideals that are based in the expectation and the assumption that everyone in their so called family is operating in the same pure motives. This thing with the pot is going to grow. People are already looking for things to import that are easier to conceal, less bulky and with a bigger profit margin. Once the money really starts rolling in these spiritual ideals will be compromised and eventually corrupted entirely. Last week I heard that one of the brothers bought a Porsche. That would never have crossed his mind as little as a year ago."

"What will happen?"

"Greed will take over Eddie and the Brotherhood will be destroyed by the government or it will eat itself alive. I don't remember a lot of the Bible I used to know but I remember this. Do not be deceived, God is not mocked; for whatever a man sows, that he will also reap. For he who sows to his flesh will of the flesh reap corruption, but he who sows to the Spirit will of the Spirit reap everlasting life. Wow, I'm surprised I remember that whole passage!"

"Well then what is your plan, you and Wayne?"

"Honestly Eddie, we want to make a lot of money."

"Do the Brothers know that?"

"Wayne and I have a legitimate business that we work very hard at, and we have developed a clientele that can afford expensive things. We have developed an eye for the things these people will want and we bring them in. We also enjoy the company of many of the people involved in this canyon community. We like to get high, even take a little acid but it's not religion to us. The opportunity to provide a service by importing products that people want is the same whether it's furniture or pot. They want it and Wayne has a good way to get it. No one is being misled here.

"Okay but back to my original question that led to all of these philosophical observations."

"But Eddie you said you liked to hear me talk."

"I do, I do, but let's bring it back to me now. Why would Wayne want to invest in me?"

"Because no one else is Eddie, not a man anyway. You're adrift, and any ship adrift without some sense of direction will inevitably run aground or sink. He doesn't want to see you sink Eddie. I know you trusted before and got hurt, but you can trust Wayne."

"What does he care if I sink?"

"Honestly? At first he only cared that I care. He loves me and he could see that you mean a great deal to me Eddie."

"You've only known me for a few weeks."

"Yes Eddie, that's true, but ask yourself this question. How long does it feel like we've known each other? How did you feel the first day we met? Don't say anything just think about it."

She reached over and wound the long hair at the back of my neck around her finger the way my little brother had and she tugged almost imperceptively, tentatively, as if unsure of how I would respond. I responded by leaning over and putting my head on her shoulder and she breathed a heavy sigh that was accompanied by a shiver, like when you first come in to a warm room after being out in the cold for a long while. You don't really realize you were cold until you feel that warmth and then an involuntary shiver just runs through you.

"I can't have children Eddie."

Tears were rolling down her cheeks and I thought how strange and unfair life was. My own mother was too busy for me and yet the world appeared to be full of women who all they wanted was to be some kid's mom and they couldn't. First Faith, and now Hope. This God really had an interesting way of operating. I wasn't sure I approved of His methods.

"He talks about you all the time Eddie, Wayne I mean."

I hadn't known many women but one thing I had already learned from Michelle is that women have all kinds of thoughts going around in their heads at the same time. They can go back and forth from one thought to another in a single conversation and somehow a man is supposed to keep track of these changes and tie them together. Its like shifting gears in a racecar on a winding road. Women's thoughts and emotions are like a bowl of noodles all winding around and piled on top of one another. You can't see where one noodle ends and another begins but they can.

Men on the other hand are more like a waffle. Nice neat little squares, you can see each and every one. Men have to make a decision to move from one square to another and that takes a minute. Each square is an entity unto itself. Okay so—— Hope can't have kids and Wayne talks about me all the time, got it.

I was getting an uneasy feeling. I didn't want to be anyone's surrogate kid. I had very strong feelings for Hope and like with Faith I had sensed in her the very strong maternal instinct that just comes with some women. I thought it very strange that the women who had kids often didn't want them and the ones who were born to mothering often couldn't have them. Me, I had a very real and powerful fear of intimacy. Any kind of intimacy. Sitting in the Cruiser driving along with my head on Hope's shoulder was sweet, it was a comfort but part of the comfort was knowing that it was just a gesture of recognition. Kind of like,

"Yeah this is a sweet moment."

Part of me was starving for a deep and committed type of family relationship but the other part of me was certain that such things were destined to fail and were best held at arm's length. Keep it on the surface, go through the motions, take advantage of the moments of the physical touch that were warm and sweet but keep it on the outside. Never, never let anyone all the way in, because as soon as you do they're leavin'.

"Eddie are you okay?"

"Yeah Hope, are you okay."

We were pulling up in front of my house and I was relieved. There was the potential for this conversation to go way deeper than I was ready for and I didn't want to hurt Hope. She had enough hurt that she was carrying around already although I had never seen it until she made that statement,

"I can't have children Eddie."

That statement opened brand new windows into her heart. No, I didn't want to ever hurt Hope. But I knew I would. I didn't want to ever love Hope. But I knew I did.

"Will you be over early Eddie?"

We both knew we had talked enough.

CHAPTER 17

I knocked on the door a little after six in the morning. She had said early and I knew they were up because I could hear music. Buffalo Springfield,

"Kind woman, don't leave me lonely tonight."

Wayne opened the door with a huge grin on his face.

"Hey my young brother, come on in!"

The house smelled amazing and it had a really good feeling this morning.

"Hope made granola, I made some insane coffee and I picked out some of the prettiest buds so breakfast is going to be unprecedented and unequalled."

I saw that three places had been set at the table: three beautiful Mexican place mats, three big hand thrown ceramic bowls with matching mugs that looked like they could hold a quart. The bowls were piled deep with Hope's granola and it smelled as if it were still warm from the oven. There was a carafe of steaming coffee, big bowls of fresh fruit, blueberries, strawberries, bananas, and a pot of honey with one of those honey dippers sticking up out of it. But the center piece of the table was a floral arrangement, all kinds of flowers from the garden, but interspersed with all the flowers were beautiful sparkling colors of the Zacatecan sensimilla. I had never seen a bouquet like it.

"I thought you were staying in the canyon."

"I got lonely at about 4:30 this morning and the place was quiet. I locked up and came and woke up Hope and we decided to do a celebratory breakfast. This 500 pound load has taken me months to set up. Meeting the right people, finding the right product, arranging the import. It went perfectly and now the first shipment is here. Today were going to package it. Some of it's going as far as Seattle. Fifty pounds are going to Santa Fe, another fifty to Denver. It should just be the tip of the iceberg Eddie. If we do it right and keep it cool we could be moving a ton at a time before too long. I want to do a ton a month if we can. But right now let's fire up this doob and get primed for Hope's granola, okay?"

"Sounds good Wayne!"

"Pull up a chair then my young friend..."

Wayne reached over and into the bouquet and extracted a likely looking bud and Hope handed him the rolling tray with its resident pack of Bambu rolling papers. Deftly he rolled a fat joint and I struck a match. Wayne took a huge hit, stifled a cough and passed the doob to Hope.

"Ladies first."

"But you took the first hit babe."

"Ahh yes, but that's the proper etiquette. Taking the first hit pulls all of the unpleasant sulfur taste from the match out of the joint thus preparing it for your precious mouth."

"Oh I see."

Hope winked at me and passed me the joint.

Man it was comfy with these folks but every time I felt comfortable, began to develop some hope, every time I felt a little faith growing in my heart towards people I remembered that it had been comfortable with Chewey. I had faith in him, huge trust and then came the betrayal. Suddenly I could feel the supremely painful tearing of my young flesh, scalding tears rolling down my cheeks, biting my lip to keep from crying out, afraid he would hit me. Then when it was over the rage in his contorted face that had once been all light and smiles as he taught me some new thing. How to make an arrow head from a piece of iron, where to find a lobster in a sea cave. All that benevolence replaced by this face of evil and the sharp report of his palm on my cheek as he threatened me not to tell a soul.

Maybe worse yet, my father's face as I told him what had happened and the deathly silent ride to the psychiatrist's office at UCLA. Him telling this total stranger why we were there and then the accusatory line of inquiry. Surely I must have done something to bring all of this about? My agony then as I ran out to the car and waited, shaking with pain and rage for my father to emerge and finally the equally silent ride home.

Suddenly we were strangers and I felt farther from all the people of the world at that moment than I could bear. A week later my pulse had finally evened out and not a word had been spoken between us. Faith had been my sole comfort coming to my room after my father slept. She said nothing of the events that had been taking place she just held me and told me she loved me. Finally the night that broke me as my father bent over to tuck me in and I kissed him on the lips, just trying to get some form of acknowledgement, some encouraging word.

"You little faggot!"

He slapped me and spit in my face then stormed out of the room and slammed the door. I slammed the door as well. I slammed the door on all of you. There was Faith and Michelle and no one else. They had pain. We shared that. Everyone else was nothing but a phantom to me. I slammed the door on any one who had not experienced the amount of pain that I had, had not suffered the humiliation of the ultimate betrayal, the supreme violation, the theft of my innocence, the very assault on the identity of my gender.

Much later I was introduced to Someone Who had experienced the ultimate pain and betrayal and I learned that He did it to erase my pain. He did it to take away all of those nights with my father's words ringing in my ears, resonating in my soul. He did it to obliterate that face of rage and hate, contempt and lust that had been my nemesis Chewey.

"Earth to Eddie, man you haven't even had a hit yet and you're already in orbit."

Yes, it was very comfortable here but I was not okay with comfort and sitting at that lovely table with these warm and welcoming people who cared about me so much I was reminded of the only truths I was sure of, love brings pain, trust is weakness.

The granola was oh sooo good! Piled high with bananas and strawberries slathered in honey. Hope had let me pour the first out of a fresh quart of ice cold Alta Dena raw milk and that first two inches in the bottle was pure cream. The best pot, the best food, the best people and yet I felt like I was only superficially there. Outside I was all good, laughing at the appropriate times, sometimes even feeling like laughing. I was feeling all the right stuff, the early morning sun coming through the kitchen window felt good on my face and my arms, but it simply didn't penetrate. It went in an inch and then fled in the face of a steely resolve and fury that was the core of my being. That cold hard inner me was the me that easily and repeatedly stabbed the driver of the Olds that night and now never even gave it a thought.

That cold hard core was the me that hacked Chewey to death with his own machete over and over in my mind lying in bed at night. It was the me that hated my father for his stupidity. That was who I was. All of this fluffy stuff was a lie and a game. Sometimes I believed in the game but my truth always reeled me back in, and I wondered,

"What if it's always like this?"

At that moment–a moment which came every day–at that moment it was time to get high.

"Its six thirty and I promised you a surf yesterday. If we leave now we can surf for an hour and still make it to the warehouse by eight thirty or nine."

"Can we run by my house so I can get my trunks?"

"Yeah but first lets go down to the garage and find you something to ride."

Hope was standing behind Wayne with her hands on his shoulders and occasionally, gently rubbing the back of his neck. She bent down and kissed the top of his head. I had never seen this kind of thing before. My dad was not an affectionate man and displays of affection were almost non-existent and when they did occur they seemed strained. My mom and John almost never showed any real loving gestures toward one another, they were just too busy, always coming or going, work, work, work.

Could this really happen between two people? I thought of Michelle and I realized that I had loved her, loved her nearness, the girl smell, her voice, and laughter. I loved looking really closely at her disfigurement. It was a mark of beauty to me. But where was she? I had no idea. She was stripped from my life and I was powerless to do a thing about it. She was taken as quickly and as completely as my childhood innocence. No, love was not at all safe, not at all to be trusted. Still I envied Hope and Wayne, envied them a lot.

"You ready Eddie."

"Simon que si, vamos."

As soon as the garage door opened my eyes went straight to the tarp covering that most beautiful thing and Wayne saw me. Like a matador performing a great sweeping media veronica he swept the tarp from that Triumph and it stood there going a hundred miles an hour. It literally took my breath away.

"Don't worry we'll get to that. I can see it's in your blood and you're definitely tall enough, but right now lets find you a board."

In the rafters of the garage were probably fifteen or twenty boards all made by Wayne except for a few made by famous shapers including a Bing Pipeliner shaped by the legendary surfer shaper Dick Brewer at his shop in Hanapepe on Kauai. It was still the longboard era although performance had escalated to such a degree that designers were being more innovative than ever before and boards were taking on a decidedly performance oriented flavor.

The board Wayne picked for me was a green 8'6", fairly thin with what you would call a hippy shape meaning the widest part of the board was rear of the center. It had a slight concave in the nose and like the Triumph it boasted pride in its construction. Wayne's logo was a rendering of the winged foot of Mercury set inside of a stylized sun with lettering that said Wave Wings inside the sun and above the winged foot and below the foot also inside the sun it simply said Wayne. We loaded that board and Wayne's in his truck and drove by my house. I was in and out like a jackrabbit.

"I'm going surfing with Wayne."

I'm not sure if anyone heard me, It didn't matter.

We pulled up to a spot called Brooks Street. There was a cluster of guys standing around at the top of the steps to the beach watching the waves. It was a beautiful morning, not a breath of wind and the sun was glistening off of the sea. There were perfect little chest high waves and about six guys were out.

"Hey Wayne, who's the kid."

"This is Eddie, my protégé. Eddie this is Howard Chapleau, that's Davie Tomkins, that's Ian Stark. This is Pat Tobin and this is Pat Sparkle."

"Hi guys nice to meet you all."

Just then I saw a guy absolutely ripping a wave to shreds but doing it with so much style that he seemed like he was lighter than air.

"Yeah Mike!"

Everybody was hooting his wave and as he kicked out he made a bow and waved up to us. Even from where I was standing his smile was humble.

"That's Mike Armstrong and nobody surfs Brooks Street like Mikey."

"See ya guys, we're gonna surf."

We carried the boards down to the water's edge and Wayne began applying wax to the deck of his board.

"Uh, any pointers?"

Wayne flipped me the bar of wax and said,

"Yeah the fin goes in the back the waxed side goes on top, if you pearl cover your head before you come up."

"Pearl?"

"That's when the nose of your board goes under water. When it does, you're going over the nose and the board is probably going up in the air, so cover your head."

"That's it?"

"You're a smart kid. You'll figure it out."

With that he launched himself expertly through the shore break leaving me standing there on the sand. On a small day Brooks Street breaks fairly close to the beach and I could hear their conversation and see each surfer clearly. There was a camaraderie amongst these guys who seemed mostly in their late teens through their twenties. I had lots of experience body surfing but nonetheless I sat down cross legged to watch how they were doing it. About ten minutes went by and Wayne yelled from the line up, "Yer not gonna learn from there man!"

With that I paddled out. The glide of the board through the water felt natural to me and I was mesmerized by the clarity of the ocean. The bottom was all rock reef covered in eel grass. I could see abalone, the big gold Garibaldi fish and the tri colored Sheepshead. The entire coast of Southern California was rich with kelp and it striated the face of the waves with its long leafy tendrils. Since I had first spear fished in P.V., I had always been in awe of the world under the sea and now as I was caught up in its beauty I didn't see the wave that suddenly broke over my head and ripped the board out from under me.

I swam back in feeling too excited to be embarrassed and retrieved my board. The world was wet and refreshing, cool, clear water and the hot morning sun. I could feel the muscles of my arms and shoulders warming and swelling under the effort of paddling and my heart was beating a steady but quick drum beat in my chest. I made it out to the line up and sat straddling my board trying to do it just like the other guys. Introductions were made between waves, Mike Armstrong, Pete Yoemans who was my age as was Douggie Brown. There was Corky Smith and Spider Wills on a knee board.

"Okay Eddie turn around this one is yours."

I turned my board around and my heart rate went up dramatically. This was it.

"Don't paddle until I say and then give it all you've got."

"Okay."

"Go, go!"

Now everyone is yelling,

"Go, Eddie, go!"

I was paddling madly and then suddenly I felt my speed increase and I was lifted up, there was a transition as I began to go down the face.

"Pop up! Pop up!

I jumped to my feet and quite by accident I made a turn, but it was a turn in the right direction and I was gliding across the face of the wave. It was a foot over my head. It was crystal clear and through it I could see the reef and the kelp fronds and all was completely silent. I felt myself slow slightly and I guess instinctively I moved a little towards the nose. I felt my speed increase until I felt as if I was flying and then I was at the sand. The wave closed out in the shore break and I was tumbled onto the beach. I jumped up and all I heard was a bunch of guys yelling at the top of their lungs.

"Yeah Eddie! Out of sight bro! Unreal man!

My very next wave I pearled and sure enough the instruction about covering my head came in handy because I as I surfaced from the white water that board clunked me right in the arm that I had covered with. I didn't care I was hooked. Brooks Street is a summer spot, only breaking on South swells and now forty two years later I still love that place. I still surf there whenever it breaks, and I still surf with some of the same guys from when I was a kid.

All day we bagged up pounds of weed, smoked joints and drank coffee. Wayne loved coffee and it was funny because all of the peace love crew seemed to hold it in disdain. I think Wayne could easily have been a redneck. For all of his color, his guitar playing, his surfboard shaping, his penchant for gypsy travel and collecting of folk ware from all areas Latin he was actually very conservative. He didn't buy into the free love thing. For him it was Hope and only Hope. He wasn't spiritual at all, and he didn't take himself too seriously.

"Eddie?"

"Yeah?"

"I know you've got some demons chasing your back trail."

"Huh?"

"Nothing. Just know that if you ever want to talk, I'm right here."

That was it, and as much as I would have liked to we never did have that talk.

All day people came to pick up packages of different sizes. Ten pounds here, twenty there. One load of sixty pounds went out. Wayne had me set a five pound package to the side and I asked him about it because I thought he wouldn't do less than ten pounds.

He gave kind of a sigh,

"Its for my brother Max. He'll be by later."

Hope came with food and beer and we took a break. It was about four in the afternoon and most all of the pot was gone. I heard it before I saw it. It was a deep throated rumble, decidedly aggressive as it decelerated on the canyon road.

'Max is here baby.'

"Yeah I heard him."

Then into the driveway turned the most amazing car I had ever seen. It looked like it was only an inch off of the ground and it was very, very black. I had never seen anything so black. The chrome of the huge grill shone blindingly, like looking right into the sun, and it growled. I learned it was a 1950 Chevy customized after a style made popular by the Chicano car aficionados of the barrios. It was a low-rider.

And then out of this apparition stepped another apparition and it was Max. He was wearing a bright white t-shirt and both his arms were covered in black and blue tattoos. There was literally no naked skin showing. He was wearing brand new Levi's 501's and engineer boots. His belt buckle was a Harley Davidson emblem and he had on a pair of very black and very small sunglasses that I later learned were called murder ones. His hair was slicked back under a bandana. He was the very first of his breed I had ever seen.

"Hey bro, hi Hope."

He came over and gave Hope a hug which she returned in spades. She kind of held him like she was afraid to let go. Almost like a kid holding onto a worn and tattered security blanket. She was holding him like someone was going to take that blanket away to give it a turn through the washer and dryer.

Wayne came over and put his arms around both of them and for just a second I had a vision of two people on the beach standing over a third person who had been pulled from the sea. It was a beautiful day and all three were wet from the ocean and glistening in the sun, but there was no life in the person lying in the sand. The two people standing were shocked and dismayed, helpless to do anything but stare in disbelief.

"How could this be? Everything was fine! We were all fine!"

As they released each other my vision disappeared but I was shaken and I knew I had to know this young man, this drowning young man. I looked his tattooed arms up and down kind of expecting to see the words, "Lost Boy", in large Old English caps. He had gravel in his voice and he moved with precision like he thought about every move. He would occasionally reach up and scratch his face or his arm and I wondered what he was on. I wanted some whatever it was.

"Are you okay Max?'

"Yeah sis, I'm okay."

"We worry about you."

"It's been almost eight years, trust me I'm okay. You got my package? I gotta go."

"Eddie grab those five elbows for Max would ya?"

Later on the way home in the cruiser with Hope I asked,

"So what about Max?"

"He's a year younger than Wayne and he was the smart one. He got accepted to U.C.S.D on an academic scholarship. His first year there he met Gloria. She was a beautiful Mexican girl and very much a scholar. Her family is deeply involved in drugs and smuggling, part of a huge cartel in Tijuana. It's through them that Wayne was able to put all of this together. Anyway her family was very proud of her and when she and Max got together the family wasn't happy but they were deeply in love.

Max's second year at school he was kicking butt and their love was blossoming. One night they were supposed to get together after a football game and Gloria didn't show up. She didn't show up for school the next day and when Max went by her apartment her room mates hadn't seen her. He called her family and they called the police but they didn't think it was as big deal and given her heritage they blew it off.

A few days later they found her in a motel room in Chula Vista. She had been beaten raped and killed. The police assumed it had something to do with her family and they made very little effort in investigating the case.

Max lost his mind, he was possessed. He started digging and learned that there had been a guy who had been trying to date her. He was very persistent but she never told any one and she rebuffed him numerous times. It was him. He had snatched her and did those things to her. Max went to the police and after an investigation that only lasted a couple of weeks they said there wasn't enough evidence to arrest him. Plain and simple Max tried to kill him, he thought he was dead when he left him but the guy survived.

Max was arrested and got eight years. The guy died mysteriously while Max was in prison.

Gloria's family took care of Max the whole time he was in prison, and to say he's connected is the understatement of the century. But while Max was in prison whatever was left of the athlete and the scholar died and the drug smuggling, heroin using, gangster

is what came home. He's still very close to her family and they hold on to each other as a way of holding on to Gloria. He can go anywhere in their world and he's untouchable. He's a saint to them. They give him access to everything they have and it's killing him, but really when Gloria died Max died with her.

He lives here in town but he hangs out in the barrios from San Diego to Casa Blanca in Riverside and Delhi in Santa Ana. He smuggles quantity but he has a few retail customers here in town. Heroin addicts with means to support their habits. He doesn't need to do it but he has become addicted to the life as much as the drugs he sells. He has a good heart, he helps people, nobody is going to go hungry if Max is around but he deals in the devil's own poison. He's tortured by the prison he has created and he hides it all behind those shades, those tattoos, that car and whatever young chick he has at the time. If you ever get him to take off those shades you'll see in his eyes he's the saddest man alive. He is a dead man walking."

I didn't say anything in response to that biography but you all know what I was thinking, another lost boy. The tree of life dripping with the bitter fruit of pain. Yes I would know Max, and soon.

As we pulled up in front of my house Hope handed me an envelope.

"See you in the morning Eddie?"

"Yeah, what time?"

"Six if you want to eat before you surf."

I got inside and went to my room and opened the envelope. Two crisp one hundred dollar bills. Man I was comin up. I had been so busy I hadn't had time to spend a penny or do anything about the pot Wayne had given me. I decided it was time to pull Philly and Drew into my world. It was time to start a little cartel of my own. I put the money in the box, shoved it deep under my bed and went to find my little brother.

I took him from Rosa and he was delighted to see me. He scampered into my arms and buried his little head in my neck. He was laughing hard and his breath on my neck and the trust in his embrace had me crying. It was moments like that one that broke into my fortress. I had no defense against that kind of innocent love, nor did I try to defend myself. There is, in that kind of love a purity that warrants no defense, requires no protection, allows no pollution. I simply gave myself over to it, although only for a moment at a time. But for that moment I was, well, I was whole, I was found.

"What do you think little man, you want to ride the skateboard?"

I took him out to the garage and got out my Hobieflex. I put him on the board in front of me and for an hour we carved turns on the driveway. I told him all about Brooks Street and Wayne, my first wave, and when he wasn't staring intently on the nose of the board and the driveway with his little tongue clenched between his lips in concentration he was looking up at me with unbridled devotion.

John and my mom pulled in the driveway at about sundown and we moved out of the way so he could pull the big Cadillac in the garage. They got out of the car and stood there. John with his arm around my mom and they were smiling. There was no admonition about Paulie's safety, no questions. They trusted me with him. It was at that moment I knew that the only thing broken here was me. I could be a part of this family, they wanted it; all of the necessary ingredients were there. Oh yeah they were busy building their business, but they were good people, good parents. I was only a few days away from starting a new school. I could start over, plug in, do the deal, be a good kid.

Then I remembered what school was like for me. I remembered comparing myself to all of those other kids. I just couldn't understand any of it. I was always doing something so outrageously weird in their minds and it was totally normal for me. I was going to be a monumental disappointment to these people.

I remembered the lunch box episode at Wonderland Avenue School, cracking that kid upside the head. I remembered how mortified everyone had been. I stopped skateboarding with Paul and handed him to my mom. He didn't like it but he calmed down quickly. Smell of mom trumps skateboard. I had an invitation here, an invitation to join. As if making an R.S.V.P. to an affair I thought,

"Thank you so much for your gracious invitation, unfortunately I have a previous commitment on that date."

It wasn't them, it was me and I never again blamed my family for the life I chose.

"I was going to make my garlic chicken, are you going to be here for dinner?"

It might seem odd that parents would be asking if a twelve year old was going to be home for dinner but what you must remember is that almost from birth I had been living according to my own agenda. I ran the streets of Puerto Vallarta at seven years old. Even today my mom is fond of telling stories about my precocious nature.

At six months old I was an expert escape artist regularly flinging myself over the rails of my crib repeatedly hour after hour. I had absolutely no regard for consequences. At four years old mom was trying to discipline me for constantly running off down the street whenever she turned her back for a moment. She had locked me in my room and I had escaped. In her exasperation after spankings and scoldings she said,

"I'm going to take every single thing out of your room and tie you up in there."

I looked her dead in the eye and said very matter of factly,

"Fine, you can take whatever you want but you can't take away my thoughts."

Add to that the guilt she felt for sending me away so she could pursue her relationship with John Stewart and she had given up trying to control me. In fairness it was all she had left to do was send me to my father, not to mention that it was God who sent me to save me from the evil being done to me, but she had no idea about that. The fact is that I went where I desired and did what I desired and I left her with nothing but worry over my possible whereabouts. She did what she had to do and the guilt she felt was misplaced but as unmerited as it was I was quick to capitalize on it.

I was quickly forming a plan. I would dine with the family and then go and find Drew and Philly and lay out my plans for them. We could roll a bunch of joints and then hitch a ride down town to Taco Bell and kick off our new enterprise. I didn't need Stevie; after all it was a simple matter. We'd pass out a few samples and then kick back for a while and see what happened. Siempre y seguro.

By setting them up at night I would be free in the morning to surf with Wayne and do whatever he had for me for the day.

"Yeah mom I love that chicken."

We all walked in the house together. There was a little garden pathway leading from the garage to the house and Paul walked between my mom and John holding both of their hands but his little neck was bent around and he was grinning at me. I was his hero and he was the only pure thing in my life. At least the only pure thing I was able to acknowledge.

I took a shower and put on some 501's, a pair of Van's and a t-shirt and went out to have dinner with the family. John was sitting in his chair smoking a Kent, a huge drink perched on the arm of the chair.

"Hey John."

"Hi Eddie. Almost time to start school, right?"

"Yeah it looks like it."

He grinned at me knowingly and said,

"Pretty exciting, huh?"

I must have rolled my eyes or something because he laughed, laughed hard.

"Well I'm pretty sure you will find some way to make it interesting."

This cat was really something. One time they had a cocktail party for a bunch of potential clients. They were all sitting around the dinner table chatting and trying to appear, I don't know, worldly, for John's approval. He was already a little buzzed and he was sitting back with cigarette smoke forming a cloud over the table even though no one smoked other than him. He was looking at all of them through his one eye and suddenly he chuckled, pushed his chair back and standing up he announced,

"You are all full of crap…"

With that he walked into the living room with his smoke and his whiskey and turned on the fights. They were in fact full of crap, and they knew it too. My mom was beside herself flitting around the table trying to clean it up. I was in the kitchen with my grammie and we looked at each other and tried to not break out into hysterical laughter. We failed. Two days later a contract showed up and they hired John as the architect for a huge project. Carte Blanche, whatever he wanted to do, no questions asked.

He was some dude, and the thing of it was that he got me and because he got me he let me go. I was sure, and would learn later about his childhood, proving my theory true, but I was sure even then that he had been a lost boy. Somehow he had channeled all of that angst and rage, he had found his peace place. He never lost his anger or his opinion that everyone was full of crap but he found a way to make it work. I think that in a way he lived vicariously through my disregard for convention because while we shared it to the ninth degree mine came out completely differently than his.

As I passed by him on my way to the kitchen he said, almost in a whisper, "School is hell Eddie, so if you can't go you gotta read. You gotta read every day. If you do you'll find it, if you don't die first."

His Kent was dangling from his lips and a long ash fell to his shirtfront.

"Damn!"

As he brushed the ashes off I was certain that the whole long ash thing was a strategic move staged to end the encounter. Yeah, he was some cat allright.

"Smells really good in here."

Gramms was setting the table and my mom was in the kitchen pulling the bird out of the oven. Even cooking she looked glamorous. At sixteen she had been a model for Neiman Marcus and that same year she began designing her own line. She was and always has been a very warm and generous person. Any good thing in me in the areas of compassion, empathy, forgiveness, or generosity came from her.

"Are you hungry Eddie?"

"Mom, I could be stuffed and still eat every bit of that whole chicken its so good."

From the dining room.

"She learned it from me."

"Yeah I know Grammie, that and the Apple Brown Betty with hard sauce."

"I'm going to make that for you soon dear."

Dinner was pleasant. It was always pleasant; that was a rule. Nothing was ever discussed at the dinner table that could possibly result in contention. It simply wasn't done. A throwback to my blue blooded family tree. Dinner was proper. Proper silver, proper linen, proper etiquette. I waited until my grandmother and mom were seated and went to pull out my chair.

"Go put on a shirt with sleeves please Eddie."

You see what I mean. Paulie was in the kitchen in a high chair with Rosa and he was pitching a fit so I went and brought him to the table. I could see my grandmother getting ready to contend this but seeing the look on Paulie's face she relented.

After dinner I grabbed Paulie and headed out to the front yard. The sky over the ocean was the color of marmalade morphing into purple as it went further up the sky. There were a lot of mint plants growing around the front door and jasmine grew all up the fence and the front gate. The beauty of the sunset and the aromas in the air had both Paulie and me in a kind of full belly trance. He was perched atop my shoulders and his little bare feet were tapping out kind of a rhythm on my chest. I thought of what Hope had said about Max's customers.

"Heroin addicts with means."

So that's what Max was on. I'm gonna have to try that very soon. Rosa emerged from the house to take Paulie down for bed. I carried him in and downstairs to the part of the house where he, my grandmother and Rosa all had their rooms. Rosa followed with his bottle. My mom and grammie were in the kitchen and John was back in his chair watching the fights. All had kissed Paulie goodnight. It took a few minutes to disengage his grip from my neck but eventually he laid down and took his bottle.

I went into my room and grabbed an ounce bag of the weed and a couple of packs of papers, my smokes and a hoodie and climbed out my bedroom window. Out on the street I fired up a Tareyton and started walking.

"Us Tareyton smokers would rather fight than switch!"

I laughed. Ninety percent of 'em had never been and never would be in a fight as long as they lived. I was going to walk up First Street to Philly's house and then get him and go find Drew but I didn't have to. Right at the corner of West Street and Monterey I found them walking towards my house. We stood there in the last of the twilight, the day quickly disappearing and yielding to darkness and lit smokes.

"I've got a little proposition for you guys. Philly is Cricket home?"

Cricket was Philly's twenty year old sister and she and her baby lived in a guest house, really more like a guest shack, behind their folk's house. Philly's room was back there also. Cricket was a full stoner but she was also a full manipulator and I didn't want her sticking her big nose in our business.

"No man she's gone for the night."

At this point I whipped out the bulging bag of bud.

"Good, we're gonna go over to your house and roll up this whole thing and then we're gonna take it down to Taco Bell and sell doobies."

"Cool, lets go."

I had one rolled up and I put fire to it and we smoked it as we walked the half mile to Philly's house.

"Man this stuff tastes good."

"Yeah, that's cuz *it is* good."

About halfway through the doob Drew said,

"Oh man, I'm getting way stoned. I don't think I can smoke anymore."

Philly and I just looked at each other and smiled. He was sure a lightweight given he was as big as he was. A couple of hits later,

"Hey don't bogart that joint guys!"

"I thought you couldn't smoke anymore."

"I'm gonna press on through, I feel a second wind coming on."

That started us laughing and I think we all had one of those, "found", moments.

Philly's house was one of those cute little beach cottages with the pretty little manicured lawn bordered by rose bushes and a white picket fence that gave rise to the term, "Laguna charm", except that there was no paint on the fence, the lawn was brown and bare, and the yard was littered with cast off children's toys and car parts.

Philly's dad was a very hard working man. He was a mechanic, and a good one. He had been at the same garage for twenty five years. The problem was that although he worked from dawn 'til dusk every day, from dusk 'til he passed out he was drunk as a skunk. He dutifully signed over his paycheck every Friday and Philly's mom kept him at home and in his Lazy Boy by buying the exact amount of cheap beer and cheaper vodka to last all week.

The fact that he had all the booze he needed and that she didn't hassle him about his drinking kept him out of the bars and coming home. In fact he was pulling his pick up in the driveway at exactly six fifteen every night and it pulled out again at exactly six every morning. He was basically a machine: work, drink, sign over the check. If she was able to buy cheaper booze by buying it in greater bulk then she would and save a little money. He was much like the vacuum cleaner, just a tool to be pulled out when needed, no conversation, no participation, just use it and put it away.

Darla, that was Philly's mom was a quiet no nonsense woman who just seemed to be doing time. She understood the futility of complaining and she just put her hand to the plow and waited for it all to be over. She was a nurse at South Coast hospital and it was there that she had a life. She was good at her job, she had a few friends and a few laughs but except for Philly's little sister Jenna home was just a place she worked and slept. In fact she often thought that her work was her home and her home was her work. Cricket was lost to her and so was Philly. Her husband was married to the bottle and only Jenna seemed to need her.

Big Philly was passed out in his big old chair in full recline position, still wearing his garage uniform and Darla was sitting on the couch illuminated eerily by the flickering light of the TV. Two people could not have been further apart while occupying the same space as were Darla and Big Philly. Philly didn't even look in the window as we crept up the side of the house to get to the guest house. He did however stop at Jenna's window and cup his hand to the glass as he peered inside checking on his sleeping little sister. Before he turned away he made the sign of the cross and kissed it to his lips which I thought was a very curious thing seeing how just like with my family there was no religion whatsoever.

We went around to the door of Philly and Cricket's little pad. It was like an unfinished add-on except it was detached from the house. I think they call them a Mother In Law. The siding was unfinished and most of the exterior walls were just tarpaper over plywood. There was no finish trim on the windows or the doors and inside the drywall had been taped but not textured. There was a main hallway with two bedrooms off to the right a living and kitchen area to the left and a bathroom at the end of the hall. The place looked as if a bomb had gone off in there. The unmistakable smell of a misplaced crappy diaper hung in the air blended with the bouquet of trash too long under the sink. It was littered with baby toys and women's clothes. Cricket was a large breasted girl and there was a bra draped over one of the chairs in the living area. I was mesmerized by the size of the cups. I looked away quickly in case Philly saw me but that image was etched in my mind for some time.

Walking into Philly's room was like landing on a different planet. Everything was in perfect order. Philly had painted the walls a dark blue color and all over them were pictures of motorcycles. His bed was made tightly and across the back wall there was a couch he had yanked in from the alley where it had been discarded by a neighbor. There was a little coffee table he had made from a plank and a couple of cinder blocks, covered by a paisley printed cloth. On either end of the table was a pair of mismatched chairs that were obviously castoffs as well. There were motorcycle magazines carefully laid out for display on the table weighted down by an empty and clean ashtray.

Philly plopped down on the couch.

"Welcome to my world."

He reached under the couch and pulled out a rolling tray and frowned.

"We need something a lot bigger. I'll be right back."

He left and came back a few minutes later with a large cookie sheet.

"Sorry I took so long. I wanted to check on Jenna."

I dumped the bag of buds in the middle of the cookie sheet and with no discussion we each fanned about a third to our respective corners of the sheet. The guys waited to see what size joints I was going to roll. After I rolled the first one Philly said,

"I think that one is just a hair too big"

"Okay we'll smoke this one later, then."

It took a couple of joints to get our sizes uniform but once we did we blew through that bag in about twenty minutes. In the end we had sixty five perfectly rolled doobies and I was very happy with the results. I divided them into three piles with the five extra in a separate pile of their own.

"There's our sample group. Philly do you have any baggies?"

"I'll get some."

While Philly was gone a thought came to me and I made two piles of thirty each out of the sixty. I decided I was just going to watch and play director where necessary.

We got to the Coast Highway and put out our thumbs and the first car to come our way was a VW bus. It began slowing down and I could see the driver was a hippie. Long hair, beard, tie dye shirt. He pulled to a stop and Philly cranked open the sliding back door. He and Drew jumped in back while I got in the front. There was a stick of incense burning in a little Buddha glued to the dash and there was sitar music playing from a little portable tape recorder sitting between the seats. Once we got underway I pulled out a doob and lit it up. I took a big hit and passed it over. The driver took a big hit as well and as he did he glanced over at me with a very inquisitive look. The doob went around a couple of times and he started laughing.

"I was going to see if you kids wanted to get stoned, I thought it would be fun to turn on a few youngsters and you pull out this amazing smoke. Where'd you get it?

"We've got some for three bucks a doobie."

"I usually buy my weed a can at a time."

"Can't do that right now, maybe tomorrow."

"Do you have ten?"

"Yep, and if you buy ten I'll give 'em to you for two"

"I'll take 'em. Where will you be tomorrow?"

"I'm going to be surfing at Brooks Street in the morning around seven."

I noticed that I said this with a certain sense of pride and belonging.

"How much for an OZ?"

"A hundred bucks."

"Whoa that's a little steep."

"Never mind then, enjoy the joints."

"No, little brother, I'll be there at seven."

We were coming up on the corner of Thalia and Coast Highway and so I said,

"You can drop us off anywhere around here."

We pulled into the gas station on the corner and I had the boys each give the dude five joints and he gave me the twenty bucks.

"What is your name anyway man?"

"Cowboy, what's yours?"

"Eddie."

While we were talking a couple of guys with back packs came up and asked if Cowboy was going much further up the road and could they get a ride. They spied the joints in Cowboy's hand and they almost started salivating. He told them sure he was going to Huntington and they couldn't get in the van fast enough. For me I was beginning to feel a sense of power I never had before. I had just completed my first ever drug deal. I had a product and people were willing to pay what I asked to have it. I had two guys working for me already and I was feeling just a wee bit taller.

We had fifty joints left plus the five sample joints and so as we walked the remaining two blocks to Taco Bell I planned my strategy. I would just sit and watch for a little while and try to pick out the people who looked like they could afford to buy and then I would simply tell them,

"Try this and if you like it I've got it."

I would sell each joint for three bucks. Two fifty if you bought five or more, two bucks if you bought ten. I had a feeling that once it got out how good it was anybody with any money would buy as many as they could and then wait until mine were gone and turn around and sell theirs.

Most of the folks hanging around the scene there were strictly consumers just wanting to get high and be a part of what was going on. Then there were those who were always looking for an opportunity. They would look for anything they could buy and sell for a profit even a small one, or they would try to act as the middle man, finding the guy with the product and the guy with the desire and bump up the price between the two. A smart guy could make a good chunk of change just hanging around and paying attention.

Looking to see who was new on the scene and getting to him before he knew who was who and what was what.

The last block before Taco Bell was like a parade of freaks. On the inland side of the Highway there was a supermarket and not much was happening over there but on the ocean side it was going off. Between St. Anne's street and Cleo street (which is where Taco Bell is) there were three head shops. The Family Store owned by a guy named Frenchie. He had a little bootleg kitchen and he made and sold crepes in the back and up front he sold whatever he thought might sell to a bunch of heads. Next was a place called Things which was short for Things For Your Head and closest to Taco Bell was Visions. Visions has weathered the times and is still there today.

Visually that block was mind-boggling as was the other side of the Highway the next block down in front of Mystic Arts World. Music and incense came pouring out on to the street from the different shops and mixed with the smell of pot, which was smoked openly on the street. There were Hare Krishnas playing finger cymbals and tambourines, twisting and turning in tight little circles as they danced and chanted their way through the throng. Minstrels with guitars played and sang in doorways. People were buying and selling drugs openly. In that two and a half block stretch of street there were probably five or six hundred people all high, all seeking to get higher still.

Taco Bell in itself was a total scene. It had been totally taken over by the throng. Tacos were twenty five cents and while many of the soul seekers hanging out there would claim vegetarian, hungry is hungry. In fact across the highway and back up the street a ways was a little restaurant called Love Animals Don't Eat Them and many times I saw people slamming tacos in their pie holes like deprived gormandizers and later posturing with the purists and tofu eaters at L.A.D.E.T.

Taco Bell had a kind of courtyard with a fire ring in the middle and a low wall all around the perimeter. It was done in Mission style, well actually the word "style" is questionable, bearing in mind that it was the source of twenty five cent meals that required no untensils. All along both sides of this wall people lounged, sitting on top of it, leaning against it, laying next to it. Every linear foot was occupied with a very colorful display of individuals.

We made our way through the crowd and I began looking for prospects. I was convinced that with my five sample joints I could sell all of what we had, come back again with more and sell all of that as well. I was right. Within two hours we sold all of what we brought and just as I had predicted, one individual bought twenty joints. He bought 'em and then went and bought a box of tacos, which he took off to the side and ate leisurely just waiting for us to leave.

When we left I had a hundred and fifty bucks in my pocket, only it felt like a million. I was feeling a rush of power like I had never felt. My mind was reeling with ideas and possibilities. I gave Philly and Drew twenty five bucks each and promised them a little stash and they were more than grateful. They were seeing me differently now. We were no longer three equals, now I was the leader. I made a promise to myself to never take advantage of that and to always be a good friend, to be fair and generous.

"You guys want to keep doing this?"

They both chimed in,

"Oh yeah! You bet bro!"

CHAPTER 18

So that was it, I was a drug dealer. I had not aspired to it; it had more or less dropped into my lap. Situations and events occurred in which I found myself propelled in a direction that I did not plan but once those events did take place I immediately saw opportunities and I was quick to take advantage of those opportunities. The sense of power and control I got from that very first night, "on the hustle", was intoxicating. It wasn't long before I had talked my way into Max's life and began doing deliveries for him. By the second month of the school year I was making five hundred a week between Taco Bell and helping Wayne and Hope. They were good mentors and advised me well, steering me into proper ways to conduct business on the street.

Drew and Philly were making a couple of hundred a week and they were both faithful and were able to keep things under their hats. All three of us had bought motorcycles and we were a little gang ripping around South Laguna only at first and then venturing out and into Laguna, Newport, and Costa Mesa. It's the strangest thing but it seems like we were almost invisible. No one seemed to notice that we were doing awfully well for three twelve year old kids. Cops didn't even seem to see us.

At first I didn't make much money running around for Max and it wasn't about the money. I was desperately attracted to the drug. After the first time I did heroin at Suede's house I became enchanted with everything to do with it. The ritual of the hype kit was enthralling to me. Even the bandana I used to tie off held an almost magical significance to me. Then there was the rush... Nothing on the planet compared to what happened when I pushed that needle into a vein and watched the blood swirl up and mix with that hot brown liquid.

Squeezing that little rubber bulb and watching that sweet nectar disappear into my arm and then the wave comes. It comes hard and it comes fast. It's supremely physical, the most intensely gratifying thing that any human has ever felt. Nothing comes even remotely close in intensity, and I mean nothing. If it were only that it would be a junkie maker, but it's so much more. It's a revelation in complete peace. It's an emotional and spiritual crescendo of joy. There is absolutely no pain it does not obliterate, no question it does not answer, no hunger it does not satisfy, no need it does not meet.

Its architect is Satan and it was created in the bowels of hell, for the express purpose of stealing men's souls as it quickly stole mine. I became so enamored of everything to do with heroin that I began posing as the grandson of an older woman from Chula Vista and would walk pieces, (a piece was a twenty five gram clod of salt and pepper heroin), across the border five at a time. It was all so easy and I never had any fear of getting busted. The truth was that I had developed a mindset that said that until you had been busted and done some time you really weren't the real deal.

So I hustled the weed, ran the border, surfed with Wayne, rode my motorcycle and by now Wayne had taught me to ride the black beast. I used heroin on a daily basis and I counted money, my money. I went to school as little as possible, got suspended whenever the opportunity presented itself and I read books. I was always reading a book.

Then one day I was at the beach at Oak Street surfing Gene's reef and about noon I went up To Gene's market to get something to eat. I got a Knudsen's chocolate milk and a Hostess lemon pie all for about thirty cents. I was coming out of the store and I saw two young guys in slacks, black dress shoes and button down shirts approaching me.

"Hey do you have a minute?"

"What do you want?"

"If you were to die today do you know where you would be going?"

"Uhh, no I guess not."

They told me about Jesus, how He had died on a cross for my sins. Did I know I was a sinner? Yes I was pretty sure that was true. They explained how much God loved me and shared with me a couple of verses they said were from what they called the gospel of John.

John 3:16-17

For God so loved the world that He gave His only begotten Son, that whoever believes in Him should not perish but have everlasting life. For God did not send His Son into the world to condemn the world, but that the world through Him might be saved.

Something was stirring way down deep inside of me and the words they were speaking had a power and authority I had never felt in all the mystic religious stuff I had read and

heard. It had the ring of truth and I learned later that it was the Holy Spirit of God bearing witness in my heart.

One of the guys said to me,

"Ephesians 2:8-9 says,

For by grace you have been saved through faith, and that not of yourselves; it is the gift of God, not of works, lest anyone should boast."

"So you mean that I can't do it on my own? I can't earn a place in heaven?"

"No man, it's all Jesus. He has done all of the work already, all you have to do is ask Him with all your heart to forgive you and come in to your life and be your Savior."

I immediately had that same sense that I had that day in front of the church in Vallarta.

"I love you My child and I will always be with you."

So much more was said that day but it came down to this,

"Do you want to receive Jesus as your Savior and have all of your sins forgiven?"

"Yes I really do."

They led me in a prayer in which I asked Jesus to forgive me for my sins and come into my heart and after we were done one of the guys told me he thought the Lord wanted him to share a passage that was just for me. It was this one from the book of Romans.

Romans 8:37-39

Yet in all these things we are more than conquerors through Him who loved us. For I am persuaded that neither death nor life, nor angels nor principalities nor powers, nor things present nor things to come, nor height nor depth, nor any other created thing, shall be able to separate us from the love of God which is in Christ Jesus our Lord.

And through my entire life that has been true, He has been there. I have run from God, I have abandoned God, and I have cursed God and yet He has never left me. He has always been there. God had a plan for my life and I had no idea what it was and I still was not a willing participant in His plan. I feel as if I have always been the rope in a tug of war between God and the devil with me changing sides as either my convictions or my lusts and self centeredness dictate but God has always had a plan. What Satan has meant for evil God has always turned around for good.

I took my new found God and my new born again life and I went to Dodge City to tell the acid princes they were wrong about God and that I had found the truth. The first person I saw was a fellow named one-armed Herbie Einstein. One of his arms was severed neatly at the shoulder and I never learned how but he was rumored to be the nephew of Albert Einstein. He was sitting on the front steps of one of the houses on Woodland.

"Hey Herbie what's up?"

"Hey Eddie what are you doing this fine day?"

"I was surfing at Oak Street and I got hungry so I went up to Gene's to get something to munch and I met two guys who told me all about Jesus."

"Oh man that is cool! Jesus was a great man and a great teacher of spiritual truths."

"Well they said He was a lot more than that. They said that He came to die for my sins and that only through His sacrifice and my belief that He is the one and only Son of God could I be forgiven and go to heaven. They said we are all sinners separated from God and so God sent Jesus to build a bridge so that we could have a relationship with God. The only way to get across that bridge is to ask Him into your heart as Lord and Savior and repent from your sinful life."

"Yeah well that's what the Bible says but the Bible has been so tampered with by men over the years that much of it can't be trusted."

"What do you mean?"

"Well just take the Bible's strong position on sex for example. Sex is a beautiful thing and should be freely enjoyed by all God's children but the Bible that we read today confines sex to just marriage. That's probably because at the time the King James Version was printed, Europe was rampant with venereal disease. The writers just wanted to protect the people from themselves. It was a noble idea but I don't believe that's what God really thinks about sex. And then the whole sin and hell thing. I think that's another way for the church to control the masses and put fear in them and thus obedience to their dogma. I believe that there are many ways to find God. There are many paths up the mountain but they all lead to the top and as long as you're seeking a spiritual path and not hurting anyone God will meet you on that path. I just rolled a doob you want to get high?"

"Uh, yeah sure Herbie. Thanks. For the advice I mean."

"No problem, young blood."

And so there it was. Seeds of righteousness and truth snatched away by the prince of the power of the air. Not in an outright condemnation of Christianity but more in a, "Yeah but," manner. Friendly opposition if you will.

Now at this time in my life I would blow holes in that argument but it was effective on a very naïve young mind.

The truth is that we can absolutely trust the Bible as being the authoritative, inerrant and infallible word of God.

2 Timothy 3:16-17 says:

All Scripture is given by inspiration of God, and is profitable for doctrine, for reproof, for correction, for instruction in righteousness, 17 that the man of God may be complete, thoroughly equipped for every good work.

And you had better believe that what God inspires He also preserves and guards. The first part of the verse says that all scripture is given by inspiration of God and the word inspiration in the Greek is the word pneustos which means breath. This verse really says that scripture is God breathed. The Bible is the very breath of God. Oh yeah, he is going to protect that from any form of adulteration or contamination and the whole host of heaven has spent two thousand plus years doing just that. The fact is that the Bible is sixty six books written by forty authors in three languages, Hebrew, Aramaic, and Greek over a fifteen hundred year period and yet it is seamless in its continuity. No other work of literature has been as well preserved or accurately transcribed in the history of the written word. The Bible makes predictions about the future called prophecy. Some of these predictions were made early on in the Old Testament and were fulfilled with one hundred percent accuracy later in scripture. Some of these predictions were made hundreds of years before they came to pass and yet they always came to pass. There has been prophecy given in the Bible concerning events that were to happen beginning in Biblical times and being completed in our day and age such as the de-nationalization and disbursement of Israel and its subsequent return to its land and Nation in 1948. There were literally hundreds of prophecies given that Jesus needed to fulfill in order to qualify as being the Messiah and yet He fulfilled every one to the letter. Many great scholars have set out to disprove the truth of scripture only to become born again Christians as a result of their research. One such fellow is the great author C.S. Lewis. There is just so much evidence to prove the Bible as being the actual, faithful, true Word of God that no one after having investigated it even nominally could deny its authenticity. Read Foundations of the Christian Faith by James Montgomerey Boyce. That will cure you of your doubtful thinking. But better yet get on your knees and ask God to forgive you your sins. Ask Jesus to come into your life and be your Lord, mean it with all your heart and the Holy Spirit of God will move in and take up residence in you.

2 Corinthians 5:17 tells us this beautiful truth:

Therefore, if anyone is in Christ, he is a new creation; old things have passed away; behold, all things have become new.

If you do these things and you read the Bible the Holy Spirit will make the words come alive and you will see a miracle.

So I sat and listened to Herbie's well meaning but uneducated opinions about God and religion for a while and finally I asked,

"Have you ever read the Bible Herbie?"

"Well no not exactly."

"What do you mean not exactly?"

"I've read parts of it like the sermon on the mount and a really cool part on love, I can't remember what else."

"Okay Herbie, thanks for the doob, I'll see ya later okay?"

"Yeah sure Eddie, just remember god is everywhere and in everything."

I went away with the feeling that all of these people were just inventing a god that fit into their lifestyle. A little pocket god they could whip out and play with. I already knew that God was way bigger and way more serious than that.

That was a monumental day in my life, the day that my name was written in the Lamb's Book Of Life but it was not only monumental for that reason but for another reason that was as dark as my salvation was light, as sinister as my salvation was pure and beautiful. Wayne had been in Mexico on a buying trip and had been gone a week. He was due back the next day and I had already asked Hope if I could go with her to the airport. Partly because I wanted to see Wayne but also because I loved to be in the car with her, it was close and I could watch her. I could see all the little muscles in her forearms as she held the wheel, all the muscles in her legs, the way her neck craned forward ever so slightly as she negotiated the road ahead.

She would reach up and tuck a tendril of hair behind her ear with perfect fingers, sometimes she would stick the tip of her tongue out the corner of her lips. I adored her, but with reserve and from a distance. Riding in the car with her was as close as I could get without revealing myself. It was close enough to smell her and it was enough.

That afternoon the world changed forever. I was on my way home on my Honda 305 scrambler. There was a nip in the air and I remember looking down at the chicken skin on my arms and being very conscious of my wet trunks under my jeans. As I came down

Monterey towards the house from the distance I could see a couple of cars parked in front of Hope's cruiser. It looked like one of them was some kind of official vehicle. As I got closer my suspicions were confirmed, it was some kind of unmarked car and in front of it was Max's Chevy.

I rolled by slowly trying to see up to the house but I couldn't make out anything so I went home. I had almost three pounds of pot that I had accumulated working for Wayne and middling a couple of deals and I wondered if I should get rid of it somehow. I decided just to wait it out and see what was going on. It seemed to me that if it was a bust there would have been a whole lot more law enforcement on site.

About a half hour later there was a tapping at my bedroom window and it was Max.

He was peering in through his little black shades and his face was unreadable. I held up a finger to indicate I'd be coming out and I did just that, I went out.

"You better come up to the house, Hope needs you there."

"What's going on Max?"

"They killed my brother."

My knees threatened to buckle under me and I felt like I was going out. Blackness started creeping in around the edges of my vision and I felt very sick.

"What are you talking about?"

Max walked around the driver's side of his car and I made my way to the passenger door realizing that I had never ridden in this car that I had coveted so much in the last few months. We got in and he turned the key and those pipes thundered to life.

"He wanted to shop around. I think maybe he felt strange using my people. I told him to stay out of Sinaloa, stay out of Culiacan. It's murderous in that place. Well, they found him last night bound gagged and shot in the head. He had been beaten and he was naked.

He had a note safety pinned right to the flesh of his forehead,

"Estancia en Tijuana perros."

"Stay in Tijuana dogs."

"They left his rental car but they took everything out of it. He had a lot of money. Damn! What was he thinking? He was way smarter than that. He must have been hooked up with somebody he trusted that I didn't know about. He had to have had somebody with him, but who? I gotta figure that out."

Max was getting really worked up and from what I knew about him he was going to go to war. If there was anything he could do he would do it and even if there wasn't he would do it anyway. We pulled up in front of the house and my sick feeling returned. What was I going to say to Hope? What could I do? Max read my mind.

"She loves you Eddie. Just be there. If she needs you to hold her then just hold her. If she needs to talk just listen. If she needs to blow up and break things just protect her. And mostly if she tries to hurt herself you save her. Do you hear me man?"

"Yeah I hear you Max."

We walked in the house and I could hear her but I couldn't see her at first. Then I discovered her on the floor curled up in a ball in front of the couch. I went and sat cross legged in front of her and I just sat there for a minute. She was oblivious to me. I reached down and touched her hair and she looked up. I have never seen so much pain in anyone's face before or since and it rocked me to my core.

"Eddie, Eddie, he's gone Eddie…"

It came out in a barely audible whisper. She pulled herself up so that her head was in my lap; her breath and her tears were hot on the front of my jeans. Suddenly I was horrified at what I was feeling. She clawed her way up the front of my Levi jacket and I lowered myself down so I was on my back on the floor. She settled in with her head on my chest and cried. I remembered the intimacy I'd felt when I'd cried on the chest of little Michelle, how that connection had been so strong, how out of those moments a love had been born that I'd always treasure, and now here I was again.

This beautiful woman who had been so much a part of my life in the last couple of months, who together with her husband had taught me so much and shown me so much love and care and now her world had been blown apart, dreams obliterated, hopes destroyed. This beautiful person, object of my youthful fantasies, but recipient of my respect and awe, she was lying here broken weeping into me. Wayne was gone, ripped right out of all of our lives in an instant. I was in a state of shock. I had grown closer to Wayne than I had to any other man in my life except Chewey but Wayne was different. Wayne represented all of the wholesome and honorable things about manhood. He had one woman and he loved her well and her only. He worked hard with his hands and carved out a life for himself. He treated his friends with compassion and generosity. He had integrity. Somehow the fact that he was a pot smuggler and therefore a criminal escaped me and I idolized him. At the moment I had little room for my own sorrow because of Hope. She needed me now and I would supply. All that my not even thirteen years could supply I would supply. Michelle had said to that bully on the playground that I was her knight errant, her protector, her guardian and that she was my princess. I made a vow to be those things for Hope.

"Max! You know I hate it when you smoke in the house!"

It had grown fully dark outside now and the house was cast in shadows, the only light coming from the bathroom in the hallway. Max had sat in the big chair near the kitchen the entire time getting up only twice. Once to put a pillow under my head, and again to go to the bathroom, and judging by the length of time he had been in there, to also do a shot.

Hope and I had both fallen asleep though I didn't know for how long nor did I have any idea what time it was. Hope's comment about Max smoking in the house was the first thing I had heard her say since she told me, "He's gone Eddie."

It seemed a strange thing to say but then I realized that she was checked out. In that brief period of sleep her mind had slammed shut on the reality of Wayne's death. It would come roaring back at any moment and I steeled myself for the inevitable cavalcade of grief that was imminent. She got up and began turning on lights and then she went to the kitchen and put water on for tea.

"Would you guys rather have coffee?"

It came then. A horrendous howl came out of her and she collapsed on the kitchen floor.

"Oh my God! Oh my God No! No God Nooo!"

She began wailing and screaming unintelligibly. Max and I both went to the kitchen and she grabbed a hold of both of our legs and clung to us as if to a life raft in a treacherous sea. I looked at Max and I could see tears streaming down his cheeks and I realized that this was the second love he had lost and I knew that he was feeling everything that Hope was feeling. I felt small and impotent in the face of their grief.

"Eddie, help me get her to the bedroom."

"Come on Hope you need to come lay down for a little while."

We walked her to the bedroom, half carrying her as she had no strength in her legs. She collapsed on the bed and pulled her legs up to her chest and began rocking back and forth and moaning.

"Come out here for a second Eddie."

He went to the bathroom and came out with a dinner plate and on the plate were about a half dozen thick lines of heroin.

"She may need this man."

"What? She won't do heroin!"

'She loves heroin fool, she's just not broken like you and me and she's too smart to go where we're going. Anyway she'll probably do some now and it will help get her through the night. I gotta go. I gotta look into some stuff. It's on you man. He handed me a few balloons of dope.

"Have you got an outfit with you?"

"Yeah I got it."

I never went anywhere without it any more.

I stood on the deck and watched Max's taillights and listened to the rap of his pipes and I felt very weary. Gone was any memory of the two guys in front of Gene's market and what had happened to me there. The world was upside down and I couldn't see it righting itself any time soon.

"Eddie?"

"I'm here Hope."

"Can you come in here please?"

I thought to myself,

"I can and will do anything you want me to do, absolutely anything. I'm here for you."

I went back into the bedroom and Hope said,

"Will you just hold me Eddie?"

I lay down next to her and she rolled into me and put her head on my chest and her leg across my body. She reached up and placed her hand gently on my face.

"It's going to be crazy Eddie. There's so much to do now. Will you help me Eddie?"

"Of course but you just shush now and get some rest. I'm here for anything you need, okay?"

"Thanks Eddie, I love you. Eddie?"

'Yeah Hope?"

"Did Max leave me some dope?"

"Yeah."

I felt really weird at this juncture because in my wildest dreams I never imagined Hope using chiva, but evidently she did.

"Will you get it for me? I really need some sweet nothing right now."

I untangled myself from her and went to the kitchen where I had left the plate of lines. When I went back in the bedroom she was sitting up on the edge of the bed and she had a rolled up bill in her hand. I handed her the plate and she quickly sniffed up two of the lines. She knew what she was doing. She looked at me with raised questioning eyebrows and extended the bill/straw out toward me.

I decided right then that I wasn't going to hide my little secret any longer. I reached in the breast pocket of my jacket and pulled out one of the balloons Max had given me and from the inside pocket I pulled out my kit wrapped in a bandana. I set it on the night stand and went to the kitchen and got a glass of water.

When I came back in the room Hope had unrolled the rag that held my works and she had the binky in her hand. She looked up at me and there was a mixture of emotions in her face. Sadness, concern, fear were there but under all of that I saw curiosity. Not a word was said as I prepared my dose on the nightstand. As I got ready to fix and reached for the bandana to tie off she took it from my hand and set it on the bed. Then she reached up and clenched both her hands around my bicep. I pumped my fist a few times and the veins popped up. I fixed, lingering because of the feel of her hands around my arm.

Things were getting very surreal and very strange especially as I began to recognize what was happening in my head. Wayne was dead and I was devastated but there was Hope and she was very much alive. It was likely that I was going to be the closest person to her in the coming weeks and I found myself jealously guarding that idea. But I was shocked and dismayed at the depth of my own selfishness, even treachery as I realized that the reason I had fixed in front of her was not at all about pulling back the covers and revealing myself in honesty it was that I wanted to turn her out. Some very sick and twisted part of me wanted to make her a part of my world, to have that power over her.

I knew she would never tell Max what she was doing and that it would be our secret. Ours alone, just the two of us.

I was sick with myself. I loathed the part of me that would think this way. I tried to put it out of my mind, to reach a loftier moral place but again and again I came back to selfish desire. We lay down on the bed, me on my back and her on her side burying herself into me, head on my chest, leg across my abdomen.

"It feels so good Eddie."

Then she began a soft and rhythmic weeping that after a little while became the gentle sound of her breathing in sleep.

It took over a week to get Wayne's body back from Sinaloa and get him cremated and in the meantime there had been a steady stream of people coming by the house to pay their respects. Almost all were sincere, some were saccharine in their sweetness and their true motives were thinly veiled. I had a list of names of people who would never get within a mile of Hope, this house, the shop or the warehouse. I may have been only twelve but I was whipcord strong and very tall for my age.

I had also experienced so much in my short life that contributed to a certain confidence in my ability to defend Hope. Most of these people had very little experience with violence. I on the other hand had been in a number of physical confrontations and I knew I was not afraid to hurt someone and hurt them badly. If there was a knife at hand I would use it. If there was a gun at hand I was sure I would use that as well. So much pain had been inflicted on me and its origins were so evil that I had lost whatever compunctions against violence that I might have once had. This may have been the peace and love generation but I was in no way shape or form a peace and love kind of kid. So I had my list and I even had outlined in my mind scenarios by which I might deal with these people. There was darkness and creeping involved.

It was Hope's plan to take Wayne's ashes to Maui and spread them half over Haleakala Crater and half over the cliff at Honolua Bay. She wanted me and Max to go with her. I had explained to my mom what had happened although I said that he had been on a buying trip for the store. She being in business in Mexico was sympathetic and surprisingly she let me go. I would have gone anyway but it was very nice to see her with so much empathy. She had virtually no clue about any of the drugs or what was really going on and she thought Wayne was just a cool guy who was mentoring me in surfing and teaching me to work in a warehouse a little bit.

Max had agreed to go but at the last minute he balked and instead just took us to the airport. He did give me fifteen balloons, a paquete, and several new needles for my rig. He dropped us off in front of the terminal and he was very grave like a deep still pool of dark water. He gave Hope a fierce hug and in an uncharacteristic gesture he hugged me too. With that we were off.

Circling high above the island of Oahu making our descent to land I was experiencing the same sense of awe and wonder I had when my mother and I had landed in Puerto Vallarta years earlier. The plane banked around the north end of the island over Kaena point and I saw the north shore. There was an early season north swell and the lines were stacked up to the horizon. There was whitewater in a crescent around the entire north and west shores of the island and I was mesmerized. Even from that altitude I could tell the waves were huge. Disembarking from the plane I was hit immediately by a wave of warm moist air filled with the intoxicating scent of plumeria blossoms. Hawaiian music poured out of the speakers in the ceiling of the terminal and I was transported to a world that would capture my heart and hold it all my life.

We waited in the airport on Oahu for about an hour until our connecting flight on Hawaiian Airlines was called for boarding. The locals were speaking what I later learned was called pidgin. It was an adaptation of the English language that the Hawaiians had developed to frustrate the straight laced and puritanical missionaries that came to Hawaii in the early part of the 19th century to convert the people away from their pagan ways.

It had for me a most beautiful sound and I immediately recognized it as sacred property belonging rightfully only to the people born and raised in this place.

Although I would spend many years coming and going to Hawaii, particularly the island of Kauai, I would never attempt to trespass into that sacred property. Oh, I may have taken on some inflections after living there for a couple of years but I made a conscious decision from the start that it was something that belonged only to the Kamaaina.

I've always marveled at the mainland guys who move to Hawaii and six months later are talking Pidgin. It's not only lame but to me it's disrespectful. No wonder so many Haoles get their butts stomped by the locals. What you need to understand is that Hawaii belongs to Hawaiians and the Portuguese, Japanese, and Chinese that were brought there as laborers many generations ago. The white man will always be a visitor and as a visitor he must treat the Aina, the land, and the kamaaina, the people, with deference and respect.

We landed at Kahului in the late afternoon, rented a car and headed out to the West side of the island to a place that had in the eighteen hundreds been the center of the global whaling industry. It was a little beachfront town called Lahaina which means Unmerciful Sun. With an average annual rainfall of only thirteen inches, it is a dry place. The west side of all the islands are very dry and have different kind of Hawaii flavor than the wetter shores. The island of Niihau just off the western coast of Kauai is only 44 miles as the crow flies from the rainiest place in the world, Waialeale, and yet Niihau is one of the driest islands in the entire world.

We checked in to the Pioneer Inn which is a beautiful old plantation-style hotel built in 1901. It was built by George Freeland when he immigrated to Maui from England, and is still operated by his family. As we were waiting at the check-in counter Hope was facing the interior of the lobby and I was facing out towards the harbor, its break wall and the ocean. Three guys approached us from the street and I knew they were looking for us, or rather for Hope and that they were friends of Wayne's.

"Hope?"

She turned around and I quickly moved up beside her, just close enough to be a part of the circle that was forming.

"Oh! Hi Les, hi Wayne, hi Bird Man. Thank you so much for coming. I noticed there's a lot of swell in the water. Is the bay good?"

She didn't care if the bay was good or not but it was her way of putting the boys at ease.

"Yeah Hope, it's going off. Wayne would have been tearing it up out there today."

"Well then what a perfect time to put him out in the line up."

"You want to do it today Hope?"

"Why not? He would have already been on his way out there to surf, right?"

"Okay, so let's put your bags in your room and head on out there."

"Hey you guys? This is Eddie and he has been working for us for the last month or two and he has become family. Wayne has been teaching him to surf and he's already pretty good."

In chorus,

"Hey Eddie, Nice to meet ya bra, Aloha Eddie."

"Hi guys, good to meet you too."

"Is this your first time to Hawaii?"

"Yeah it is, but I love it already!"

"How long are you going to stay?"

We were walking over to the staircase. I looked over at Hope who said, "Three or four days. I want to put half of Wayne at the bay and half of him up country in the crater. At least I think that's what I want to do, nothing is carved in stone and I may change my mind when I see the bay."

Les made a comment.

"Sounds like you're already having second thoughts and if I could offer my humble opinion I think Wayne would want to be 100 percent at the bay. That was where his heart was most deeply invested in this island. This swell is a freak early swell, and we do get North swells in September but this one is huge, almost as if it was sent just for Wayne."

Hope just nodded her head and smiled at Les.

These same three guys were in a number of pictures in Wayne's photo album and I knew a lot about them. I knew that they had all lived together. When they all first came to Maui they had camped on Mala wharf, an abandoned wharf at the edge of town that had holes all along its decking that you could easily fall through at night. They had eventually rented a little crash pad from Fred Kobitake, Lahaina's slum lord. If you were a surfer and had spent any time in Lahaina you knew Kobitake. The two Wayne's shaped boards together and all of them had been in Wayne's band.

When Hope showed up the three of them had been living the single surf bum life on West Maui for a couple of years and they were resistant to her. It took all of about a week before Hope was a cherished part of their little tribe and so I knew that while these conversations appeared somewhat superficial when we got to the bay it was going to get heavy. We dropped the bags off in the room, which was looking straight out at the harbor and agreed to go out to the bay in Wayne's VW bus.

I looked out of the window and saw the hull of an old whaling ship called the Carthaginian moored right in the middle of the harbor and just out beyond that the North swell was wrapping around the island and bending in to the harbor. Perfect little shoulder high waves were peeling across a reef. Crystal clear and stunning in their beauty they beckoned to me and I suddenly hoped I would get to surf here in Hawaii. Hope came up behind me put her hands on my shoulders and whispered in my ear.

"Of course you will Eddie."

All of the guys were watching me and Bird Man exclaimed,

"Check it out! He's land surfing!"

They all laughed and I realized that I had been twisting and turning my body as if I was surfing the wave I had been watching. Les slapped me on the back and said,

"You're about to see one of the most beautiful sights in the world. Let's go you guys!"

We went out and hopped in the van. Wayne driving, Hope riding shotgun and me, Bird Man and Les in the back.

"Wait, stop Wayne-o!

"What, did you forget something?"

"No, it's just that Eddie's never seen any of this before, he should be up front."

Wayne stopped the bus and Hope and I switched places.

We headed northwest down Front Street through Lahaina, a sleepy little village filled with tourists. There were lots of little shops selling souvenirs, particularly black coral jewelry. Black coral diving has always been a big deal in Lahaina.

It is extremely dangerous. The trees of black coral found at depths of two to three hundred feet putting the diver at a huge risk of contracting the bends as well as being exposed to a myriad of other deep sea dangers. Huge tiger sharks being one of them. Front Street also had a number of restaurants and bars that were all doing a brisk trade. As we made our way out of town I saw Mala Wharf not realizing at the time that I too would sleep on its deck of rotting timbers many a night.

We wove our way up the highway through the little villages of Kaanapali, Honokawai, Kahana, Napili, and Kapalua and we then we were in the country. The terrain had gone from dry west island sparse, to semi tropical lushness along the way and once we passed

Kapalua the road became a winding ribbon of rises and dips. On the rises there would be glimpses of the ocean and at one point Wayne said,

"Get ready, here it comes."

We were in the deep of a valley that bisected the highway and it ended in a huge bay and through the trees and brush I saw a cliff off in the distance and the air around that cliff was heavy with the sea mist generated by the breaking of huge waves. I could both hear and feel the surf as the road rose out of the valley. We ascended the grade for a little while and went further from the ocean but as we neared the top of the hill the road veered back toward the sea.

We crested the top of the hill and my excitement rose as I realized that at any moment I was going to see the legendary Honolua bay. I could see the top of the cliff and the sea beyond the point and the reef but as of yet I could not see the line-up. Then suddenly it was there before me. We pulled up to the top of the cliff where a number of cars were parked and there it was.

It was very late afternoon and the sky was beginning to take on the nuances of dusk, the sun was low on the horizon. It was a little bit obscured through the mist of the breaking waves and the face of the cliff was partially hidden by that mist which was lit in golds and oranges. The waves were stacked up like corduroy to the horizon and as they marched in to the point they jacked up on the reef and threw themselves out into perfect barrels, backlit in turquoise and orange. They were bright and splendorous as they ran down the reef, not a drop of water out of place. At different spots along the break they would belch forth a blast of compressed air and often they would spit out a surfer who had been deeply ensconced in the tube.

"Well what do you think?"

Les was asking me as he passed me the joint he had lit when he stepped out of the bus.

"I want to live here forever."

We were all standing in a line at the top of the cliff with Hope holding the urn that was Wayne's ashes pressed tightly to her breast. I noticed that there was a line of surfers climbing up the cliff and that no one was left in the water. Wayne held out his hands to Hope for the urn and as she passed it to him she said,

"All of him please Wayne."

"Hope, can we make it so he never leaves this place?"

"What do you mean?"

"Do you trust me Hope?"

"Of course Wayne."

"Okay then, just watch.

He went to the van and came back with a sheet of cardboard two diver's five pound belt weights and a tube of epoxy. He began mixing up a batch of the epoxy on the cardboard.

"I'm gonna mix it up pretty hot so it will dry fast."

Once he had the mixture done he opened the urn and inserted the two weights. By this time there was a group of surfers standing around watching. Some seemed to know Hope and were paying their respects but it was clear that they all knew Wayne. Wayne smeared a gob of glue around the rim of the urn and the inside lip of the lid and screwed it on tight.

"Now we wait."

There were probably twelve of us standing on the edge of the cliff watching the surf silently. Perfect empty waves were peeling off with machine like precision. Hope pulled out a joint, lit it and passed it and she did that until about four or five joints were making a cloud of smoke over the group. There we were standing on the edge of this cliff watching, smoking, and waiting. Someone down the line from me began a story about a surf session he had had with Wayne. Someone else said, "Yeah I remember that day."

And it began like that. For half an hour until it was nearly dark people shared about Wayne and then Bird Man said,

"Let's paddle him out and put him on the reef where he can be the first to feel every set wave that ever comes in to this bay again."

All the guys filed down the steep trail on the face of the cliff with Wayne in the lead carrying the urn. It was his plan to carry the urn out past the line up and dive down with it placing it in a hole in the reef. The skindiver's weight belts would insure that it remained in place. I've surfed there many times in the forty years since that day with the knowledge that that urn of ashes is still out there cradled in a pocket of coral.

It isn't Wayne. Wayne is someplace else altogether. It's the memory of Wayne and the community of people who loved him. When we got to the bottom of the cliff all the guys grabbed their boards and prepared to paddle out. One guy whose name I never even learned approached me and held out his board.

"I didn't know him that well, you go."

"I don't know if I can make the paddle, it's really big."

"Just stay with the boys, they'll time the sets right so you don't get caught inside."

I was scared. Getting out was one thing and I was doubtful about pulling that off but if I was successful then I had to get back in again and the thought of trying to catch and ride one of these big Hawaiian waves and with it getting dark it was frankly horrifying.

I was generally not afraid of anything but something in me told me this was not the day to try to prove myself.

"Thanks man but I don't think I should try it."

"That's cool bra, just thought I'd offer."

They were all lined up knee deep on the rock shelf that lined the inside and as the last wave of a very long set broke outside they set out. They dug deep with strong arms and sinewy shoulders and I was surprised at the speed with which they propelled themselves toward the now setting sun. Surfing in Hawaii takes you to another level of fitness and mental readiness. There's a lot of water moving and the consequences for not being up to the challenge are severe, so the sense of community in the water is very high.

When you live and surf a couple of winters in Hawaii you develop a deep reverence for the brothers who have been raised in those majestic and yet sometimes treacherous seas. I'm known there and I'm accepted there, always treated with aloha and it's because I understand who they are and who I am in relation. I'm not less, nor am I more, but I *am* a guest.

I was surfing a very large day at Kalihiwai on Kauai and I got caught in the lip on a take off. I was drilled head first into the trough of the wave as the lip came down and pounded me mercilessly. Tons of water snapped my head to the side and I was sure I had broken my neck. I had no feeling in my body and was completely paralyzed. I was about to drown and was powerless to save myself. Out of nowhere the arms of Josh Kamalani reached down and pulled me to the surface.

He and another local boy, Kala Alexander somehow got me to the shore through a devastating shore break with waves fifteen feet high slamming the sand. Josh asked when we made it in,

"Shoots bra, you okay? You give 'em one big scaea!"

All I ever heard after that was how well I had ridden the wave before that one. It's just what they do. With no thought for their own safety, they just go in the face of danger and help.

Those two brothers saved my life that day and I will never forget that but Hawaii has saved my life many times. It has been a place of refuge and healing for me when I've been in the deepest despair. The land there has been a mother to me cradling me in her arms of fragrant mystical breezes, waterfalls and rainbows and the seas of Hawaii have been a father to me, awesome and humbling in power, sometimes stern in discipline but always giving me a sense of wholeness and accomplishment.

We were all gathered back at the top of the cliff and the night had settled over the North Shore. I could still make out the huge black lines marching relentlessly toward the island. There was soon to be a full moon on the rise and Bird Man brought that to all of our attention.

"Wrap around swell in the harbor and a full moon to boot, who wants to surf tonight?"

Hoots of acknowledgment made a cavalcade of raucous noise and I felt a surge of excitement course through me. I looked to Hope and she was smiling at me and in her eyes was a deep joy and more than a little pride. I knew she was full of sorrow at the loss of her husband and her best friend but I also knew that she was, at least at that moment, supremely glad that she had brought me to this place. She could see that my heart fit here and I think she knew what kind of place Hawaii would be for me.

It was quiet in the van on the way back to Lahaina and I was lulled to a sweet place by the sound of Wayne going through the gears in that old bus. A VW engine has always sounded cool to me. Bird Man and Wayne were in front and Hope was between Les and me in the back. I had Hope on one side and the window on the other and it was as fine a place as I had ever been.

The island smells and the warm breeze coming over me from one side and the feel of Hope pressed against me on the other. She was very much closer to me than she was to Les and I knew that I was what she was clinging to in her pain. Her investment in me, bringing me to this place, watching me experience the islands was what was sustaining her. I made a bold move and I reached over and put my hand on her knee giving a light squeeze and when she looked at me I whispered,

"Thank you Hope."

She laced her fingers through mine and whispered back,

"Anything for you Edward."

Les watched this exchange with a smile on his face and put his hand on her other knee and she grasped his hand as well. It was a precious moment with only one thing gnawing away at it. I was getting dope sick and really needed a fix.

"We can throw a barbecue at Banyan Tree Park, play some tunes and then surf when the moon is highest."

"Man its already dark!"

"So what bra? It's a huge day, Hope is here, we're sayin' goodbye to a brother and we gotta show this youngster how we do it here."

"Yeah okay. We'll drop you guys off at the hotel and go round up all the stuff and come back and get ya, cool?

"Yes Les that would be good. Eddie and I can get cleaned up and get unpacked."

We got up to our room and it was about eight PM. The room was on the side of the hotel facing the water as I mentioned before. It had a queen bed and a single with the door to the bathroom between the two. It was plantation style with a hardwood floor and all white rattan furnishings. The beds were covered in white chenille spreads and there was a ceiling fan turning lazily in the middle of the ceiling.

The room spoke of an uncluttered simplicity and I was coming to understand that this was the way of the place and its people. The simple white wooden shutters were open and even though the moon was still low and as yet behind the hotel, the night was bright and the moonlight shimmered off of the water of the harbor like Swarovski crystals brocaded across the front of a debutante's dress.

"I'm going to take a shower Eddie so if you want to get a glass of water could you do it now please?"

She knew what I was about. She knew what I was needing.

"Sure, I'll get it right now."

I set the glass on the night stand by the single bed and retrieved my works from my duffle bag. A junkie's hype kit or "works" is generally not the most hygienic looking affair. Usually wrapped up in a bandana it includes a binky, which is an eye dropper with the needle pushed on to the end. These work okay but the problem is that the needle often slips off of the dropper barrel and the dropper itself, the squeeze bulb part, just doesn't have enough oomph. They're generally designed to distribute just a drop of liquid at a time, thus the name dropper. Most junkies used to build their own, and like a mechanic has his favorite wrenches and a chef his favorite cooking tools, the binky also gets highly personalized.

Nowadays the binky is a thing of the past and hypes just use disposable insulin syringes, but back in the day we used to lovingly build our works. I would take a glass on glass 3 cc syringe and grind the flanges off of the end leaving a perfectly straight barrel. For the dropper part I would use one of those decorative rubber table grapes. Inside they always had a funny white powder but once turned inside out that nice clean shiny outside would then be the inside surface exposed to the dope. Also turning it inside out provided a nice little lip at the opening.

The syringe barrel would be fitted inside that opening on the grape and that lip provided a good solid base for a careful winding of thread tightly joining the two parts together. A knot and a drop of cement and viola' a high power injecting device. These things had enough power to shoot a stream of liquid across a room and in fact I've been in shooting galleries where users would shoot their rinse on the wall making a mural of bloody graffiti. It's really no wonder that so many have Hep C today. Every hype I know from the old guard has it. Miraculously I don't and it truly is an act of God which I will explain later, maybe. So the binky is the first item in the kit. The second item, the cooker, is equally steeped in ritual.

Today most hypes just use a spoon or a torn off coke can bottom, but we all had some kind of ornate antique soup spoon. The handle would be bent around in such a way as to make the bowl of the spoon sit perfectly level on a table. The bottom of this spoon was wiped off after every use because the matches or candle or whatever the heating element was would leave a thick black soot residue. The dope side of this cooker was never cleaned. Until you ran out of dope.

Every time I did a shot I would leave the cotton a little bit wet and leave just a teeny bit in the spoon. It would dry and turn crusty and at the time of my next shot I would scoot that old cotton up to the edge of the cooker and put in a new one. It was kind of an emergency account, or maybe overdraft protection. If times got lean for a day or so there was always enough residues in the cottons and the cooker for a really good hit maybe two or three if I was lucky. Both of these items would be carefully wrapped in a piece of plastic and then wrapped again in the bandana.

Sometimes needles were hard to come by and so the necessity of prolonging the life of these things resulted in some very ingenious methods of maintenance. A needle could be sharpened on a match book cover. You would make a few strokes and then drag the needle across the sensitive skin on the back of the hand checking for, "barbs", and repeat the process as necessary. If a needle got clogged, as they were apt to do from little bits of cotton or undisolved product, you would break open a light bulb and remove the filament. This filament was small enough to go through the tiny hole in the needle. Kind of a mini pipe cleaner.

I say all of this for your education but also to make a point; as I had said, this room was very white and spoke of simplicity and purity. The island had gotten to me in such a way that a spell had almost been broken. As I opened my set of works I saw them for the first time not as the carefully constructed and lovingly kept tools of a spiritual ritual. Because whenever I looked at them I was intent upon the minutia. The carefully wound thread on the barrel of the binky. The ornate inlay on the handle of the spoon and the condition of its contents. Full and crusty signifying abundance and clean and dry signifying draught.

But rather I was seeing them open and waiting, set upon this white nightstand in this white room with this fragrant warm air caressing my neck where the chicken skin of my early withdrawals was already spreading its tendrils to my guts. They were a filthy bloody blade in the chest of truth and beauty, they were for the first time dirty to me. Yet I knew that I must take them up and use them for their intended murderous purpose.

I had the paquete, a chicano term for fifteen balloons of dope, wrapped in a cigarette cellophane and I pulled out a single green balloon. A paquete of multi colored balloons always looked so festive and indeed it was. Kind of, "Yippee look at all that dope! Not gonna run out today!" I stretched the neck of that balloon and bit through the knot with my teeth.

Upon pouring it out into my cooker I had a thought and put a smidge on a saucer for Hope. Everything was the same as I cooked up my shot. I pulled a little cotton from the chenille bedspread and wadded it up. Into the cooker it went. As I watched my blood register in the mixture and just before I squeezed off on the bulb a light gust of trade wind blew the scent of jasmine and a few words of pidgin spoken on the street in through the window and I was unsettled. Something was wrong, something was different.

And then just for a brief instant I saw that cross and I saw a bloody beaten man hanging on it. He raised His bowed head and looked right at me and He said something I could not make out. I shook my head, the chicken skin of my withdrawals raised by that breeze on my skin said to me, "Squeeze it man!" and that I heard clearly. So that's what I did and a few seconds later I was in that place. That place of counterfeit perfection.

"Oh nice Eddie you saved me a taste."

She was wearing little jean cutoffs and a tube top and her long hair was wet from the shower. She smelled clean and fresh. I on the other hand felt dirty and stale.

It had only been about an hour since the guys had left us and so I was surprised when there was a knock at the door. I opened it and Les was there.

"You guys ready for kau kau?

"Huh?"

"You ready to eat?"

We walked out of the hotel and over to Banyan Tree Park where the guys had set up a barbecue. There were a couple of guys playing guitar with another guy playing a ukulele. The music they were playing was very similar to the music I had heard in the airport and Wayne told me the guitar style was called slack key and that it was a Hawaiian thing. It was so beautiful. One of the guys playing guitar was very Hawaiian as was the uke guy. The other guitar player was Les.

The center of this park was a huge Banyan tree which was first planted in April of 1873 to mark the fiftieth anniversary of Christian missionary work in Lahaina. When it was imported from India it was only eight feet tall. It's now over sixty feet high with twelve major trunks in addition to its huge core trunk. It covers an area of two thirds of an acre. The setting was spectacular and I fell deeper under the enchantment that has always been Hawaii for me. We ate, listened to music, smoked, and everyone, "talked story." I mainly listened and got educated. Most of my childhood I spent around considerably older people and the friends or acquaintances I had that were my age seemed so much younger than I. About eleven o'clock Bird Man started passing out mushrooms.

"Here kid, eat these cuz in an hour we surf."

"I don't have a board."

"Oh man, do I look stupid to you? Of course you don't have a board, that's why I brought you one."

He began walking over towards Wayne's van and I just stood there.

"I might have been wrong about you, at first I thought you were a smart kid. You comin' or what?"

His harassment was good natured and he made me grin to myself and of course I hurried to catch up with him. As I came along side he slapped me affectionately on the back. When we got to the van Bird opened the rear hatch and pulled out one of the four boards that were inside. It was deep red and I immediately saw the winged foot that was Wayne's logo.

"Wayne called this a hotdogger, its only seven six. It should work really well for you."

He handed it to me and I hefted it feeling its balance and then I put it under my arm.

There's something you feel when you hold a board that you were meant to ride. I don't know what to call it but there's an immediate connection. I've ordered brand new boards from really good shapers and gone to pick them up at the glass shop and known immediately that they weren't my boards. This board and I connected.

"Can you feel it man?"

"Oh yeah I can feel it. That's not all I can feel, those shrooms are comin on right now.'

"Time to surf then."

Bird whistled and Les and Wayne excused themselves and made their way over to the van. Hope was deep in conversation with a very large Hawaiian lady with hair that went down to her knees. I don't even know if she saw us leaving.

"This is a fun wave and we surf it every full moon if there's swell. You just need to enjoy this Young Blood."

I stepped in to the water and was amazed at the warmth. It was at least as warm as the air.

"I'm going up to bed Eddie, have fun."

She was standing above and behind me on the breakwall.

"Okay Hope, I shouldn't be that long."

She gave a little chuckle and said,

"Yeah right, I'll leave the door open for you."

It was 1967 on Maui and you could do that then.

We all pushed off and began the paddle out the channel. I had never surfed a break that was so far out. I was used to reef breaks but those in Laguna were close to shore, here it was a bit of a paddle to get to the line up. Surfing had come easy for me mainly because I had already been body surfing for quite some time so I understood the principles of catching and riding waves. That and the fact that I rode a skateboard every day. It was just a matter of putting it all together. There was more than adequate light with the full moon and the lights from the hotel and as we got into position I felt confident.

The mushrooms had come on completely now and everything was full of color and my body felt very connected to the sea and to the board I was on. It was so beautiful. The water was inky black and reflected the night sky perfectly. I could look down at the water and see the stars and the moon. The waves were consistent, about head high and perfect. Bird Man caught the first one. Wayne said,

"Your wave Eddie."

I turned and stroked into a head high left hander. As I popped to my feet I threw a quick top turn and got in trim. This board was phenomenal. It made me twice the surfer I had been. I raced along the face of that wave climbing and dropping as I went. The wind was in my face and I felt like I was flying. I heard someone yelling and I realized it was me.

"Hooooeeyyy!!!"

We stayed out until probably four in the morning and at that point I was satiated. When we got to the van and I had carefully placed my board inside I turned around and all three of the guys were facing me like a wall. Wayne said,

"Be careful with your life little brother, you might be going just a little too fast. Slow down don't be in a hurry and whatever you do keep surfing. It will keep you pure."

Bird said,

"If you ever need to come here we will be waiting for you. Don't even think about it, just get on a plane and show up."

They each gave me a huge hug and Les said,

"The swell is dropping so tomorrow you need to ride the bay, you're good enough. We'll come for you in the morning, well late morning or noon-ish, seein' as how the sun is coming up in three hours."

I don't know what Hope had told them but it was apparent that she had told them something and that it was because she was scared for me. I was thankful for that.

There was moonlight spilling across the bed where she lay sleeping when I came into the room. She was so peaceful looking in her slumber. There was no evidence of the pain she was trying to process, trying to hide. There had been two pillows on her bed and now there was just the one under her head. I found the other between the bed and the wall and it was soaking wet from her tears. She had tried to hide it from me. I held it to my face. I held her tears to my skin and I tasted their salt mixed with the smell of her hair. I needed a shot of dope.

I placed the pillow back on the other side of her bed and prepared a fix. Once again I was struck with the contrast between the soot blackened appearance of my outfit and the pure white simplicity of the room. The uneasy feeling I had did not stop me from doing what I needed to do. That's just how it is. A junkie knows that however he may be feeling when he's in need, as soon as he hits it, it's all gonna be just fine. However this time it wasn't just fine, no not fine at all. I rinsed my rig and suddenly a cavalcade of sorrow washed over me and I felt the need to pray. I didn't even know how to pray but I remembered one of those young men telling me,

"Just talk to God from your heart"

I got down on my knees by the side of Hope's bed and I gently placed my hand on her back. My heart ached with love and compassion for this woman.

"God I am so lost. Please help me."

I was twelve years old and I felt like an old man. I felt worn out and tired. I was already so accustomed to loss that Wayne was quickly becoming an afterthought. Life was all about people leaving, that's what people do, they leave and they never come back. As for me I never fit in the places where I should have been and I fit perfectly in all those places I should never be.

My safe place was in knowing that nothing was to be trusted and my strength came from a recklessness and an anger that had been bequeathed to me through the lust of a sick and perverted man. I hated my father for the way he treated me after he knew. I hated him for taking Faith from me and I was full of rage over losing Michelle. What was Wayne but another in a long list of losses?

I was on my knees on the side of Hope's bed and my head was resting on her calf under the sheet. I would lose her too, of that I was sure. In spite of the fact we were here on a dreadfully sorrowful mission it had been one of the best days of my life. But I was sure that times like these could not be held. Maybe today would be a good day to end all this silliness. I could cook up four or five balloons and take my rig over to the park. No one would find me until it was too late.

Maybe then the constant strain of living out of step with the rest of the world would end and I would have peace.

"What are you doing Eddie?"

She reached down and laid her hand on my head and began to stroke my hair.

"I was trying to pray."

"You don't try to pray Eddie, you just talk to God."

Yeah, I would lose her, I knew that. I was just a kid. No matter how much I had done or had been done to me, I was a kid. But the feel of her hand on my head and the sound of her voice strengthened me. I could not be so selfish as to abandon her now. She needed me and I needed her.

I was crying into her leg, it all just weighed so much. I had a hundred years worth of experiences in my twelve years of life and it felt heavy.

"Come up here Eddie."

I climbed up on the bed and she put her head on my shoulder. I was weeping openly now.

"Shhhh its okay Eddie, I'm here. I'm not going anywhere."

She was stroking my cheek as she spoke comfort to me and slowly my agony gave way and I succumbed to her ministrations. It wasn't long before her breathing took on the regularity and rhythm that signified sleep. I bent down and kissed the top of her head and then finally and with all of my heart I prayed,

"God can you help me? Will you help me? I don't know which way to go to get someplace safe."

I saw that cross off in the distance of my mind's eye and I saw that beaten and bloody form on that cross. Again He raised His head but this time I was able to make out what He was saying to me.

"I love you my child and I will always be with you."

CHAPTER 19

"Eddie, wake up son. You should probably eat something."

I was on that big old couch in Joseph Miller's living room and I had fallen into a deep sleep. I seemed suspended in the place between the dream and the reality, the past and the present. I could almost still feel Hope's head on my chest and smell the Plumeria blossoms dancing on the trade winds and yet at the same time I was aware of the sound of a crackling and the shadows and lights that danced across the walls and ceiling from the fire in Joseph's huge hearth.

How long had it been since I had thought of Hope or Hawaii? I was so deeply entrenched in this life of inland biker towns and drug addicted convicts and gunslingers that I had completely lost the loves of my youth. But that seemed to be the one reoccurring theme of my life, losing things or maybe throwing them away.

Fundamentally I think I knew that a person's journey was one of decision making and all of us were free to make right decisions regardless of what had happened to us but another driving force in me was the wounded one. Angry and rebellious maybe feeling like I was getting what I deserved and therefore determined to play it to the darkest depths.

I lay suspended in that wondrous place between two distinctly separate worlds, floating ethereally in the not quite awakeness of dream and drug but very suddenly I was assaulted by a wave of pain that came over me like a thundercloud, dark, loud and ominously oppressive. I was propped up in a semi sitting position with my right hand in a bucket of ice water and I had definitely not been in this position the last I recalled. Joseph picked up on my confusion.

He chuckled,

"You were in some shape when I came in Eddie. At first I thought you had left the land of the living but you were breathin' regular and after I was in the house a few minutes you were talking up a storm. Boy you have had one crazy life if I could make any sense of what you were sayin'! But anyway I thought you'd better ice that wrist and you were like a sack of potatoes when I picked you up and turned you around to get your right hand on this side of the couch. I like you, but not enough to put a bucket of water up on my sofa."

"How long was I asleep Joseph?"

"Bout four hours I guess."

"Yeah that sounds about right cuz those pills are just plain worn off."

He passed the tray over without blinking an eye and I promptly shook two pills out of each bottle. I didn't want to get as loaded as I had on that first go round. Even so his eyebrows went up as I gobbled the pills but he didn't make a comment. He had said something about eating and I wanted the pills to go in first so as not to be made less potent by mixing them with food.

Looking down at my wrist I saw that the swelling had diminished a great deal, enough so that the broken bones were now distinguishable as they pressed against the skin. Two of the metacarpal bones on the back of my hand were sharply defined as well as some bones I don't know the name of on the inside of my wrist. Foolishly and predictably I might add I tried to move my hand. The lighting bolt that shot up my arm and into my brain was more than sufficient chastisement.

"So son, are you hungry? I got some left over pot roast with carrots and new potatoes heated up and one thing I learned is you gotta fuel the body to heal the body."

Suddenly the mention of pot roast, which by the way is one of my very favorite meals, well it turned my stomach upside down with hunger and I realized all I had had to eat was drugs and booze since the barbecue the night before. Well that and a splash of iced tea.

"Joseph, I love pot roast especially left over, and I am starving. Also I am left handed so I won't be suffering from any limitations when it comes to wrangling a fork."

We both chuckled and as he got up to go to the kitchen I heard the weary sound of his old bones. It sounded like someone pouring milk on a bowl of Rice Krispies. Snap, crackle, pop. The warmth of those six pills began to seep into my pain and I laid back and relaxed. The wear and tear on Joseph's body was the result of a life well spent. He carved out a life and raised a family. He had a legacy of integrity. The wear and tear I was placing on my body was the result of a life spent running and hiding burying my pain in destruction. I had a daughter I hadn't seen in months. I thought about the prayer I had prayed that night on Maui and the thousands of prayers I had prayed since then.

God always showed up.

I always ran.

How far could I run before there was no place left to run to?

How far could I take this hellbound train and still escape with my life?

Tonight could be my last night, and then what?

What would I leave behind but pain and sorrow?

Even the expense of my funeral would be on others.

"Let's eat son."

Joseph placed a tray on the ottoman between his chair and the couch and passed me a plate piled high with great smelling food. He took his own and then he folded his hands and said,

"Let's thank the Lord."

The tears poured down my face and punched me right in the gut.

THE BEGINNING

EPILOGUE

Eddie is in the fast lane headed for nothing good and Eddie is the proverbial rope in a tug of war between good and evil, God and Satan, heaven and hell. It could go either way for Eddie. God is trying to work in Eddie's life but so are supernatural forces opposed to God that manifest themselves experientially in Eddie's life. Those actions by those forces give rise to traits that define Eddie, fear, anger, abandonment, pride, all things that are in direct opposition to the fruits of the Holy Spirit listed in Galatians 5:22.

But the fruit of the Spirit is love, joy, peace, longsuffering, kindness, goodness, faithfulness, gentleness, self-control.

Although deep inside of Eddie he has some of those traits as well they have been buried in the muck and the mire of Eddie's experiences many of which are the result of a seriously broken decision maker.

Eddie represents a demographic. A huge segment of our culture is lost and confined to prisons and institutions some literal and some figurative. Eddie is the guy doing life in prison in Pelican Bay. Eddie is the guy who used to be a bad dude that has lost his mind from drugs and alcohol and now pushes a shopping cart around talking to himself. Eddie is the guy who died of an overdose so his friends threw his body in a dumpster. Eddie is the girl caught up in a web of prostitution brought on by her addiction which was brought on by sexual and emotional abuse as a young girl. But Eddie is also the tall strong overcomer serving God with a clean conscience and a purified renewed heart. This story and the ones about Eddie to follow I wrote for the men and women who have tried over and over to change. Everyone has given up on you. Family, friends, even the church have had enough of you. You will just never get it. Well you can get it, because God loves you and his heart is for you.

1 Timothy 2:3-4.

For this is good and acceptable in the sight of God our Savior, who desires all men to be saved and to come to the knowledge of the truth.

All means all baby!

Keep an eye out for the continuation of Dead Man Waking and find out how things turn out for our Eddie.

May God bless you and keep you,

Peter Cropsey

I was raised in Laguna Beach California which in the late sixties and early seventies was the epicenter for the free love drug culture. The streets were full of people fully in the throes of the hippie movement. By the time I was twelve I had taken LSD with Timothy Leary and was a daily user of hash and marijuana. By the time I was fourteen I had been arrested for felony drug charges, and burglary. I had also overdosed on heroin. It was at that time in my life when two guys from Teen Challenge shared the gospel with me on the street and I knew I was hearing the truth. I accepted Christ as my Savior but it would be many years before I submitted to Him as my Lord. I spent the rest of my childhood, my teen years and my early adulthood addicted to heroin and meth and in and out of jails and prisons. God had His hand on me the entire time and He was faithful even though I was not. By the time I was in my thirties I was so deeply involved in gangs and drugs that I didn't have one relationship that didn't revolve around drugs, prison or gang activity. I had developed a reputation as a dangerous person and I did my best to cultivate that reputation at every opportunity. I was so far from God I thought that I would never find my way to a life outside of the bondage I was in. I paroled in 1989 from Corcoran Prison and somehow I found my way to a twelve step meeting. I saw people there who had recovered from a seemingly hopeless state of mind and body.

I kept going back and it stuck. After I had about a year clean I went to church and God was waiting for me there. I realized that He was what I had wanted all of my life but that I was so deeply in bondage to my sin that I was unable to be accountable to any relationship let alone a relationship with God. Since I was sober I was able to be accountable and I recommitted my life to Jesus. In 1996 I began attending Calvary Chapel Laguna Beach and in 1999 I enrolled in the Calvary Chapel School of Ministry. I graduated in 2001 and went to the North Shore of Kauai to plant Calvary Chapel North Shore. I pastored there for two years and then returned to Southern California. My dear friend Pastor Steve Rex took over for me and the church in Hawaii is flourishing under his leadership. I still get the blessing of teaching at their church when my wife and I visit the islands. In May of 2006 a friend suggested that we begin a Bible study in our home and Brave Heart was born. I pastored that church for three years and then underwent another dramatic change in my life and realized it was time to take a step back and reevaluate the direction God had for me. It was time for me to finish this book, an undertaking that began some three years previously. Through it all what I have learned is not only is Jesus Lord of all but He is a God of repair and restoration. He is deeply interested in our lives moment to moment and there is no part of our lives that is too big or too small for His healing touch.

He doesn't say He just wants those who are nice, or smart, or pretty. He never says He is looking for people with character or integrity. No God wants us all. In fact He has a special interest in those of us who the world would esteem as maybe less than.

1 Corinthians1:26-28

For you see your calling, brethren, that not many wise according to the flesh, not many mighty, not many noble, are called. 27 But God has chosen the foolish things of the world to put to shame the wise, and God has chosen the weak things of the world to put to shame the things which are mighty; 28 and the base things of the world and the things which are despised God has chosen, and the things which are not, to bring to nothing the things that are.

2 Peter 3:9 expresses the heart of God perfectly.

The Lord is not willing that any should perish but that all should come to repentance.

He is so full of grace and all He asks of us is that we make an honest evaluation of our lives from His point of view.

1 John 1:9

9 If we confess our sins, He is faithful and just to forgive us our sins and to cleanse us from all unrighteousness.

Man, that is all that is required to be made as pure as snow in God's eyes.

I have a dirty, dark past but what Satan had meant for evil God has intended for good.

My King has turned my rut into a groove.

God has taken a man with a reputation of darkness and made a man with a reputation of integrity.

1 Corinthians 4:1says;

Let a man so consider us, as servants of Christ and stewards of the mysteries of God.

It is only by His grace and His power that in my heart of hearts I desire this more than I desire any other thing from life.

Romans 3:10 says;

As it is written: "There is none righteous, no, not one;

Also in Romans 3:23 it says;

For all have sinned and fall short of the glory of God,

Man, oh man, this has got to be the hardest thing to swallow, the idea that by nature we are sinners and that nothing good dwells in us.

I like to point at all of the cool things I have done for others and say, "See I am a good guy!"

And in fact if we judge ourselves by man's standards we may just be pretty good compared to say an armed robber or a kidnapper.

But when it comes to God we are judged by His standards and unfortunately there is no sliding scale.

God is totally holy and cannot allow any sin in His presence.

Romans 6:23 tells us;

For the wages of sin is death, but the gift of God is eternal life in Christ Jesus our Lord.

Look, here's the thing. I have tried to get around this whole Jesus deal. I have studied a myriad of religions and philosophies looking for the truth. They all just came up short.

When I learned that the Bible was an integrated message system written by the Spirit of God as He gave it to the minds and hands of men over approximately a millennium and a half. When I realized that these sixty six books written by forty authors as they were directed by the Holy Sprit were so perfectly interwoven that science, history, and archaeology were unable to disprove the truth contained in its pages I was amazed.

Then there is the miracle of prophecy. There were literally hundreds of prophecies about Jesus in the Old Testament that needed to be fulfilled for Him to be the Messiah and He fulfilled each and every one to the letter. Prophecy is God's fingerprints on the Bible and provides irrefutable evidence for the truth of Christianity.

Still, I have to tell you that in spite of all of the evidence the thing that is the true proof is the change God brings to the hearts of all who receive Him.

You can ask the believer who has only been walking with the Lord for a couple of days.

He will not know all of the theological defenses for the gospel but he will tell you that he is no longer the same. He will tell you that a hunger he had suffered from all of his life has been relieved and in its place is a fullness of joy that is quite inexplicable.

Romans 5:8

But God demonstrates His own love toward us, in that while we were still sinners, Christ died for us.

That is the most wonderful thing, the idea that God's grace provides a way for us to be reconciled to Him that is in no way related to our efforts.

All we have to do is receive this wonderful gift and then walk in it.

The work has already been done on the cross.

God cleans His fish after He catches them.

Romans 10:13

For "whoever calls on the name of the Lord shall be saved."

Come on and call on Him right now. It is no accident that you picked up this book.

If you are sick and tired of being sick and tired then today is the day you can enter in to a relationship with a true and living God who cares for you and has been calling you to Him all of your life.

Jeremiah 29:11 says this;

For I know the thoughts that I think toward you, says the Lord, thoughts of peace and not of evil, to give you a future and a hope.

If you want to spend eternity in heaven with Jesus and if you want to have all of your sins forgiven you then please pray this prayer.

But remember Acts 4:12 says;

Nor is there salvation in any other, for there is no other name under heaven given among men by which we must be saved."

So if you are ready to turn it all around and enter into a relationship that is eternal and full of peace and passion, joy and truth then please just pray this simple prayer.

Lord Jesus, I know I am a sinner. I believe that you died for my sins. I believe that you rose from the grave forever defeating sin and death. Please forgive me for my sins and

enter my heart. I invite you to be my Savior and also the Lord of my life. Please give me a hunger for Your Word and the company of other believers. Please plant me in a church that is rightly dividing Your Word of truth. Thank you Lord for saving me. Amen

Congratulations you are now a member of the family of God.

Galatians 3:26

For you are all sons of God through faith in Christ Jesus.

COMING SOON

"EDDIE"
BY PETER C. CROPSEY

Ephesians 4:22-23
Put off concerning your former conduct, the old man which grows corrupt according to the deceitful lusts, and be renewed in the spirit of your mind, and that you put on the new man which was created according to God, in true righteousness and holiness.

The Apostle Paul

"When you get up in the morning two guys are gettin' up with you, the old man and the new man. You're gonna sit down with both of em at the breakfast table. What you gotta do is take the oatmeal away from the old man and pass it to the new man giving him a double portion cuz the guy that eats good is gonna be the guy with the strength to win the day. In fact then just take the old man out back and bust a cap in his head and then go in and pray with the new man."

Eddie Wilkins

CHAPTER 1

As you may remember from the last time we were together I had left the club run, which was at a lake about thirty miles east of Modesto CA, supremely stoned on mescaline, heroin, and meth, not to mention at least a half pint of Jim Beam. It was a beautiful summer morning and I was flying down that gently curving country road. I was rippin' along at about sixty when a subtle noise coming from my open belt drive insisted on my attention. Normally a quick glance would have been all I dared risk at that speed and knowing my bike better than I knew, well, anything, it should have been all that was required.

But to my dismay, when I looked down I discovered there was a dachshund sized dragon flying along next to my bike breathing flames and smoke, it was common for me to see things like that in the late sixties and even the early seventies but this was nineteen hundred and eighty one, so it distracted me, particularly when it looked up and announced,

"You are about to eat it bad, boy!"

Yeah, I got distracted and when I looked up it was just in time to see my front wheel leaving the edge of a twenty foot embankment. And eat it bad I did...

An old farmer whose field I landed in, was the only one to see my wreck and he pulled me in out of the field. His name is Joseph Miller. From the moment I first laid eyes on Joseph Miller the simple presence of the man brought me face to face with the truth. I was nothing but a punk in a tattoo suit. I was a waste of space and air armed with a pistol, a grip of bad habits and a broken decision maker.

This man represented everything good and true, represented everything a man should represent. A love for God and country, an unflagging loyalty to his family, and the values that it takes to raise that family. He had carved a life out for himself in this world by the sweat of his brow and the integrity of his heart. His hands were busy hands, workman's hands, rough and strong hands. He was a rough and strong man, being around him clearly illustrated how far off the beam my life had gone and yet in spite of my tattoos, my dirty boots and 501's, my whiskey sour stench, and my saucer sized pupils he was disposed kindly towards me.

It seemed as if he saw me for what I could have been and not what I was. He had raised two strong sons, perhaps it was in his mind that if I had been his son I could have been like Bo and Billy, I would have had some direction, some guidance. I might have been solid and right, not broken and addicted. I know that as I lay there on the big leather couch and looked around the living room of his old farm house, a house that was made by his hands and showed love and attention in every beam and stone, as I looked at the beautifully framed photographs that chronicled the life of his family it surely crossed my mind,

"What if I had been this man's son instead of the son of a pot smoking, hippie nudist who really had no interest in being a father?"

I had been on his couch and under his care for the last twenty four hours. Joseph's wife Joanne had died of cancer in their home five years before and Joseph had given me three bottles of her left over pain meds. Even years after the expiration dates they still packed a whallop and it was under their ministrations that I had taken a soul searching trip through the past.

This salt of the earth, self made man who had carved out a life for his family on this 120 acre farm, and who had shown me a kindness when he didn't have to, well, he had caused me to think about the self centered , debauched life I was living. I mean how did I become this heroin addicted, prison bound fool riding full speed ahead on a hell bound train? Laying there on his couch and riding that wave of opiated semi-consciousness I took a trip back to the beginning of it all. I took a trip back through the file cabinet of painful memories and bad decisions, I revisited people and places that had shaped me, and after all was said and done I had come to the realization that I was one seriously broken individual. Not just the broken from the accident but a marrow deep soul kind of broken.

I had remembered one recurring vision I had had all my life, but that hadn't visited me in so long I had almost forgotten it. It was the vision of a man hanging bloodied on a cross and he would look up and say to me,

"I love you my child and I will always be with you."

I hadn't seen that man for a very long time and I wondered if I had just gone too far or if He became tired of my seemingly endless cascade of poor decisions and selfish actions.

I was marinating on all this stuff when I saw the Ranchero trailing a plume of summer dust making its way down the long dirt road that led from the highway to Joseph's farm house.

As we pulled away from the farm I could feel the anxiety coming off of Stormy as powerfully as you can feel the angst when you're standing right in front of the PA column at a punk show. She was gripping the steering wheel of the Ranchero so hard her knuckles were white and she was chewing her bottom lip vigorously. This was totally out of character for Storm who was usually in complete control of her emotions.

"I'm strung out Eddie."

I had to think about that revelation for a minute before I answered. I had known of course, all the signs had been there plain to see. The next door neighbor Jack was a light weight dealer and I had seen Storm slipping out to go over to his place a couple of times. When she returned she was different in a way only another junkie can know. Storm's husband Ricky had been killed on his Panhead by a drunk lady and left Storm behind with two little girls, Margie and Ruthie. The grief she lived in had found its relief in the heroin that came from helpful neighbor Jack.

"Yeah I thought so, and you know I'm gonna beat Jack blind dontcha?"

"Eddie you are not in any condition to beat anybody in any way, and besides Jack is no longer the problem."

In the wreck I had gained a broken wrist, collar bone, and a few broken ribs so Storm was right it was gonna be a couple of days before I was in any kind of shape for beatin' on Jack.

"Then what is the problem sis?"

The dams that were her bottom eyelids gave way and rivers began to pour from her eyes. I knew this was the beginning of that bone deep soul weeping that overcomes every fiber of your being.

"Pull over."

She did, and when she had stopped she slumped over on me and it began. The pain of her weight on my wreck injured frame was monumental but it was nothing compared to the pain I felt in her shrunken little body. I hadn't really noticed how skinny she had gotten since Ricky was killed. Her tiny frame was wracked with spasms of emotional agony and I realized that I hadn't seen her cry since the accident. She had been stoic at the funeral, her face set and filled with the resolve that she was going to mother the girls and weather the storm. At first she only used the chiva to get through the darkest moments of that storm but the spirit of heroin is a cunning demon and he whispers sweetly in your ear from the very first shot,

"C'mon you know you want me right now? I'll make everything all right I promise."

She desperately needed everything to be all right and so she gave in to his solicitations. Now he had her in his vice like grip. All of the pain she had been denying, stuffing way down deep inside of herself and burying with syringes full of deception came vomiting up out of her and she just wept into me, her little back heaving as she was wracked with sobbing. I just held her and waited. After quite a while she shifted her weight so she could look up at me. She must have seen me wince. She sat up suddenly.

"Oh, I'm so sorry Eddie. Are you okay?"

"I'm fine girl, can you talk to me? What's going on?

"Two guys have been staying at Jack's and they have taken over his house."

"Who are they?"

"I think they just got out of Folsom. One guy is really big and his name is Billy and the other guy is a lot smaller but he is way more scary and his name is Chris. He has death in his eyes Eddie."

She began crying again, big giant tears. I could almost see my face reflected in them they were that big.

"He came to the door and introduced himself but it felt like a threat. He was really staring at the girls like he was weighing the liability of them being there. I'm scared of him Eddie. It's like he's casing my house for some kind of evil thing"

I knew who they were. Billy Wills was a born and raised Sacramento boy. From what I knew he came from a good family who lived in Orangevale. He had been raised right, played all star football in High School and then one day he did a shot of dope. He was smart and he had breeding but that didn't keep the cops from busting him for assault and robbery when he was eighteen. Now at almost thirty years old he had earned a reputation in the prison system and on the street although he was rarely out for more than a minute.

Chris Dalton was a completely different story. He was raised in Modesto by seriously alcoholic parents who communicated by beating each other with whatever was close at hand. Chris got more than his share of the beatings and by the time he was twelve he was in reform school. He was made a ward of the state at fourteen and grew up in youth institutions until he was old enough for prison. He was mean, cunning and smart.

"Stormy turn the car around we gotta go get Blue."

It was about noon, close to twenty four hours since I rode my bike off of that twenty foot embankment. The old farmer Joseph Miller had seen me flying through the air but no one else had. He hooked a flat bed trailer up to the tractor he had been disking his alfalfa field with and came and hauled my broken body to his farm house. My bike was left where it lay and I wasn't concerned. No one could get to it without going right by the house. Joseph and Storm had loaded my twisted scooter on the trailer Blue and I towed up from the O.C.

We must have been a curious sight as we slowly made our way down the dirt road to the lake where the club run was in progress. I say this because a little crowd was forming around the twelve gauge toting prospect at the entrance. Down into camp we went, a hotrod Ranchero with a beat and bandaged guy riding shotgun, a chick driving and a twisted and broken Harley trailering behind. It took a moment for the boys to recognize me with the turban of bandages on my head and the makeshift sling on my shoulder but when they did it caused a ruckus.

Monkey Man and Danny Mac charged the truck and were practically in the window before Storm could even get stopped.

"Oh man, what happened bro? Look at you, and oh no! Man yer bike…. It's… it's bad!"

With bikers there was always more concern for the condition of the bike than the person. People heal on their own or die, bikes have to be remade. That takes time and money, both of which are often in short supply in the life.

"I never shoulda' let you gobble that tablespoon of Cocoa, man I knew it."

Monkey Man was the purveyor of a substance we called Nestle's or Cocoa and it was Nestle's Quick mixed with lots of mescaline. We might have called it Quick except then it might have been confused with the meth that along with Kessler's blended whiskey was the staple diet of the club. I had eaten a good tablespoon of that chocolate mescaline before I left yesterday.

"No man, it's all on me. Hey Monk, we've got an emergency in Sac town where's Blue?"

" I dunno' man, 'Prospect go find Blue right now and do it runnin'. "Hey Stormy it's good to see you. I was really sorry to hear about Ricky he was a righteous dude. If you ever need anything you know who to call, right?"

"Yeah I know Monkey, thanks a lot."

The boys were a little uncomfortable with Stormy's grief so after a minute or two of boot shuffling in the dirt they just kind of sauntered off mumbling their goodbyes. My mind was already working overtime at the news of these latest developments at the place Blue and I had been head-quartered since we left the O.C. a few months ago.

Billy and Chris both making parole at the same time was not fortu-itous for us. Sacramento was kind of on loan to us because when we had shown up all the serious white boys were locked up, leaving the town wide open. Predators are very territorial over the areas inhabited by their prey. To guys like me and Blue, or Billy and Chris the prey were always the bottom feeders, the addicts and two bit hustlers that didn't have the heart for prison and therefore wouldn't take the kind of chances that yielded the big paydays.

For guys who lived a large part of our lives in prison these lesser crea-tures provided a myriad of services. They moved out of their bedrooms and onto the couch when we showed up at the door, they ran errands that were too troublesome for us. They provided intel on who was up to what on the streets, they forfeited whatever they had to shoot, eat, drink, or drive until we could make that big hit and get into a nice hotel.

Sometimes the cuffs would go on again before the big hit came and all we were left with was the satisfaction of knowing that we had our way with the neighborhood and our ability to terrorize the poor white trash ghetto was alive and well. We were, after all, the undisputed kings of the trailer parks and the low rent apartment projects. Once we were again tucked neatly in our six by nine cells the bottom feeders would get to parade like roosters saying,

"Yeah the boys were stayin at my pad this time until they got gaffled up again."

I realize I sound a bit condescending and so let me clarify. I have taken that fall from champ to chump, left alone on the street, the last one not busted. Without Blue my game would quickly slip away and I would find myself living in garages or some stolen, broken down camper on the side of some house, barely hustling enough dope to stay well and drinking cheap screw cap wine when the cottons were too dried out to beat again. Oh yes indeed, I was a gangsta... Alas I digress...

The look on Blue's face as he came running up from the lakeshore was one I had rarely seen. He looked incredulous. His eyes were wide open as was his mouth and I could tell that the sight of my twisted bike on the back of the Ranchero and me all bandaged up in the shotgun seat had shocked him badly but the news I was about to deliver would land the final blow in this sudden sobering up process.

"What happened to you Eddie, oh man yer bike is toast!"

Always the bike...

Something about Blue never failed to put me at ease, make me feel comfortable so I replied,

"Who goes swimmin'with their boots on except someone who is scared of little squishy crawly things getting between their toes?"

Blue was stripped to the waist and lake water was collecting in a puddle at his feet around his well worn Chippewas. Droplets glistened in his hair and his beard and dripped down across his bare chest. The deep concern he had for me was etched into his features. Suddenly everything became very still and my awareness of the summer sun, the gentle breeze rustling the leaves of the gnarled old oaks in this meadow, the melody of the bird's songs intensified. I became acutely aware of Blue and Storm, I could almost feel their heartbeats. I was overcome with a deep love for these two friends.

Now Blue was leaning in the window of the Ranchero and Storm was leaning over me towards Blue. I was right in the middle, with both of them just inches away and the moment manifested itself to all of us. It was a monumental moment. It was a sense of family and belonging so intense it was tribal. It was a very brief glimpse into purity and perfection that those of us living in the life rarely if ever get to feel. Nothing was said but everything was communicated.

"Yeah, my feet are sensitive so what?"

Storm had shown up full of anxiety, but now she knew that everything would be fine and I knew it too. Like I said something about Blue put me at ease, made me comfortable. There was a synergy with us, we were more together than we were apart. So much more...

Blue had a girl named Crissy once. Relationships get twisted up and convoluted when everybody is living on speed and heroin so she split one day. About a month later she called from a little town north of San Francisco. She said she wanted to come home but she had hooked up with some dude in a motorcycle club and he wouldn't let her leave. Blue asked her,

"What motorcycle club?"

She replied,

"The Puddle Butts"

I'm kidding, but who cares about the name, it was just some small club in a small town trying to be outlaws. Blue asked me,

"You ready for a little ride?"

"Naturally."

We put pistols and ball peen hammers in our bedrolls, filled a dozen syringes with heroin and speed and put them in the little black case, (you remember the little black case from Dead Man Waking, right?), a couple of pints of Kessler's in each of our vests, we gassed up, did a shot and hit the road. We left the O.C. at about ten in the morning and rode 90 miles an hour all day.

Stopping only to gas up, take a leak and do a shot, the pints we passed back and forth at freeway speed, we were pulling into that little town about midnight. Crissy had given Blue directions to the club house and we were about a block away when we stopped to transfer the ball peens and pistols to our waistbands and we just rode on in.

The prospect at the front door got a hammer to the breast bone for his attempt to deny us entry and surprisingly he was the only security they had. Like I said, small town, small club, overconfident in the false belief that they were the biggest fish in the pond.

Identifying the president was easy. There were only three patcholders besides him in the club house and he was the one with the puffed up chest. As quick as a water moccasin slippin' through a bayou swamp Blue had his pistol rammed into the side of this cat's head.

"If things go south here you have only yourself to blame cuz I just came for one thing. Where is Crissy?"

"I can have her here in ten minutes."

"You do that, and make sure she has her gear with her cuz she'll be leavin' with us."

Blue and I were back to back, I could feel his commitment to this course of action right through his leathers. Man, he was always a cool character! He had his pistol all up in that dude's grill and I had mine trained on the rest of the room. There wasn't gonna' be any fight here. They didn't know who we were or who might be with us, they only knew that this had gone down fast, and the dark quick energy we brought to the room was something they were unfamiliar with. It was the real deal. Something they thought they had but seriously didn't.

"Hey man, we're cool, just take her and split."

The prospect with the caved in chest kind of crawled in the door and Blue told him,

"Prospect, get up and put everybody's guns, knives or whatever on the table here."

That yielded a couple of Buck folders, a Bowie and that was it, nary a pistol in the place. The "P" made a phone call and after about ten minutes of these guys all starin' at the floor a bike pulled into the driveway. Crissy came flyin' through the door and jumped into Blue's arms.

"You came, you came!"

Trailing along behind Crissy came a somewhat dejected but resigned looking young biker who I recognized immediately as having salt. I didn't figure Crissy would be with some poop butt but this guy carried himself like upper crust. He was young but I could see him callin' the shots up here one day. He walked right up to Blue and put his hand out.

"Rowdy Ralph."

"Blue."

"Sorry man."

"It ain't on you Young Blood."

We live in a different world, a very different world indeed.

As we were preparing to say our sad farewells and Blue was strapping Crissy's bag to his bike I heard him say to her,

"Good looking kid, you sure you wanna split?"

"At least he doesn't have a needle in his arm before his feet hit the floor in the morning."

"Like I asked, you sure?"

"Yeah, yer my man Blue, for better or for worse."

Three months later Crissy was dead from an overdose.

We checked into a motel down the road and headed back south on a bright clear morning. So that's how it was for me and Blue. When we were together we had the juice card in a very big way. We just had a thing, a synergy, we knew there was nothing we couldn't do and no place we couldn't go.

COMING SOON

LIVING LIFE 365/24/7
BY
PETER C. CROPSEY

Ephesians 5:1-4
Therefore be imitators of God as dear children. And walk in love, as Christ also has loved us and given Himself for us, an offering and a sacrifice to God for a sweet-smelling aroma. But fornication and all uncleanness or covetousness, let it not even be named among you, as is fitting for saints; neither filthiness, nor foolish talking, nor coarse jesting, which are not fitting, but rather giving of thanks.

Here is a complete picture of the contrast between the new man and the old man. It makes it clear that there really is no grey area in God's economy. There is no neutral territory, you're either in or you're out. You're either living the life Jesus prescribed for you or you're not. So many times we want to act as if there is wiggle room and we accomplish this in our minds by subscribing to a cheapened sense of grace. We take scriptures like 1st John 1:9 If we confess our sins, He is faithful and just to forgive us our sins and to cleanse us from all unrighteousness. We take those scriptures which are intended to put on display God's immense desire to have us in fellowship with Him, we take them and adopt an attitude that says, "God will forgive me." Well of course He will but let us remember what it tells us in 1 Samuel 15:22 "Has the Lord as great delight in burnt offerings and sacrifices, As in obeying the voice of the Lord? Behold, to obey is better than sacrifice." God makes provision in His grace for our failures but it is so much better to live in the power and authority over the sin nature that is our inheritance in Christ. Colossians 1:12-14 says we should be; Giving thanks to the Father who has qualified us to be partakers of the inheritance of the saints in the light. He has delivered us from the power of darkness and conveyed us into the kingdom of the Son of His love. If we have been qualified to be partakers in the light and delivered from the power of darkness then what excuse could we possibly have for continuing to fall except our lack of understanding of the power we have been given? Either that or we live in this cheap, "God will forgive me," mindset that cripples the ability of the Holy Spirit to raise us up to where God wants us to live, in true righteousness and holiness. If we have been conveyed into the kingdom of the Son of His love then there is no temptation to sin in that place. I am not saying we will become masters of sinless perfection but what I am saying is that we will live in the distinct awareness of close proximity to absolute purity, His absolute purity. We are then to become imitators of that purity. Therefore be imitators of God as dear children. Watch your children, they absolutely adore you and want to be just like you, unless of course they are teenagers. But see how they just stare at you and then attempt to do the very things that you are doing. Do they do them perfectly at first? Of course not but their little hearts are bursting with desire to be just like you. That is why Paul uses this analogy. He goes on to say, And walk in love, as Christ also has loved us and given Himself for us. It is always the result of any goal that we set for ourselves spiritually or that the Bible sets for us. Love. Love, love and more love. It is the supreme manifestation of God in the world and in the life of men. It is the fruit and the evidence of our true position in Him. If we are not loving then we are not imitating Him as dear children.

"Lord, today I will live in obedience rather than sacrifice. I will be an imitator. I will seek that my thoughts are thoughts that dwell on Your great sacrifice for me and I will seek to live sacrificially and love whole heartedly, amen."

Ephesians 5:8-10
For you were once darkness, but now you are light in the Lord. Walk as children of light (for the fruit of the Spirit is in all goodness, righteousness, and truth), finding out what is acceptable to the Lord.

What a powerful indictment! Paul doesn't say we were in the darkness, he says we were once darkness. Not that we were groping around in some frightful place looking for the light switch but rather we were that actual blanket of blackness. We were the very thing that prevented sight. Thinking about it like that I can see it. Pride, arrogance, rebelliousness, self-sufficiency, fear and anger, all of those things created in me a smothering covering over the life God had created for me. Somehow God penetrates us. His grace, His longsuffering, His great love for us, somehow the Holy Spirit is able to penetrate us, darkness, and shine a sliver of revealing light into our hearts. It is God's goodness that leads us to repentance. What a glorious moment, that precious day when awareness came flooding in. Where were you? I was in a worship service that I had attended out of curiosity, (so I thought at the time), and in the middle of a chorus God made His move. His presence and His great love flooded me in such a way that I was brought to weeping instantly. There was no denying that I was caught in the velvet chains of His love. Hebrews 10:31 says; It is a fearful thing to fall into the hands of the living God. Not fearful in the sense of harm coming to me but fearful in the sense of I had just experienced something so magnificent, so incredible that I was afraid of ever losing it. I was awestruck and filled with wonder and I didn't want it to ever go away. For our God is a consuming fire. He wants to consume us. He wants to devour us as darkness and then convey us into the kingdom of the Son of His love. For you were once darkness, but now you are light in the Lord. He doesn't just want to take us out of darkness and bring us into the light, He wants to devour the darkness that is us and then make us into light. Not just living in the light, an illumination from another source but actually being a source. We are to become light, but light in the Lord. The moon's light is reflected light, reflected from a sun that is far far away. God wants to make us the source of light to a lost and dying world. Light in the Lord. We are too close to be reflected light, we are so close to Him that we become His light imparted supernaturally. We are made in the image of His Son. Jesus said in Matthew 5:14-16

"You are the light of the world. A city that is set on a hill cannot be hidden. 15 Nor do they light a lamp and put it under a basket, but on a lampstand, and it gives light to all who are in the house. 16 Let your light so shine before men, that they may see your good works and glorify your Father in heaven. We are the light of the world and we have a singular and awesome charge and that is to glorify our Father in heaven.

"Lord, make me shine so brightly that I will be seen from a great distance. That my life would so clearly exemplify Your great grace that from far off people would see that I am Yours. Cover me Lord with Your Holy Spirit that I would not stumble and that I would not allow even the slightest bit of darkness to ever tarnish this light that You have caused to shine from me, amen."

Ephesians 5:17
Therefore do not be unwise, but understand what the will of the Lord is.

Here it is again. It is constantly recurring in scripture. It is the, "Don't do this but do this other thing instead", admonition. God knows that there are more than just a few of us afflicted with, "the broken decision maker syndrome." This verse could be translated, 'Don't be stupid, think, think, think, what would God have you do?" Most often it's not that hard to determine. Most decisions really require very little thought. "Should I go out and get drunk tonight?" What would God say? "No you should go to a Bible study or stay home and put on some praise music and worship Me." Or, "Should I sleep with this guy in the hopes that he'll like me enough to marry me and become a Christian?" What would God say? "No, you should seek me with all your heart and let me take care of that lonely place and I will bring you a man who loves me to love you." In the event that the decision is too difficult for us James tells us what to do, James 1:5; If any of you lacks wisdom, let him ask of God, who gives to all liberally and without reproach, and it will be given to him. God is ready to give an answer to our deepest and most confusing questions but He often speaks in a still small voice and so we must really be listening. If we are asking God for something and at the same time mass texting five or six friends with the same question planning on acting on the advice that most closely fits our desired outcome then we will not hear from God, All preconceived ideas must be put aside vehemently and our hearts must be lifted up to God as Isaac's breast was to the sacrificial blade of Abraham. You see James continues by saying this; James 1:6-7 But let him ask in faith, with no doubting, for he who doubts is like a wave of the sea driven and tossed by the wind. 7 For let not that man suppose that he will receive anything from the Lord; 8 he is a double-minded man, unstable in all his ways. But let him ask in faith. Sounds easy but so many of us have failed so many times and with such terrible consequences that we have become calloused and untrusting. But has it ever been God who failed us? Think about it. Can't we look back and see where every time we have asked God for strength to face our temptations and we have fallen that in truth we had already made a decision to fall? I remember going to church with it in my mind, "I want to get high." I'd be in church, "Lord please help me to not get high." I'd leave church and go get high. "Well I guess God wasn't listening to me today." Did I tell anyone what I was thinking? Did I say to anyone, 'Can I hang out with you after church? I really think I might get loaded if I'm alone." No I did not do those things. God uses people and we are only as sick as our secrets. Following our verse in Ephesians it goes on to say this; Ephesians 5:18-21 And do not be drunk with wine, in which is dissipation; but be filled with the Spirit, speaking to one another in psalms and hymns and spiritual songs, singing and making melody in your heart to the Lord, giving thanks always for all things to God the Father in the name of our Lord Jesus Christ, submitting to one another in the fear of God. It is clear that this Christian thing is a "we" thing and that we are to share our lives with others. That means coming to the brethren with our struggles and then submitting to their ministrations. We must remember that the battle is always won in the mind and most of our minds left alone are in very bad company. I am speaking for myself here.

"Lord help me to make right choices, I know that often you speak through others, help me to find good people in the faith to trust and confide in, amen."

Ephesians 6:10
Finally, my brethren, be strong in the Lord and in the power of His might.

Over the next few days we are going to explore Paul's, "armor of God" treatise which opens with this magnificent statement. He says, "finally", because he has laid out beginning in chapter 1 the entire Christian experience. He begins with our salvation, "Just as He chose us in Him before the foundation of the world", the supernatural beauty of the gift of grace, "For by grace you have been saved through faith, and that not of yourselves; it is the gift of God". He then moves on to the actual means of our salvation, "But now in Christ Jesus you who once were far off have been brought near by the blood of Christ." After all of this, which we can say is God's part, he addresses Christian living which we can say is our part. Walk in unity, put on the new man, walk in love, walk in light, and walk in wisdom. Then like a symphony gathering itself and rising up into a crescendo he delivers instructions for the most supernatural part of the Christian life, the fight against the prince of this world. The spiritual war of God and satan that has raged for eons and in the fall touched down to earth and brought man into the fray. Mere man limited by his own mortality suddenly brought into a murderous war fought in a spiritual realm by supernatural beings. How could God have done such a thing? How could God have given us over to the deadly danger of being susceptible to the wiles of satan? How could he have given demons the ability to have an influence in our lives and even our thinking? To allow His crowning creation to be exposed to such a dangerous scenario is almost unthinkable. The answer is astonishingly simple, it is dependence. God wants us completely dependent on Him for everything. Peter says this; Your adversary the devil walks about like a roaring lion, seeking whom he may devour. Satan is walking, he can only be at one place at a time. God on the other hand can sweep the entire universe in a glance, and what is He looking for? 2 Chronicles 16:9; For the eyes of the Lord run to and fro throughout the whole earth, to show Himself strong on behalf of those whose heart is loyal to Him. Dependence. God is looking for a loyal heart and it is that heart for which He will manifest His might. It is that heart for which He will pour out the oil of victory and cause that heart to be the heart of a champion, a victor. Paul definitely saved the most challenging aspects of negotiating life for last. So he says, "Finally." "At last." "Most importantly." "Pay attention ya'll." Finally, my brethren, be strong in the Lord and in the power of His might. Be strong, "in the Lord." That is the operative phrase in the entire imperative. Dependence. Proverbs 3:5-6 Trust in the Lord with all your heart, and lean not on your own understanding; In all your ways acknowledge Him, and He shall direct your paths. Trust in the Lord with all your heart, Finally my brethren, be strong in the Lord and in the power of His might. Dependence. What is it to be in the Lord? It is to be out of ourselves, completely. Jesus said, "If anyone desires to come after Me, let him deny himself, and take up his cross, and follow Me." So to be strong in the Lord is to be absolutely convinced of the inadequacy of, "Me." We must commit spiritual suicide if we are to live the victorious abundant life.

"Dear Lord, teach me all about it... Point me in the direction of my own grave. I want to depend solely on You for my very breath. I want to be strong in You and in You alone God.

Thank You for calling me out of the darkness and into the kingdom of the Son of Your love, amen."

Ephesians 6:11
Put on the whole armor of God, that you may be able to stand against the wiles of the devil.

Yesterday Paul told us; Finally, my brethren, be strong in the Lord and in the power of His might. That is because our own resources, our own strengths are insufficient to fight in a battle that is supernatural in every sense. Oh, it is true that the outward manifestations of this battle may often be physical, but they are always completely spiritual in origin. So it is only the strength of God that can give us the victory in this battle. Today Paul tells us to put on the whole armor of God. When David was to fight Goliath King Saul wanted him to wear his armor and to wield his sword but David knew that the armor of a king was not sufficient to bring down the enemy. David had already established what I like to call a conqueror's bank account.

1 Samuel 17:34-37 "Your servant used to keep his father's sheep, and when a lion or a bear came and took a lamb out of the flock, 35 I went out after it and struck it, and delivered the lamb from its mouth; and when it arose against me, I caught it by its beard, and struck and killed it. 36 Your servant has killed both lion and bear; and this uncircumcised Philistine will be like one of them, seeing he has defied the armies of the living God." 37 Moreover David said, "The Lord, who delivered me from the paw of the lion and from the paw of the bear, He will deliver me from the hand of this Philistine." This conqueror's bank account is something we all need to invest in. Victories in the Lord that we recall to boost our trust in Him in the face of our, "Goliaths." With those we can truly say that His past faithfulness demands our present trust.

So we must put on the whole armor of God which we will detail soon but let's look at the rest of the verse. Put on the whole armor of God, that you may be able to stand against the wiles of the devil. We want to be able to stand. We can't take this lying down. This means that we can't have a complacent attitude toward the enemy. He is very real and we must be wide awake and focused. 1 Peter 5:8; Be sober, be vigilant; because your adversary the devil walks about like a roaring lion, seeking whom he may devour.

Be sober, be vigilant, be able to stand against the wiles of the enemy. What is this word, "wiles?" It means to beguile or lure away from, a trick or strategy meant to fool, trap or entice. Is the devil going to walk up to you in his little red suit with his tail twitching and his pitchfork pointing at you and say, "I have every intention of causing you to fall into sin and forfeit your inheritance in God's kingdom because I want you to suffer forever with me in hell. So how do you like me now?" No, this is why we need to be ever so aware of his devices. He has spent years studying our weaknesses and proclivities, taking notes and patiently waiting for an opportunity to catch us in an unguarded state. Satan will always use the weaknesses of the natural man that still struggles to find life inside of us to get his way. James 1:14-15 But each one is tempted when he is drawn away by his own desires and enticed. Then, when desire has conceived, it gives birth to sin; and sin, when it is full-grown, brings forth death. Our armor is cheap and weak, tarnished, compromised. God's armor is shiny and new and constructed of indestructible materials. God's armor must be

our defense in this battle we are in.

"Lord, today I will invest in my conqueror's bank account. I will put on Your armor and I will trust in You. Your past faithfulness demands my present trust. I love You my God, amen."

Ephesians 6:12

For we do not wrestle against flesh and blood, but against principalities, against powers, against the rulers of the darkness of this age, against spiritual hosts of wickedness in the heavenly places.

When I was a lot younger I loved the martial arts. Brazilian Jiu-Jitsu became very popular and the sport of MMA really took off. I was deeply involved spending at least four nights a week at the gym training. I trained in Muy Thai kick boxing, western boxing and grappling or wrestling. While the stand up aspects of the sport were strategic and called for planning and thinking nothing came close to the mental involvement required of ground fighting. It was constant concentration and the implementation of strategy. Before every move you had to think of the opponents reaction to that move and plan a counter move. "He could potentially do this so I had better be ready to do this." Paul is right on the money when he uses wrestling in his analogy. But let us realize this, For we do not wrestle against flesh and blood, We are in a battle for which we are totally and completely outgunned. But against principalities, against powers, against the rulers of the darkness of this age, against spiritual hosts of wickedness in the heavenly places. When Israel was taken captive in Babylon Daniel was God's man in that time. Daniel was praying for knowledge of the future of his people and the angel Gabriel came to him and said this, Daniel 10:12-13 Then he said to me, "Do not fear, Daniel, for from the first day that you set your heart to understand, and to humble yourself before your God, your words were heard; and I have come because of your words. 13 But the prince of the kingdom of Persia withstood me twenty-one days; and behold, Michael, one of the chief princes, came to help me, for I had been left alone there with the kings of Persia." This is speaking of angels and demons, they are real and not just the subject of some novel written to entertain us. But against principalities, Gabriel couldn't come to Daniel which was his assigned mission because he was being delayed by principal demons also assigned to keep Daniel from receiving the knowledge that he sought. Satan is extremely strategic and he is very concerned with interfering with the communication between God and His people. His methods for accomplishing this range the gamut from our own sense of unworthiness, "You are such a stinking sinner, God doesn't want to hear from you.", to just putting up supernatural roadblocks as he did with Daniel. But let's look at this aspect, against spiritual hosts of wickedness in the heavenly places. What is a host? Two definitions are provocative. First a host is one who entertains guests. Satan loves evil, he loves to make evil comfortable in his domain. He does all he can do to promote it and feed it and entertain it. Satan is the harbinger of every evil thing that ever existed. Secondly a host is an organism that supports a parasite. Everything about Satan and his kingdom, which is this world, and all of its present systems is designed to be a host for the parasitical nature of evil. Don't be weak kneed about this and say, 'Oh it's not that bad." Yes it is, and all this world's system includes capitalism, government, entertainment, and advertising. Condense this verse and see this. For we do not wrestle against flesh and blood, but against the rulers of the darkness of this age.

"Lord, open my spiritual eyes to see the darkness that weaves its deceptive web around me. Cause me to identify it and step out into the light. I can claim my victory by Your Spirit, amen."

Ephesians 6:13
Therefore take up the whole armor of God, that you may be able to
withstand in the evil day, and having done all, to stand.

We are still a day or two away from addressing the, "whole armor of
God, "but suffice it to say here that Paul says we should take up the whole
of it. Part of the armor just will not do. It is the same with our entire Christian walk. We must subscribe to all of it. We must adhere to every aspect
of doctrine that is laid out in the pages of scripture. We do not get the opportunity to pick and choose which aspects of our religion we get to adhere
to. 2 timothy 3:16 -17 says; All Scripture is given by inspiration of God,
and is profitable for doctrine, for reproof, for correction, for instruction
in righteousness, 17 that the man of God may be complete, thoroughly
equipped for every good work. It doesn't say that the part of the Bible you
like is profitable to you. Besides which if we truly love God then all of the
Word is a lamp unto our feet and a light unto our path. 1 John 5:3 tells
us; For this is the love of God, that we keep His commandments. And His
commandments are not burdensome. The greatest joy in life comes from
living out the words of scripture day in and day out and seeing it mold us
and shape us into the image of our precious Savior. Paul says; Therefore
take up the whole armor of God, that you may be able to withstand in the
evil day, and having done all, to stand. Withstanding in the evil day is a
promise of God in response to our faithfulness to take up the whole armor
but the very most beautiful part is this; and having done all, to stand. This
means that because we have been faithful to live the Word and obey the
Lord that in the end when the dust clears having done all we are standing.
We are the conquerors. Psalm 24 says; Who may ascend into the hill of the
Lord? Or who may stand in His holy place? He who has clean hands and
a pure heart. Because we have done all, meaning that we have taken the
entire prescription that the Doctor Jesus has given us we can stand in His
Holy place. In the rubble of the battlefield that is now holy ground we are
standing with our arms raised up in praise and a cry of victory on our lips.
Enemies that at one time had dominion over our lives are now the casual-
ties of a God imparted righteousness. They lie dead and defeated at our
feet. The addictions, the constant poor choices, the anger, the sorrow, the
unforgiveness, all of it lies defeated at our feet and over us flies the banner of

Jesus Christ. It flies in glorious splendor in celebration of our transformed lives and we will never ever be the same.

"Dear Lord, Having done all I will stand! Teach me to do all. Teach me from Your Word. Speak into my life the strategies of Holy victory. Place in me the heart of a conqueror. I will trust in You and in You alone today and forever more. I love You Jesus and I thank you for saving me! Amen."

Peter Cropsey and his wife Dawn are the pastors of First Love Church in Costa Mesa California. The website firstlovechurch.net features all the sermons and entire church services including the worship music streamed in crisp video and audio reproduction

For a daily devotional that puts legs on the Word of God please visit firstlovechurch.net or visit First Love Church on Facebook.

ABOUT THE AUTHOR

Peter C. Cropsey lives in Costa Mesa California with his wife Dawn and their two daughters Paige and Harlow. He hasn't been in the back seat of a cop car since 1987. Prior to that he stole everything he drove, lived in Motels and gang clubhouses, shot dope every day and never stepped outside without a pistol. He paroled from Corcoran state prison Sept 3 1989 with a deep desire to change. He immersed himself in a program of recovery and the change came. In 2001 he graduated from Calvary Chapel School of Ministry and was ordained a pastor at Calvary Chapel Laguna. For twenty years he has helped men stuck in the life of drugs and prison to turn it around. During that time he has been a heavy equipment operator, custom motorcycle builder, cattle rancher, the co-founder of a men's treatment center and a pastor.

Peter C. Cropsey is a man who believes that God can turn the rut into a groove every time and that it is possible to change even the darkest lives into lives of hope and light.

He has a saying,

"Two things I have learned. One, that as long as you are breathing there is hope and two, with God all things are possible."

76482103R00126

Made in the USA
Columbia, SC
26 September 2019